"The other night we had a freak dew-fall that might not happen again for weeks—and it cheered us all up and we started building an airplane, of all things, just because Stringer sold us an idea that only a lunatic would think of. Now I've seen straight for the first time. How long d'you think Kepel's going to live? And Harris? And when they get near the end, are we going to watch them suffering without giving them half our ration to try keeping them alive? So where does that leave us? I'd sooner look at things as they are than kid myself."

He wanted to say more but he could hear the sound of his voice coming through distorted lips; he sounded like an old man without dentures in, comic and enfeebled. They were all old men, old in that they were nearing the end of life.

He didn't want to talk anymore. He wanted to lie down and sleep.

THE FLIGHT OF THE PHOENIX

The Flight of the Phoenix

Elleston Trevor

HarperEntertainment
An Imprint of HarperCollinsPublishers

HARPERENTERTAINMENT
An Imprint of HarperCollins*Publishers*
10 East 53rd Street
New York, New York 10022-5299

ISBN: 0-06-076222-5

HarperCollins ®, 📖 ®, and HarperEntertainment™ are trademarks of HarperCollins Publishers Inc.

First HarperEntertainment paperback printing: November 2004

Printed in the United States of America

Visit HarperEntertainment on the World Wide Web at www.harpercollins.com

10 9 8 7 6 5 4 3 2 1

To the great
WALLY THOMAS

There are certain men who, when faced with the choice of dying or doing the impossible, elect to live. This story is written in honor of their kind.

CHAPTER
1

THE WIND HAD FLUNG THE SAND THIRTY thousand feet into the sky above the desert in a blinding cloud from the Niger to the Nile, and somewhere in it was the airplane.

Two hours before, there had been nothing on the weather map, nothing like this; but the meteorological bureau in Jebel Sarra had a reputation for being forty-nine percent right, and the plane had taken off into a pale-blue sky with a pilot, navigator, twelve passengers from the Jebel oil town and a cargo of worn tools and burnt-out drill bits for replacement. It was a Salmon-Rees Skytruck passenger-conversion freighter, a twin-boom shorthauler on the Sahara runs.

Out from Jebel the navigator had checked his track, height and position overhead El Tallab in the Koufra Oasis Group. A minute later a wind gust tore the aerial out of its socket.

The noise was heard all over the aircraft, and the pilot told his navigator, "Go back there and tell them what the noise was. Tell them everything's fine."

Moran ducked through the bulkhead and spoke to three or four of the men halfway down the cabin. The man at the rear still had the monkey tucked inside his jacket: you could smell it from here, so what was it like for the man? He told them what had happened but they didn't seem very interested. They had got into this plane to get somewhere, and they weren't going to worry about anything that happened on the way. Moran knew only a few of them by sight: Cobb, chief driller at Station A Jebel, a huge man with red hair and a face screwed into a wrinkled map of all he would like to forget (they said he was being shipped home for psychiatric treatment, and you could tell it from his face); Loomis, a thin quiet-eyed Texan, who'd had a cable, something about his wife; Crow, the Londoner who looked more like a monkey than the monkey at the back, going home on leave; and Roberts, out of the oil camp for the third time this year and still healthy looking, already home, in his mind, with the rain on the windows already washing the sand out of his soul.

The others were strangers to Moran, but he would see them again. Maybe it was just the money, but there was something about an oil town that kept hold of people until they died in it. He went back into the control cabin, wondering if the psychiatrist would ever let Trucker Cobb see Jebel again.

He looked at Towns, who was carefully check-ing landmarks. Fifteen thousand feet below the Skytruck the desert looked like a sandpit where children had left their toys scattered: among the dun wastes rose the dunes and spurs and massifs, and between them lay oases like weeds sprout-ing, and the abandoned oil drillings and camp towns half-covered with the drifting sands of the last great storm. From south to north ran the Oum el Semnou pipeline, parallel with the camel track where a puff of dust marked a caravan on the move.

Moran put his headset on and said: "We going on, Frankie?"

Towns turned his head an inch as a sign that he was still in thought; his eyes moved across and across the pattern of the land below; then they scanned the horizon.

"What's the risk?"

The habit-phrase was reassuring to the naviga-tor. He said, "I don't see how we can get lost. We live here. The only risk is if the weather clamps down."

Towns let a minute go by before he said, "We're bigger."

Moran was satisfied; not with his dead radio or the weather report that was often wrong as hell, but with Towns. He had flown the oil runs with him for three years. But they should at least go

through the motions of reaching a considered decision. "What alternate did you nominate?"

"El Aouzzad."

"Christ." Two dozen mud-built sweatboxes
with doors stuck fast with crushed flies, a mosque
like a dog kennel, and three wells, two of them
filled with salt water and the third with drowned
rats. Visit the ancient kasbah of El Aouzzad, a
palm-fringed haven amid the vast stretches of
sand—and bring an elephant gun, it's the only
thing the termites won't eat providing you can re-
load fast enough.

"Fort Lacroix is under repair," Towns said,
"and I didn't fancy going into Pic Tousside over
the Kemet range if we got into trouble. You persuade me to lob down in El Aouzzad for a couple
of nights while they find some aerial wire, and
we'll do that, Lew." He was keeping on track by
visual reference to the north-south pipeline and the
long brown spine of the Kemet Massif on the other
side. Moran said:

"I'm happy as I am."

"How are they at the back?"

"Okay. Did you see Trucker get on the plane?"

"Nope."

"He's being shipped home to a mental clinic. He
looks far gone. You know how they start to look."

Towns nodded, watching the Kemet Massif
turning slowly on the horizon and waiting for

4

Tazerbo Oasis to come up on the starboard wing.
If the weather kept clear for two more hours, they
would be north of the central desert and within
running distance of the Djalo Oasis Group.

He began humming inside his headset until
Moran told him to shut up or take it off.

An hour afterward they hit a wind-shear and
dropped a hundred feet without touching the sides.
Moran leaned against the perspex trying to sight
the Radaou-Siffi camel track, the only landmark
they would be able to pick up in this area where
the central desert opened up from east to west. Either he was anticipating or the sandstorm of a
week ago had covered the track completely. The
wind sheared again and Towns brought the plane's
nose up, looking across Moran to the west where
the horizon was boiling up dust. His ears automatically monitored the note of the engines and
found it perfect. But he wished they had a radio.

Moran checked the directional gyro against the
compass and reset, and peeled off a strip of chewing gum, which Towns had not often seen him do.
It made a disgusting squelching noise in the headset. No one had been in to see them, from the back.
There was nearly always one of the drilling engineers on the flight deck, in here to kill off the boredom by telling them how to fly the thing. In a
passenger-freighter like this there was no cabin
staff to keep them out.

He asked Moran, "They still got that monkey back there?"

Moran gave a studied sniff. "You didn't think it was me, did you?"

There was still no sign of the camel track. The storm would have covered it. A storm like that would have wiped out a whole oil camp with driven sand, except for the derrick. The west horizon was still curdling up, brown, yellow and hard blue sky. Within twenty minutes the gyro had wandered and Moran reset it, chewing busily on his gum. He hadn't spoken for a long time. He knew what his pilot knew: another hour now and they'd be able to run for Djalo even if the bottom fell out of the sky.

A flight of migratory geese crossed the wake of the Skytruck ten minutes later, coursing eastward at about ten or twelve thousand feet. Behind them there was a veil of rising sand where a wing of the wind had broken away from the main drift.

Moran stayed hunched against the perspex, looking down at the spread of the central desert. There were no toys lying scattered there now, and no weedlike tufts of palm. The afternoon sun cast shadows across the scimitar-curving dunes, and pools of dark light swam on the eastward lees of the plateaus. It was lunar landscape, dead and un-knowable. Down there you would find not a leaf, not a grassblade, not a footprint of any living thing. The plane's shadow haunted a dead world.

Moran bumped his head as the Skytruck fell into a pocket of air and Towns worked to keep her stable. There was no horizon now to the west: desert and sky merged in a swath of yellow. Sand began touching the perspex and Moran sat upright on his seat, checking the gyro and allowing for compass deviation caused by the iron-bearing rocks northwest of the Koufra Group.

Within ten minutes the sun went out and they were headed into a darkening yellow void. Towns went down to three thousand feet, as low as he dared, because of the table mountains of sand that reared sometimes two thousand feet above sea level in this area: but there was no freak break in the wind. The sand was boiling up from the land with the consistency of steam from a boiling vat. In fifteen minutes he had climbed to twenty-five thousand and was flying through yellow murk. The desert was no longer below them; it was in the sky.

"Check heading, Lew."

"You're plumb on."

The sand hissed against the windscreen like dry rain.

"There's a ten-degree drift," Towns said.

"I allowed for that." They were headed north and the wind was out of the west, up from Fezzan, maybe rooted even as far as the Hoggar Range. They were in a dead crosswind of thirty rising forty miles an hour or more. The chewing gum tasted foul in the mouth. The one risk had come off; the weather bureau in Jebel Sarra was proving forty-nine percent right again. But Frank Towns had said they were bigger, and in three years he had been zero percent wrong. Behind those three years, before Moran had known him, there were another twenty-seven, a total of forty thousand flying hours. That was real size, bigger than almost any risk you could think of.

The sound from behind made Moran start. It was one of the men from the back, a stranger to him. He swung his right earphone free.

"If the aerial's gone," the man said in a pitched but reasonable tone, "and there's no visibility, how is your pilot going to find his alternate?"

Moran looked up into a thin young face with mild eyes magnified by rimless glasses. He looked more like a student chemist than an oil driller. Maybe he was. Moran resisted the impulse to tell him that their alternate field at El Aouzzad was now some hundred and fifty miles behind them. And it was no good trying rough humor on a face like this. The question had been put very formally, even to the extent of "your pilot."

"We are on course and on schedule," he told the young man. "If there's anything interesting to report, we'll be letting you know."

The magnified brown eyes blinked slowly like a lizard's.

"Thank you." He went back into the main cabin, slipping the door catch deftly and nudging the panel to make quite sure it was properly closed. He had to climb awkwardly across the big man's legs because he wouldn't move them. Conversation with the big man, whose name he had learned, had not been easy so far on the flight; but he resolved to try again. "I've just spoken to them on the flight deck, Mr. Cobb. They assure me that the flight's going according to plan, but I must say I would have expected them to be turning for their alternate airport by now." After a moment he asked, "Wouldn't you?"

Trucker Cobb swung his great head slowly to gaze into the soft questioning eyes. There was the awareness that people were trying to get into Cobb's world, and he had to make the effort of meeting them.

"You from Jebel, son?"

"My brother's there. I've just paid him a visit. He's an analytical geophysicist. Do you know him? Our name is Stringer." He edged his eyes away from the rather intimidating stare.

"I've seen enough of that stuff. I've seen enough." Cobb was staring now at the window; it was an opaque panel of yellow. He knew that it was sand. He could recognize the color of sand, anywhere; it was the color of sickness.

Stringer said, "Anyway, they have assured me

that the flight is going normally. I suppose the pilot knows what he's doing, though frankly he looks an old man, to be flying still. He looks all of fifty, which is old to be still flying. Don't you think?"

He looked hesitantly into the lost blue eyes that had yellow squares set in them, the reflection of the windows. Cobb didn't seem to have heard him. To go and talk to anyone else would mean climbing over the big inert legs again, so he sat still and watched the particles of sand flying at the window and jumping away. There was something fascinating in sitting here and realizing that if the thin pane of plastic were not there one would have to squinch one's eyes and duck one's head to avoid being blinded.

Behind Cobb, Captain Harris lit another cigarette and felt the plane lurch as the pilot corrected the drift. He would have liked to take a draught from his water bottle, because the stew he had eaten before take-off had been heavily salted; but he was in uniform and one should try to exert a little self-discipline. The thirst would be the more urgent by the time they landed at Sidi Raffa, and its quenching the more enjoyable. Besides, Watson was here, a man to note the smallest weaknesses in others.

The plane lurched again and someone called out in mock alarm, and another man laughed.

Sergeant Watson, immediately behind his officer,

gazed at the lean straight neck. It was scrubbed pink between the khaki collar and the patch of white skin where the sun hadn't colored it yet after yesterday's haircut. It was a neck, thought Sergeant Watson, fit for a chopper. He had been thinking this for some time now, and enjoying it. You could stare at a man's neck in absolute safety—by the time he'd screwed his head round you'd be looking somewhere else. Safe from the danger of an answering glance (in terms of answering fire), you could get a man right in your sights and rattle away till he was riddled. This bastard had been dead meat for two hours now. It helped. It helped a lot, no bloody error.

Sated at last with the sweetness of victory, Watson looked around him again, and thought again that for two pins he'd sling it in with the Army as soon as his time expired, and mob out with blokes like these, got up dandy in civvies like they wore, jeans and boots what color you like and tartan shirts and all—and the *money* they must pull in . . . not one of them without a gold wrist watch the size of a bloody alarm clock, and pockets full of Parker pens! Two hundred nicker a month, some of these boys knocked up, with a company-paid air trip home every three months for a full month's leave . . . it didn't bear thinking about. And no bloody upstart officers with their fatherly approach, treating you like some snotty-nosed back-street slum kid just because nobody'd ever learned you how to say "old boy" in the right kind of tone. No bloody Harris.

He stared back at the exposed pink-and-white neck and gave it a couple of short-range bursts to soften up the muscle.

Kepel, the German boy, stared at his own face in the blank yellow window, listening to the unceasing hiss of the sand. Beside him, the tall quiet Texan never moved. The cable had said "urgent you come," and he had spun the words around in his mind until it meant nothing, because it might mean everything.

At the rear end of the cabin, Crow was making no headway. Roberts wasn't budging.

"Look, you can easy pick up another one the next time out." He poked his long tapering nose into Roberts' face, pecking at it as if it were a coconut.

"For that matter, so can you—"

"I've *told* you, it's his *birthday*—"

"He'll have plenty of other birthdays." Roberts kept his hand on the button of his jacket in case the monkey tried to get out. It looked as if Crow meant to grab it from him anyway, given half a chance. He didn't know how Crow, with all his Brylcreem and after-shave lotions and Talc de Fougère Royale under his armpits, could bear to get this close to poor old Bimbo. It'd be all right at home, because they said if you soaked them in Milton and smothered them in coal-tar soap once a day your best

12

friend would never know they were in the house. They'd cross that bridge, anyway, when—

"Twenty quid, then, but that's my limit, Rob!"

"No takers."

"Are you daft? Twenty quid! You can get a bran'-new locomotive, ten trucks an' a whole mountain cutting for that!" He knew Rob was a train man, in fact he was a bit that way inclined himself.

"I'm getting them anyway." Roberts grinned. A check for close on five hundred had gone into his local bank ahead of him.

"I know if I got offered twenty nicker for a flea-'appy little perisher like 'im—'alf-dead, you can smell that—I'd take it an' run."

Beside him, Bellamy watched the sharp face with its long pointed nose; he had met Albert Crow five or more years ago when they'd both been kids of twenty and fresh out from green England to scratch for oil under the burning crust of the earth, because the money was good and because dark skins and palm trees and the lurching grace of camels were right out of a legend. Hassi-Messaoud . . . Edjeleh . . . then far south to Jebel Sarra with the drillers who came from everywhere—French, Americans, Greeks, Italians, Englishmen like themselves, men who fell in love with the very name *Sahara* and then gradually fell in hate of it and the baking wastes of nowhere that hemmed in the oil camp with the confines of terrible distance. Sahara, the biggest open prison in the world with walls of sand a hundred miles thick and as high as the sky.

This was where they'd been educated, Albert and him, together; and for five years there'd hardly ever been a time when he couldn't look up and see this pinched beaky face with its missing-nothing eyes taking it all in and turning it all over and weighing it up. You could see life just by looking at Albert looking at it, and you'd never miss a thing.

"Twenty quid," said Crow, "fleas an' all."

The cabin heeled badly, then leveled. Tilney lurched out of his seat and came up the aisle.

"I'm not keen on this," he said. His good-looking boyish face was blank: he was too frightened to express his fear. Crow looked at him and away. The yellow of the windows had gone darker; the sand hit the panes like gravel.

" 'E's right, y'know. We're in dead trouble!" He went forward and opened the bulkhead door, ignoring the "Keep Out" notice, pushing his long nose into the control cabin. He had to shout twice before the pilot heard him. "Listen, skipper, 'ow we goin' to land, in this lot?"

Towns glanced up to identify the voice and said, "The same way as I've landed half a million times before, starting from before you were born. You'll see a notice on the other side of that door. Read it on your way back."

Crow blew him a silent raspberry and went out,

shutting the door. Moran got up and checked it, slipping the lock. The cramped flight deck was filled with yellow light. He said nothing to Towns as he took his seat again in front of the gyro.

The starboard engine didn't cough more than twice before it cut off. Towns corrected automatically for full port thrust and then feathered the starboard airscrew.

There was no sandscreen made that could stand up to this liquid cloud. The jets had choked up and there was no point in trying the Coffman starter.

They were both reading off the instruments, the first thing that any crew does in a flight-deck crisis. The Skytruck was in perfectly stable flight with a five- to ten-degree drift easier to control now that the full thrust was on the windward side. In clear air the port engine might keep going at peak throttle for hours without overheating and seizing but in this welter of sand it could shut down any second; then it would mean a dead-stick landing with visibility fifty yards. The answer was very simple.

Moran sat praying that Towns wouldn't be unthinking enough to ask a routine question of his navigator: what what was their position? Because it was unknown.

Towns was turning the aircraft into wind.

"We putting her down, Frankie?"

It had gone quiet now, because the sand was

meeting them head on and in line with the slip-stream, and the starboard engine was silent.

"The only thing. Before they both cut." He had the control column forward and the altimeter began dropping toward the fifteen thousand sector. "Keep your eyes skinned—it'll get thicker as we go." The cabin was darkening.

They were down to five thousand feet when the second engine went dead, and there was no sound but the soft crackling of the sand.

CHAPTER 2

IN THE UNNATURAL HUSH OF THE CABIN TOWNS' voice was loud. "Tell them to prepare for a crash landing."

Moran got up, spitting out the soft pip of chewing gum because now it could be dangerous.

While his navigator was gone, Towns worked things out again carefully.

With no radio signals reaching them for the past hour, and with no visual reference to landmarks below for the past thirty minutes, their position was unknown. If he had corrected accurately for drift since the last visual reference they would have remained on track; overcorrection would have taken them too far west; undercorrection too far east. There was no means of telling. From the moment they had turned into wind a few minutes ago at upward of fifteen thousand feet they had started a course due west. How far it would take them could be read from the airspeed indicator and clock: but without signals from ground stations they couldn't know the actual wind velocity. The indicated airspeed showed 200. Reckon the wind-speed at 40, give or take 10, they were in a glide descent of 160 mph. The wind sounded stronger now, but it was probably the same strength, because the silent engines and the thickening of the sand clouds nearer the ground increased the noise: allow for that too.

They were going to put down somewhere in the Central Libyan Desert, so that one image filled his mind. Water. With fourteen men on board there was maybe enough for a couple of days, with their water bottles plus the sealed emergency drinking tank. That would do. They wouldn't be on the ground for long: they would land, cover the engines, and wait for the storm to die. That would take from three to six hours: at this season the storms were frequent, violent, but short. When the wind died they would take down both carburetors and clear the jets of sand. Reassemble—start up and take off. Fuel situation good. Could even re-rig the aerial wire if the rear socket was still there.

The risk was the terrain. Without power there was no question of snooping around at nought feet looking for a smooth stretch: they'd have to go down cold and make it first time, whatever the terrain. It might be flat hard sand, or *fech-fech* with a hard crust and rotten underneath, or broken-up scree, or a powdery dune, or the sheer side of a thousand-foot plateau. In this yellow spume he wouldn't see much of the terrain anyway; but the undercarriage must be left down or they'd never take off again.

The temptation to retract and put her down on the hull was very strong. He would resist it. She had to be flown in and flown out again. She was an airplane. The final consideration must be kept right out of his mind: it was, if anyone got killed it would be his fault. He should have followed the rules and made for his alternate at El Aouzzad when the aerial went.

Moran came back. He had left the bulkhead door wide open and latched back: access might be needed after a bad landing. His neat, correctly shaped face expressed nothing of his thoughts. If they were going to hit the side of a plateau, then that's what they were going to do; if they were going to wreck the undercarriage on rocks and no one ever found them, then that was what would happen. It was easy enough to turn fatalist at a time like this: it took fear away and let you concentrate on getting through alive. Easy, too, to put your trust in Frank Towns.

People called Frank a failure. In a way that was true: graduating from wartime flying for Transport Command, he had captained his first main-route airliner within a year of the war's end, and was flying Constellations for U.K.A. until the company switched to the new Supers. He passed his conversion course without a hitch: there wasn't much difference in the two types. Then he began thinking of himself as a veteran, and sent in a complaint questioning the competency of a route-check examiner on the Cairo run, who had twice failed him on emergency equipment tests. Most pilots resented the policy of route checking but few of them ever countered a failure with a complaint; and Frank's record got its first black.

He failed two more flight checks and a base check within a year; although U.K.A. knew that he was a first-class flyer they warned him that his attitude toward what he called "going back to school" would bring him more failures. He straightened up, then failed a conversion course from a twin-jet to a big four-jet DC. U.K.A. passed him on to the branch lines with Viscounts. In a year they let him try converting to the Comet and again he failed. He'd told Moran, "You know how many instruments that damn thing has? They cover the ceiling. I'm a flyer, not a theater organist."

In 1958 Frank was working for the fringe operators: short sea crossings, desert lifts, jungle runs, flying all kinds, whatever they'd let him have: and for six years his record had been unblemished. He made no conversions—never "went back to school"—and he flew through weather that would have kept other men on the deck, flew machines out of swamps and bush strips and desert pockets that were fit only for birds.

It had been true what Frank had said: he was a flyer of the old school who could use the sky for a playground; but the new school wouldn't take him because he was too old—not so much in years but in his attitude of mind; he had to fly a plane by the seat of his pants and not by reference to a battery of instruments.

Moran had never navigated the main-schedule routes but he'd been on the short hauls for fifteen years and flown with scores of pilots, and there was one he could willingly put his trust in, above all others; and he was flying with him now.

He took his seat again and Towns asked him, "How are they back there?"

"Fine. No complaints." Most of the passengers were from Jebel, and oil drilling was dangerous; to be in danger was not new to them. "Rob says good luck."

"Got their belts on?"

"Yes, Frank."

"You check the freight?"

"Tight all round." He watched the altimeter. "You timing the glide?"

"Yep. Clock 3:10, airspeed 200 as we turned."

Moran wrote it on his pad, tore off the sheet and folded it into his pocket.

"Figures are in my pocket," he said. The pad might land up anywhere, or get burned, and if anything happened to him, Towns would know where the figures were; and they could be very important: even a rough check on their final position would be better than none. The moment they saw the terrain coming up at them he would take clock and ASI readings, note them and pocket them.

The sand was hitting the windscreens black now; they must be running into their own shadow thrown by the remaining light of the sun against the screen of particles. It had the look and sound of black rain. Beyond, the world was still yellow.

Towns had the control column steady and leaned forward over it, as if a fifty-yard visibility range could be improved by these few inches. He was ready to throw the controlled-slot lever the instant he saw ground.

When the altimeter showed fifteen hundred feet Moran said:

"We going in with our shoes on?"

"Have to, or we shan't get up again."

"Oh, sure." He stopped automatically reading off the instruments. They meant nothing now. Towns was going to fly her in with his head and his hands. He would have liked to tell him, at this moment, for the record Frank, there's no one I'd prefer to fly with. But it would be embarrassing to say aloud and anyway Towns wouldn't care: there were only two people here in the sky: this man and his machine.

"I'm looking" was all he said.

"Do that."

Moran leaned forward too, resting his arms comfortably along the foam-rubber crash pad. There would be time, right at the end, to pull back and duck. He couldn't see anything beneath them, any change of coloring, any lightening or darkening of the sand haze. The altimeter, set for sea level, could read a thousand feet out of true: they might still be two thousand high, or they might now be skating in across the terrain at derrick height.

The Skytruck was losing airspeed. There was no burbling and thank God no wind-shear as yet, but Towns was having to deal with slight pitching. With nothing visible below, there was coming the sensation of land nearing—the "nought-feet feeling" made up of many small factors: pressure on the eardrums, the rump settling into the seat, the body's reaction to decreased airspeed, the heavy feeling of the whole machine that was sensed even without a hand on the controls. Moran started to take long slow blinks to avoid fog hypnosis. He thought now that the yellow was darkening.

"I think we're near."

"Yep."

Everything was going limp and metal jointing creaked as the lift slackened under the mainplanes.

"I think—"

"Plateau—"

"No ground yet—"

"Coming up now."

Moran thought, We didn't hit the plateau. We could have.

A shape fled past and Towns hit the controlled-slot lever and they felt the lift coming on but there was nothing they could see below the windscreens until another shape came curving past, a crescent dune. Dead ahead of them the sand haze was opaque and Moran knew that even if they were sitting here with the plane at a standstill on the ground they still wouldn't see anything because the wind was scooping the surface into the air and the air was so thick with sand that there was no line of demarcation.

They had cleared the plateau and now ran between low dunes with the landing wheels plowing through a top scum of blown sand and the main slots wide open to give them lift as the speed died toward stalling point, the point where nineteen tons dead weight would flounder and drop flat and break up.

Moran took readings from the clock and ASI, noted them and put the sheet into his pocket with the first one. The surging noise of rough-sea surf began and he said:

"Touching, Frank, touching—"

"Still high."

Moran looked to see if Towns' safety harness

was tight, then adjusted his own, bringing his knees up with his feet on the seat rung, hands folded loosely on his lap, forcing his limbs to relax while his nerves tried to tense them.

Thick sand washed against the undercarriage and Towns braced the column back as the nose went down. The surf roar lightened but now the whole machine was staggering and the dark of a dune flowed past the windows as the main wheels hit ground and the hydraulics took the first shock and the second and the third until sand blew up in a yellow explosion across the windscreens. The cabin shook like a dog and the instrument panel blurred to a haze on the antivibration web. Someone in the back was shouting.

The Skytruck hit ground for the last time and slewed badly and then a wheel struck something and she spun like a boomerang and ran wild with the main legs buckling under and the hull taking the weight. Somewhere a spar cracked in the roar of sand. Moran heard the freight break loose and smash through the skin of the hull as she spun again in her own length, then he passed out as the blood piled to one side of his head. A man was screaming and then the scream stopped.

CHAPTER
3

OUTSIDE THE WRECK, WHERE TILNEY HAD RUN
sobbing with his hands to his face, gold light filtered
down through the haze of flying sand. The ring of
dunes made humps of shadow. An undercarriage leg
lay across the trail of furrows that the plane had
churned. The wind tugged at Tilney's thin body.

Some of them came out, to move about, staring
at the thick gold sky and the humped beast shapes
of the dunes; they moved to and fro, silent.

Roberts sat on the ground, pressing the monkey
against the warmth of his chest, trying to stop its
quivering. It had its mouth open in a grimace of per-
sisting terror; he could feel its sharp teeth through
his shirt. It had fouled on him, but he did nothing
about it, simply repeating, "Bimbo . . . it's all right,
Bimbo," and stroking the small coconut head.

Moran had come to as soon as the lurching
swing of the plane had stopped. He had hit the re-
lease of the safety harness and got out of the seat,
surprised to still hear the patter of sand against the
windscreens although they had stopped moving.

Towns freed his harness and for a moment sat, stiffly, looking straight in front of him at nothing. His face was ashen.

"You all right, Frankie?"

After what seemed a long time Towns said, "Yep." He stood up and staggered through the bulkhead doorway, and Moran remembered hearing someone screaming. He went to help Towns.

The light was dim in the main cabin. Someone had got the door open and it swung in the wind. A rock had ripped open the hull and Moran's shoes grated on sand. A man asked:

"I suppose the lights don't work?"

The switches were lost among impacted sheeting and Moran went back to the flight deck and tried the emergency circuit, but nothing happened. Crow and Bellamy had an electric torch, and with its light they examined the man on the floor where the rock had gashed up through the hull. Then Crow swung the torch away and they took another look round. Moran and Loomis began working with them; Towns fetched the emergency torch from the flight deck that Moran had forgotten about.

Later they laid the two bodies side by side at the rear of the main cabin. Some of the heavy drilling bits had come unshipped and one whole crate had broken through the freight bulkhead to smash across the rear group of seats. It took an hour to

free the German boy. Towns had given him morphia from the crash kit and he was quiet now.
When they had propped him across two of the forward seats, strapping him lightly with the safety
belts, Crow and Bellamy went outside and lit ciga-
rettes, shielding the lighter from the wind; they
leaned together against the hull, smoking and saying nothing. They could hear the Army chap, Harris, giving orders all the time to his sergeant, inside.

Crow said, "It's letting up, Dave."

"What is?"

"The wind."

"Bit late."

A figure was wandering in the haze of sand not
far away; now it became lost and Crow said,
"Who's that bloody fool out there?" He left the
plane and Bellamy followed, and they brought
Tilney back. "Start loafin' about in this lot, Tilly,
and you'll lose your little self." The boy couldn't
keep his hands from his face. He moaned all the
time, and they sat him down next to Roberts and
Crow said, "There's another one for you to nurse,
Rob. Christ's sake don't let 'im go wanderin' off
again. This lot, you go ten yards and never find
your way back."

Inside the wreck Captain Harris was talking to
the blond boy, Kepel, using the few German words
he knew. Kepel's eyes were clear and steady, though
the pupils were still enlarged from the drug. For

some reason he insisted on speaking English, probably because it was better than Harris' German.

"Please do not give me any more drug. It is not bad pain now, thank you." He smoked the cigarette busily as if pleased that he could move his hands. There had been remarkably little bleeding, but Loomis, who had examined him with long gentle hands and quiet eyes, had told them that the boy's pelvis was smashed up and both thighs broken. He was not to be moved.

The first gleam of the sun's light was now falling through the gap where the window had been, shining on Kepel's thick bright hair. Captain Harris said to him, "When you need anything, call me or one of the others. There's a gap we've made between the cushions underneath you, and a canvas bowl. You mustn't move, you see, so when you want to go to the lavatory, all you have to do is to let go. It's all rather neatly arranged." He gave a doctor's smile. "Now we're going to make plans to fetch help here. Rescuers."

"Thank you, Captain. It is captain?"

"That's right. Name's Harris. This is Sergeant Watson."

"Oh, yes. Otto Kepel. My name."

Sergeant Watson, upright against the cabin wall, nodded down to the boy and thought: God Almighty, a proper gents' jamboree, introducing each other like they was at a party, with this kid lying here smashed up to hell. And bloody Harris playing the little M.O. and loving himself. It was fit to beat the band.

"I understand, Captain, that there are—" The boy's face contracted until the skin was stretched against the bones; his eyes fell shut, then slowly came open. "That there are men now dead."

"Er—yes. Yes."

"How many?"

"Er—two. Poor chaps." He straightened up. "You were lucky. Now we have to get things organized all round. But we'll be back."

He stood Sergeant Watson outside and began detailing procedure: they would use what they could find to lay out SOS signals on the sand as soon as the wind died completely. He thought that Watson seemed rather quiet, but then he always was, perhaps. A sterling fellow, provided you handled him correctly. Good to have him along.

As they talked, the young man who had said his name was Stringer stood nearby, listening, apparently taking it all in; and Captain Harris was glad of the audience, because they would all have to pull together now, and most of these fellows probably didn't have a clue about desert survival.

When the wind dropped at five o'clock, sheared as if by a blade, the sand haze fell and the sun struck from the west across the dunes.

Moran had told Towns, "We're going to have to

sleep inside there, Frank." The "Frankie" didn't come too easily now, because Towns' face was shut, as if he'd slammed a door on everything he was thinking. Moran knew that he was thinking of the inquiry. Two words were going to finish a career of thirty years. Pilot error. The ruling was perfectly clear: in the event of radio failure and all absence of contact with the ground, captains of aircraft will at once head for the nearest nominated alternate airfield and land there, regardless of fuel reserve and landing-weight restrictions normally imposed.

"If we're going to sleep inside," he said to Towns, "we'll have to move those two out. Right?"

Towns made an effort to listen. In the returned glare of the sun his face looked old, older than fifty, older than any known number of years. He didn't answer, but went with Moran, taking the spade from the crash kit and digging two shallows in the sand. Loomis, tall and unspeaking and with his quiet eyes everywhere, saw what they had to do, and helped them.

All the others kept away, as if it were a private occasion. The bodies had been swathed in the white silk panels of Frank Towns' parachute, for they would be taken from the sand and flown out when rescue came. With an urgency that choked him Towns wished he could tell Moran and Loomis what was on his mind, to hear his own voice putting it into ordinary words that would be so much cleaner than the shape of nightmare thought. He would have said, I killed them, as if with my hands.

The spade was bright in the late sun. The wind had left a breathless silence in which voices carried clearly. When the spade was still, Loomis said, "I guess we need to put something here, so we can find the place." He went to the wreckage and came back with a piece of buckled tubing that happened to have the shape of a cross.

The sun touched the ridge of the long dune west of the wreck, and Captain Harris came up to Towns.

"I think we should get things organized all round, do you agree?"

Towns' face had lost some of its blankness, but he heard himself asking, "Why me?"

"Well, I have to consult you, of course. As captain of the aircraft."

Sergeant Watson spat into the sand.

Moran watched Towns' face and saw the surprise come into it, the first expression to be seen there since he had sat stiff in front of the control column with his skin ashen. Towns was looking at the smashed hull with its mainplanes jutting out like broken bones; and then he laughed, terribly, throwing back his head and shutting his eyes while Moran had to turn away.

Harris watched the pilot. The fellow was still suffering from shock, as most of them were. They would have to rally their spirits. He turned to the navigator, who seemed to have taken things rather well.

"First of all," he said to Moran, "how long do we estimate having to stay here? I imagine there'll be an air search under way before long?"

Moran said, "We're due in at Sidi Raffa just about this time. It'll take a few hours for them to work up interest because as far as they know we might have come down almost anywhere, at any one of a dozen water points where there's no telephone or radio. I'd say the air search'll begin about dawn tomorrow." He couldn't find a cigarette, and didn't want to ask Towns for one.

"Thank you," Harris said cheerfully. "We know our rough position, of course?"

"I've been working on that. It's rough, all right, and it's nowhere near our planned track because we came down from it at a right angle due west, from near enough twenty thousand feet. I can tell you our *exact* position: Central Libyan Desert." For some reason he hoped the smooth pink face of the captain would look shocked. How long had the man been on desert duty? Did he know what it meant, to be in the middle of the Central Libyan?

"I see." The smooth pink face merely looked

contemplative. "Well, we have to get flares ready, in case. I take it we have petrol and oil available?"

Sergeant Watson thought, Why not make out a form and take it to the bloody stores?

"When we hear aircraft," Moran said, "we can set this whole thing ablaze in two minutes."

"But that lad's inside—the German boy!"

"I didn't mean it literally, Captain."

"Er, no. Well, I'd like to have your permission to drain a certain amount of petrol and oil from the aircraft, and get flares ready."

"Okay, but don't set the tanks on fire."

"Sarnt Watson! Oh, there you are. See what rag you can find—any kind of fabric, and some shallow dishes. Make some out of the metal panels if need be."

In a couple of minutes Moran followed him into the wreck and found the tool kits, helping him to slacken a fuel-pipe union. Harris was trying to do his best and there was no need to obstruct him. There was also the danger of what the medics called "post-crash inertia" setting in: the disinclination to make any effort once the worst had happened.

He wished Towns would straighten up.

By midnight the temperature had dropped to ten below zero.

They put jackets over the sleeping Kepel. Outside the wreck Harris had set a dozen flares ready for lighting in the form of an arrowhead. He had been trying to interest the others in the idea of survival.

"Towns tells me we have an emergency drinking tank holding ten gallons of water. With our water bottles and the two tins of orange juice we've found, there's a bit over eleven gallons all told. At a minimum of one pint per man per day, we have seven days' supply. I'd like to suggest that we institute a rationing scheme at once."

Watson had made a small oil lamp that could burn all night in the hull. They sat silent with the reflection of its flame bright in their eyes; but this, the only sign of vitality, was borrowed. No one answered Harris.

By the light of his electric torch, Bellamy had written in his diary:

I suppose it could have been much worse. The pilot brought her down like a feather, but we hit the only few rocks in the whole of this area. If the freight hadn't shifted we wouldn't have lost Sammy and Lloyd. I can't get them out of my mind, nor can anyone, I think. I wouldn't like to be the pilot. Thank God Albert's all right. I don't think I could have stood it if he'd bought it. Anyway they'll find us tomorrow. We're lucky.

Earlier, he had seen blood on Crow's hands.

"You get hurt, Albert?"

"Eh? Yes. Not much."

Afterward Bellamy had seen that someone had

been cleaning the blood from the smashed seats; he knew that would have been Crow. He never could bear untidiness.

"Re food." Captain Harris had tried again. "There's none on board except for the dates."

"Keep 'em, Cap," said Crow. There were two whole crates of the stuff, dried, packed and labeled, among the freight. He'd lost his appetite for camel crap the first month in Jebel Sarra.

Harris' pink face swung about in the light of the oil flame as he talked. "Even in their dried state there's some little moisture, of course, and if necessary we can last out for weeks, re food. We have to think very seriously about water, though."

He hoped it didn't sound as if he were panicking, but the instructions in his desert-survival pamphlet were quite clear: in the event of a party's becoming lost, the strictest rationing of water must be instituted forthwith, even if it were anticipated that a water point could be reached within a few hours or that a search party could be expected in the area.

"I'd be glad of your opinion, Towns." It was extraordinary that there should be so much difficulty in interesting these chaps in their own salvation.

"The few times I've been down in the desert," Towns said with an effort, "I've been seen within twenty-four hours."

"Then we'll hope for as much good fortune tomorrow." One or two of them were lying curled up against the cold, trying to sleep; and Harris gave it up. He asked the navigator, last thing, "Have we any wire cable we might use for an aerial?"

"I checked the radio soon after we landed. The valves are smashed."

"I see." Harris went outside, taking his sergeant with him. They began lighting the flares, because it would be hopeless trying to sleep unless something, at least, was being done toward the idea of staying alive.

Inside the wrecked hull Moran heard Trucker Cobb turning in his sleep, and wondered what state the man would be in tomorrow. According to Crow and Bellamy, Cobb had been going slowly round the bend at Jebel without telling anyone or even showing it for quite a time, preferring to fight it alone. It was the usual thing: mistakes made and, in this case, covered up; then hitting the bottle; finally the hallucinations—owls diving at him, lights weaving about in the dark on the far side of the derrick. They'd even sent out a search party from the camp one night to look for Trucker's lights: and that was when it all began to show.

On top of that, now, the crash. And Trucker was a big man. He would take some holding down if the rest of the screws got loose.

Moran heard movement on the other side, and murmured, "All right, Frankie?"

"Yep."

The flame of the lamp moved shadows about the curved hull roof. Cobb stirred again, trying to rid his head of something hard inside the duffel bag that was his pillow. It was the little transistor radio, and he nudged it to one side.

* * * * *

At midnight Cairo Radio reported calm air conditions reestablished over the main desert areas from the Hoggar Range in Algeria to the Red Sea.

Shipping along the southeastern seaboard of the Mediterranean was still meeting with very heavy swell, but the wind had eased to Force 5. The crippled tanker *Star of Egypt* was now making into Alexandria with an escort of two other ships.

During the successful rescue of the crew of a fishing vessel five miles north of Tocra off the Libyan coast, helicopters had reported sighting aircraft wreckage in the area. It was believed to be that of the Sahara Air-Freight Company's Skytruck, now overdue six hours at Sidi Raffa. A spokesman for the company had confirmed that the machine would have faced extreme difficulties in landing at Sidi Raffa during the sandstorm and in the absence of radio guidance. It was feared that the Skytruck had overshot the airfield on the coast and had come down in the sea, since its course from Jebel Sarra would have taken it across the coast at this point and into the area where the wreckage was seen.

Libyan Air Force planes embarking upon a night air search for the missing freighter had been recalled to base.

* * * * *

Starlight, falling across the ring of dunes, silvered the hoarfrost that was forming from the dew a little before dawn.

The lamp inside the dark hull had been put out some time ago, but the arrowhead of flares burned on steadily in the still air, signaling the empty sky.

CHAPTER
4

THEIR EYES WERE RED FROM WATCHING THE sky all yesterday, and stubble was on their faces. Already they had the look of the lost.

In the white noon heat of the second day, Captain Harris came into the shade of Moran's parachute that they had spread across the wreckage, and told Towns:

"It's time we tried marching out."

Towns screwed up his long eyes against the light. The parachute gave shade but its white silk glared as badly as the sky. He said conversationally, "I'm sticking."

"For how long? There's a limit, you know."

"For that long, then."

Harris squatted on the sand, lighting the last cigarette he possessed. "Of course you must do as you choose, but I shall leave at sundown this evening. I'm taking Watson and anyone else who wants to join us."

"Which way," Towns asked, "are you 'marching'?"

"That's where you and your navigator can help

me. How far are we from the nearest water point?" He looked at Moran. "You said you'd be making a second check."

After a moment Moran said, "How many will you be taking along, d'you know?"

"Not yet."

"Now is the time, maybe, to find out."

A group of them sat nearby, below the broken boom. Harris told them what he intended to do; and after a while he had all of them round him except for the injured Kepel and Trucker Cobb, who had not spoken a word since yesterday. Moran told them:

"I've spent a bit of time on this. It's not accurate but it's not far out. When I give exact figures you can take it there's a margin of error of ten or at most twenty percent." He gazed across the flat waste of sand where they had worked six hours yesterday digging out an immense SOS. In the night a small wind had softly obliterated it. "I put our position at 27 degrees North by 19 degrees East. We're in the middle of a circle of some hundred and sixty miles radius. Radius—not diameter. The circle goes through the three nearest water points: Marada, north; Tazerbo, east; and Namous, south. West of here the nearest place is Sebha, two hundred and eighty miles off. Can forget that. Nearest caravan track is the one going north-south between the Djalo and Tazerbo oases.

The nearest point of the track from here is two hundred miles off, due east. So we can forget east and west."

Towns had pulled a map out of his wallet of papers, and they spread it on the sand. Moran showed them Marada, a small water point inhabited solely by Africans. "A hundred and sixty from here. Say, London to Sheffield."

Harris tightened his mouth.

Loomis thought, New York City to Albany.

"That's the objective, then," said Harris. He hoped nothing untoward sounded in his voice.

"Or south, to Namous. About the same distance." Moran scratched at his stubble, unused to it. "Have you done any marching in desert terrain, Captain?"

"On exercise, that sort of thing."

"How far?"

"Oh, ten miles or so. Full pack, of course."

Moran nodded. "And plenty of water."

"Sufficient."

"I've done a bit of marching," Moran nodded, "in desert terrain. A bit more than you. It wasn't on exercise. I don't know what your practical navigation's like, but mine's not bad." He looked across the shimmering haze of the wastelands where they flowed through the horseshoe ring of dunes, as water flows through a harbor mouth and flows on until it meets the sky. "That's an ocean out there and you wouldn't get me to march ten paces from here because in the daytime it's hitting a hundred and twenty in the shade, and out there there's no shade. You'll be taking a pint of water a day with you, and you'll sweat ten."

He noticed that Sergeant Watson was listening hard to every word.

"We intend marching by night," Harris answered.

"Fine. In what direction?"

"We shall take a compass, of course."

"Tell me one day what it was reading when you passed the Jebel Haroudj Mountains here." He tapped the map. "They're mostly magnetic rock. Have you ever seen a compass do the twist?"

"One can steer by the stars." He had all the necessary instructions in the desert-survival booklet.

"Fine. And you know where you're aiming for. But you don't know where you started from. My calculations could be twenty percent in error. If they were *one* percent in error, Mr. Harris, and you marched a hundred and sixty miles by the stars, you'd pass the Eiffel Tower without even seeing it, in daylight. Look where Marada is, here. You miss that little bunch of trees and you wouldn't stop till you hit the coast anywhere between Sirte and Derna, three or four hundred miles off. You try for any of the other places, say the Tazerbo Group or Aozou, southeast, and miss them, and you'd finish up in the Sudan, a thousand miles from here. But you wouldn't miss them. You wouldn't even know where they were, to miss, because the stars move, and your compass would swing, and you'd go in a circle. Are you right-handed, Mr. Harris?"

"Of course."

"Then you'd go in a left-hand circle, because your right leg's more developed than the other one and it takes a longer step, and there's nothing in this world you can do about that. Nothing."

Under the glaring shade of the white silk, beautiful as an emir's tent, the others listened to Moran. Apart from his level voice there was the intense silence of the desert where there are no leaves for the wind to move, no birds, no animals or machines or any trace of man. It was a silence hardly ever found even in mid-ocean.

From where he sat, Crow could see the big hunched form of Cobb, crouching in the shade of the tailplane, quiet as a rock. Crow was beginning to worry about Trucker Cobb. Last night he'd had them all out of the hull because he'd seen lights on the horizon. And this time he'd insisted they were real. It had taken four of them to drag him back when he'd tried to walk to the horizon, and it had taken Loomis an hour to talk him out of a mood of smoldering anger. He'd been angry that they didn't believe the lights were real. All this morning he'd said no word to anyone.

"If you still mean to try marching," Moran was saying to Harris, "you should consider a few other things. This wreck and this chute are the only patch of shade in an area of some fifty thousand square miles of sand, so you'll need your cap. If another sandstorm blows up, you'll drown in it, because your reason will go. If it's sunshine and starlight all the way, you can walk straight into a patch of *fech-fech* and drown in that just the same. I saw a man do it, an Arab on a camel, and he never even had time to yell out." He watched Harris burning his fingernails on the butt of his last cigarette before he dropped it into the sand and circumspectly buried it with his foot. "You ever hear of a man named Joe Vickers?" Moran asked him.

Harris said, "No." But he was quite prepared to hear anything, except that he shouldn't try marching out.

"I knew Joe," Bellamy said.

"Then you tell the cap."

Bellamy said reluctantly, "He was on his own at the main derrick at Jebel after sundown, stowing some gear. The derrick was lit up and so was the camp, a mile away. A sandstorm got up—not a big one like the one we've just had, but it got up pretty quick, you know how they do—and he tried to walk back to the camp. A mile. We found him the next day, five miles into the desert, dead as a duck.

There's a big new lamp at the top of the Jebel derrick now—see it for miles even through rising sand. When it's switched on we call it 'lighting up for Joe.' We say it without thinking."

Harris stood up, tucking his uniform shirt in neatly at the belt. "What killed him?" He wasn't as tall as Cobb or Loomis but his head touched the dipping white silk canopy and he looked unkillable.

"The desert," Moran said.

"He must have panicked, of course."

"Sure he panicked. Once a man knows he's lost, his chances are halved. The desert does the rest. It's not always hunger or thirst or the heat or the distance you have to go. In the end it's the desert that kills."

"I see. Poor chap." And Crow suddenly admired the pink-faced robot standing in the middle of them with its principles clicking away like clockwork; because from any other man the "poor chap" would have been said in sarcasm. But you could tell he meant it. He was sorry for poor Joe Vickers.

"I must make a few preparations," Harris said to nobody in particular. "If anyone wants to think it over, I'll be delighted to have him join us at sundown when we leave." He ducked below the edge of the silk. "Sarnt Watson!"

*   *   *

In the brass heat of the afternoon Towns stood in the open with his sunglasses casting green shadows across his eyes, looking at the sky.

"I don't get it. I don't get it, Lew." He had said it all yesterday when he had stood staring at the sky like this.

"They're searching our track," Moran said, "that's all."

"We'd see them from here."

"We don't know where 'here' is, Frankie." He asked, "Would you say Harris has gone nuts in some quiet way?"

Towns looked down from the empty sky. "He won't go."

"He'll go."

"He can't. Christ Almighty, if *they* die too . . ."

He walked back to the wreck, alone; and Moran let a minute pass before he followed. It was no good telling Towns again it wasn't his fault but the meteorological station's. He had tried telling him but Towns had looked him in the face without friendship—"You want to get some conviction in your voice when you say that. Convince yourself first, and when you do, you'll still be wrong."

When Moran reached the canopy, Crow asked:

"What 'appened to the air search, Lew?"

"It may be on now."

"Christ, 'ow can they miss?" He and Bellamy had worked all morning, laying out another great big SOS on the sand with bits of ripped metal, seat fabric, anything handy. They'd got Tilney to help but he wasn't much use. He just kept on saying, "They'll find us, won't they? Won't they?"

It had made Crow sick to listen.

He watched Stringer, at it again.

One or two of them had noticed Stringer, and couldn't weigh him up. He didn't speak to anyone; he didn't seem to understand they were all in a bad spot; he was interested only in the wreckage, wandering round and round it, looking at the damage, hands stuck into his pockets and a handkerchief on his head. Stringer was the only one to have shaved. He had an electric shaver with a built-in transformer so that you could use it in the car; and it worked on the Skytruck batteries.

No one else had shaved, or washed. Towns had agreed with Captain Harris and the rationing scheme had begun already: one pint of water per man per day, no washing or shaving, with an extra allocation for Kepel if he needed it. They didn't think much about it; if you kept in the shade and didn't exert yourself you didn't sweat too much; but most of them knew this was partly an illusion: even in shade the heat evaporated the sweat as it sprang to the skin.

Loomis was another quiet one, saying little. The cable had come from Paris direct through the Jebel Sarra radio post. He had an apartment overlooking the Seine, and they had lived there for a year now. He flew back every month or two; and although they had been married for twelve years it was a succession of honeymoons; and because of this, and the interest of the work at the prospecting camps, he could stand the desert and its terrible size and loneliness. The desert he would not be able to stand was perhaps already opening in front of him, because the cable had said *urgent*.

He saw the word wherever he looked, huge against the sand, bigger than the SOS, while the minutes and the hours went by, and he was no nearer her.

The German boy complained of no pain today. He answered politely when they took it in turns to talk to him, and some of them left him after a minute or two, seeing that it was an effort for him. Bleeding had started again, perhaps because he had moved. A gold stubble was now on his face, but it made him look no older. He looked very young. He had asked only once how long it might be before they were rescued, and Towns had just said, "Not long." Every time he went near the boy he was afraid of the sour-sweet smell that would begin to rise from him if gangrene set in.

It was about the middle of the afternoon when Roberts came to Crow and said, "You can do me a favor if you like."

He had the monkey with him, tucked inside his

jacket. It still quivered in regular long-drawn spasms, its bright brown eyes slowly closing and then snapping open in renewed terror. When he had got it to drink some water for the first time since the crash it had gripped the rim of the metal mug with its miniature fist, to stare down at its reflection for as long as Roberts' patience had held out. Afterwards he'd tried to interest it in a mirror, in the likeness of its own kind whose company it lacked, but it hadn't worked.

Now he stood stroking the hard little head, asking Crow:

"You want to look after him for me, for a few days?"

Crow took an instant to think; then he said, "Christ, 'ave you gone daft?"

"He's only on loan, remember." He unbuttoned his jacket. "I can't very well take him with me."

Crow reached up his sharp bony hands and took the monkey, and Roberts' eyes had an odd smile suddenly in them. "There's quite a likeness. You might be brothers." He went to find Captain Harris, to tell him he'd be ready at sundown.

None of them thought, looking back, that there was any connection between Roberts' decision and Sergeant Watson's. It seemed pretty clear that Watson would have done what he did even if it had meant that Captain Harris would set out alone.

Hearing him shout, Towns went across to him.

Watson was sitting on the sand, flung out awkwardly, one foot buried in it. Sweat trickled from his temples and his dark-red face was pinched in pain.

"Twisted it," he said through his teeth, "twisted the bugger."

Some of the others came over and he was half carried back into the shade of the canopy, where they sat him down. Harris came up and Watson said between bouts of pain, "It's where we dug out the signal, sir—I fell in, see—sand covered it an' I didn't see it—" His breath hissed in through his teeth as Harris felt the ankle. "Twisted," he managed to get out. "Went right over."

Harris nodded. "Keep it still. I'm afraid we can't make a cold compress. But it's not broken."

In half an hour he came back to where Watson was still sitting propped against the hull, and eased off his boot.

"Try moving your toes, Watson."

It was an effort, but he managed.

"You're all right. Just a sprain." He straightened up. "I'm sorry this has happened. You won't be coming with me, of course."

Looking up at him, Watson decided to play it the way he'd often played it, the way these pipsqueaks liked it. They never saw through it, because they never wanted to.

"I wouldn't be much use to you, sir. I'd be lettin' you down, an' I wouldn't like to think that, never."

"Of course not. Accidents happen, Watson."

"As if this lot wasn't enough, eh, sir?"

"It's very bad luck. Don't let it worry you. It's you I'm thinking of—heaven knows how long you'll have to stay here before we can send help." He went back inside the hull, where Roberts was studying the map.

An hour before the sun went down, Trucker Cobb came to Harris, lumbering, his great hands hanging as if nerveless, his red hair unkempt. "You're leaving, I'm told."

"That's correct."

"I'm on, then. Who else is going?"

Captain Harris looked at him obliquely, aware of slow fright within himself. So far as he had ever found out, one thing could scare him above all others: the mere presence of a man who wasn't "quite right." He still remembered, too sharply, Cobb's wild eyes in the night when they had to stop him from walking to the horizon where he could see the "lights."

"I'm taking Mr. Roberts. Just the two of us." He fiddled with the small kit he was packing, aware of the presence of the huge man beside him in the baking heat of the hull. It was like being shut in with an unexploded bomb.

"And me," Cobb said. He didn't appear to understand.

Harris found himself listening to the ticking of

his own watch. He had no idea by how little or how much this man was mad, or how much it would take to send him over the edge. All he knew was that he would no more walk into the desert with Cobb than he would ride into it on a tiger. Moran had said, "It's not always hunger or thirst or the heat or the distance you have to go . . ."

"There's a risk of our getting lost out there." He heard his words forming without having thought them out properly. He noticed that Cobb's breathing was heavy. The heat, of course. "All the other chaps, except Roberts, have definitely decided to stay on, and I'm sure they're right." He mustered a tight smile—"Call me the restless type"—and the smile became frozen as he looked into the eyes of Cobb.

"They can do what they like. I can do what I like." He flung a big arm toward the open door of the hull and his shout rang in the confines, *"Jesus Christ, I've seen enough of that stuff, I've seen enough! You get that?"*

Harris spoke quietly, knowing now that he was committed to a risk he had never even considered; it was like diving into the sea from the breakwater and realizing that just below the surface there were rocks that you hadn't noticed. You couldn't stop or go back.

"We mustn't disturb poor Kepel. We'll talk outside." He laid a hand on the man's arm. It felt like a beam of living timber.

"He's as good as dead." Cobb stared into his face. "We all are—you know that. That's why you're going." He put his hand over Harris' that still lay on his arm; the great loose fingers were running with sweat. "You're taking me with you, son. You know the way."

Harris pulled his hand free as if from the gap of a slamming gate. Without moving Cobb bodily he couldn't get past him to the door of the hull. Beyond the door the sun was nearing the dunes. The coward's way out shamed him even as he took it. "We'll go and talk to the others before we leave."

"Fuck the others." Cobb's stare was bright, as if he were growing more and more pleased with the wonderful idea of going home with Harris. He looked like a man saved.

Harris saw, on the edge of his field of vision, the bright polish of his revolver holster. He had been of two minds, packing his basic kit, about taking the gun. In the open desert there was just a chance of running into a *razzia* of Bedu raiders. There weren't many left, and they never tried attacking an oil camp; but cattle raids were common, and the *razzias* were always armed. Two Christians alone in the desert would be dead meat. Not that one revolver would be any good. But there was the other matter. If he and Roberts got lost, and had no more water, the gun would enable them to die decently and still sane.

It was within reach of his hand, but he thought Cobb was near the edge: beneath the tousled red hair was the face of a child who has been promised a treat—the bright blue eyes were alive with anticipation. Thwart him now and he'd charge at a tank, let alone a revolver. And there was of course no question of shooting; it could be used only as a threat, a bluff.

Cobb must weigh fifteen stone and he was well over six feet high, the type of man to die quickly in the desert even with a double water ration. Harris himself was of average build, and Roberts was almost thin. Cobb would be the first to die if they got lost, and he wouldn't die sane; he wasn't sane now. They would have to give him part of their ration, have to wait for him when he lagged, to support him when he weakened. To no avail, in the end.

Even if he were sane, they couldn't take him.

Harris did something he had never done before. "All right, Cobb. Let's go."

CHAPTER 5

THE DUNES WERE TURNING MAUVE AS THE DAY ended. The sand still burned underfoot but the air was cooler.

They watched Captain Harris buckling his Sam Browne and settling the holster. They were all standing up, even Sergeant Watson. The gash on Loomis' cheek had darkened, the blood drying on the stubble. Cobb was somewhere on the other side of the wreck; it was worrying to hear the sobbing from such a big man.

Deceiving him deliberately—an action so strange to Harris that his voice had faltered—he had given Cobb ten minutes to pack a kit. It was the only way he could get out of the hull to talk to the others. They had agreed without any discussion; and it had been Loomis who had chosen to tell Cobb that he must stay with them. Cobb went wild and Loomis was down before the rest came in a pack; and the sand was still churned from the struggle. When he had begun sobbing, his eyes squinched within the big doughy face and his arms

56

flung out on the sand, they had left him, one by one. He had picked himself up, to trudge with his back humped and his eyes still shut in the hopeless rage of a child, knocking into the tail unit before he passed out of their sight.

Crow had made to follow, to comfort him, but Bellamy had stopped him. "He'd half kill you."

Harris had said stiffly, "I'm sorry; but we couldn't have taken him along, could we?"

"Would've been suicide," said Towns. "He'll be okay with us here."

Moran looked at the captain. "Set a good pace for the first hour. We shan't be able to keep an eye on him so easily when it's dark."

The sun was resting on the rim of the dunes when Harris said brightly, "Well, good-by, Watson. Up to you to hold the fort now!"

They called out good luck and then Harris and Roberts were walking side by side toward the gap in the dunes, their long shadows rippling across the sand.

Until the two of them were out of sight, the others remained standing, as if at some ceremony at sundown.

Towns' thick legs were astride and he gazed across the purpling sands with a kind of longing for those two men to get through alive; because two were dead and Kepel was going to die, and the score was mounting against him.

Moran, beside him, had his narrow head on one side as he watched the two men nearing the mouth of the dunes. He wondered what they had in common, that they alone should have chosen the long way home.

Loomis, with his long curving body against the side of the wrecked hull, looked away before they were out of sight, because already they looked halfway lost in the falling night; and the message he had given Harris to cable, if he could—*My darling, I am coming. Kim*—would never reach the house by the Seine.

The monkey was quiet in Crow's arms, and he didn't dare move in case it was sleeping. He'd offered twenty quid for little Bimbo, and now he would have offered twenty quid for Rob to keep him and stay here with him where there was a bit of safety.

Bellamy stood with his eyes half closed, his wrist still throbbing from the struggle with poor Trucker. In his mind he was putting the words down in his diary: *Tonight Rob left us, and Harris with him. I don't think we shall see them again.*

Tilney had his thin fingers trembling on a cigarette; there'd been no question what to do—go or stay, because if they reached anywhere they would send help back, and if they didn't, help would have to come anyway, would have to come. You could see a wrecked plane more easily, from the air, than

58

two or three men on their own. His mind trembled on the very words . . . *God, dear God, send help*.

Watson's face was shadowed in the fading light; his eyes gleamed in his dark face. *That'll take some of the piss out of him once he gets out there— that'll take the shine off his bloody Sam Browne.* He gave his officer a long-range burst in the back of the neck. If that didn't kill him the desert would.

Stringer stood alone near the port boom that he had been inspecting most of the day. His eyes blinked slowly, unseen behind the reflection of the sundown.

Then the gap in the dunes was empty. They moved their feet, looking at one another.

"There's ten of us now," said Crow to no one, and no one answered him.

* * * * *

The flares burned all night under the cold eyes of the stars. The sky and the desert were silent, and the only sounds in the expanse of what might have been a lifeless planet were those of men fitfully sleeping inside the dark wreckage of the airplane.

It had been too cold to sleep outside, but when the first tinge of rose colored the eastern slopes of the dunes there was no white of hoarfrost, because there had been no dew.

As the sun's light flowed against the hull, some of them awoke, to see the pink oblong of the doorway; and because their dreams had been of towns and trees and ordinary things they woke to the nightmare of the new day, remembering that the sunlit doorway led out to nowhere.

Some of them lay thinking, and trying not to think, trying to fall asleep again and lose themselves in the dream of being found. Tilney lay shivering, already dying his little deaths as the day began. Towns had dreamed of the future, and its voices had been shouting at him over and over again, shouting *pilot error . . . pilot error . . .* Kepel gazed at the now red oblong of the doorway, trying to remember a time when he had not lain here with his body broken and the smell of his sweat and his dirt sickening him. Crow looked along the distorted perspective of the hull at the litter of seats and the ripped metal panels, at the others who still slept or stirred or sat propped in the seats like passengers who were going somewhere; then he rolled over quietly and got to his hands and knees, crawling over the hunched shape of Bellamy and going through the doorway into the dawn.

The arrowhead pattern of flares burned weakly and a small wind, unfelt against his face, drew from each flame a thread of black oil smoke, making a skein across the smoothness of the sand. The sun's half-circle was enormous on the ridge of the dunes, and rays of its red light slanted down through, the last shades of night, as in a biblical painting.

As he made his way round the wreck he touched its metal, brushing his fingers along it, but it was dry; there'd been no dew. When he had looked everywhere, under the low shelf of the starboard mainplane and in the troughs and hollows where the hull had plowed into the sand, he went back into the hull, and found Bellamy awake, and said:

"Cobb's gone."

The sun's light was in Bellamy's eyes and he moved his head away. He'd been dreaming of rain on windows in the house in Reading.

"Cobb?"

"He's gone."

Bellamy's mouth was stale and dry and he began fishing for his water bottle, and remembered that there'd be a single mugful for the day. He took one swig to rinse his mouth.

"Where?" he asked Crow.

"Where is there to go, for Cri' sake?" Crow left him, and walked away from the wreck as far as smooth sand, and urinated. Watching the stream of water, he thought what a shocking waste it was. Couldn't you distill this stuff somehow, get even an eggcupful out of it, enough to keep you alive another few hours? It was shocking, like peeing gold.

When he came back to the wreck, Bellamy was outside, the sun bright on his stubble. "We'd better have a look round, Albert."

In the low sun the sand was heavily marked near

the wreck, and they picked up three trails, two of them side by side. Harris and Roberts. The other one joined them, halfway to the mouth of the dunes, and then merged with them.

"Oh, bloody murder," Crow said. "That's it, then. Gone after them." They followed the trails to the far side of the dunes, and stopped. Ahead of the trails the desert lay flat and gold and unbroken, and Bellamy remembered how Moran had said, "That's an ocean out there." It was the first time he'd seen land so empty, and so vast. At Jebel Sarra and the other drillings there had always been something for the eye to hold on to—the derrick, sticking up like the skeleton of a church, the roofs of the camp buildings, the trucks and stationary engines scattered about, and even, at Jebel, the Maffa-Soud Oasis right on the south horizon, its date palms like a puff of green smoke. Here, when you turned round, there were only the dunes, and inside them the wreck of the plane.

"God, it looks small from here, Albert."

"Even from 'ere. No distance. N' wonder they 'aven't seen us yet from up top."

"They haven't even looked." Since the plane had crashed there'd been no sound, anywhere, louder than a man's voice.

Crow turned again and looked along the line of the trails. "I s'pose it'd be a bit daft to follow 'em, Dave."

"In this?" The sun had been up less than an hour and the sky was already a blinding glare more white than blue, and their stubble itched with sweat.

"He must've left quiet," Crow said. "None of us 'eard 'im."

"I thought I heard someone go out, sometime in the night. I supposed he'd gone for a pee." He remembered Trucker's dreadful sobbing, last night on the other side of the wreck, no sound of a sane man. But with people like him, who went round the bend, there was often a lot of cunning left in their heads. Trucker had meant to go with Harris and Rob; they'd stopped him, but he'd meant to go; and now he'd gone. There was no telling when he'd left, how much start the other two had on him since sundown last night. He must have taken a torch, though even by starlight the tracks would have been clear enough to follow.

Crow was saying, "If he's caught up with 'em, that's their lot, Dave. And his."

"We should've watched him closer." He turned his back on the north, where the trails led, not wanting to think about those three, Trucker sweating his heart out under the killing sun and seeing mirages of his own mad making, giving the other two no peace, shouting at them with his eyes wild and that awful look of a lost child in them, till Captain Harris would wish he could just pull his gun and shoot in self-defense—because that's what you could call it. Alone, the two of them stood a chance of hitting a water point, if Moran's calculations were wrong: and that was what Harris was staking his life on. With a man already mad before thirst set in, there wouldn't be a hope. You could shoot poor Trucker and get away with it in any court; but Harris wouldn't shoot, because a man like Harris would never get away with it in his own conscience.

"Come on," Crow said. "We got the 'ousework t' do."

They began walking back through the mouth of the dunes. Even from here, small though the wreck looked, they could hear voices coming from it, as the others woke and talked; and there was another sound on the air.

Crow heard it first and stopped in his tracks, hitting Bellamy's arm. *"Dave!"* in a hiss of breath. They stood still, listening to the thin steady drone, disbelieving it; then Crow was spinning round with his hand up to his eyes to shade them from the circling glare of the sky as he stared upward, seeing the black dot of the plane wherever he looked, seeing it even when he was forced to look down at the sand with his eyes streaming from the glare.

Bellamy hooked his fingers into cylinders like field glasses to cut out all the glare he could, squinting through them in a slow arc as he turned full circle, sighting the low sky just above the horizon, where a plane would first appear.

The thin drone was not loudening, but it was still there in the air. Now it was drowned by Crow's laughter and Bellamy took his hands down and stared at him. The tears were shining down Crow's face and he couldn't move for laughing.

The words came out in jerks. "That little bleeder—it's that little bleeder at it—Stringer—'avin' a bleedin' shave."

Bellamy listened again. It was right: the sound was coming from the wreck. Stringer's electric shaver. He gave Crow a push that sent him staggering.

"Shuddup, for God's sake! I must say you've got the most peculiar bloody sense of humor!"

They walked back, side by side, to the mess of the airplane. Stringer was standing in the doorway like a bird on a perch, blinking through his glasses at the world outside. His face looked cool and smooth, and Crow looked up at him.

"You 'ad a nice shave, 'ave you then?"

Bellamy took him away before he began laughing again about how bloody funny it was that it hadn't been a search plane up there looking for them. A perfect scream, with five days' water ration left and no hope of getting more.

They did the "housework" before the noon heat

65

drove them under the canopy; the others, except Stringer, helped. The huge SOS sign had sand on it, blown up by a breeze in the night; they brushed it and stacked away the magnesium panels that were kept near the flares at night, ready for burning to give an intense white light. Now it was day, and in their place they put the heliograph reflectors ready, the odd panels they had taken from the wrecked starboard boom that Harris had told Watson to polish with the button polish in his kit. Towns kept the box of emergency flares ready just inside the door of the hull, the pistol with them.

It was like spinning a spiderweb, Crow said, in the hopes of catching a fly.

At exactly noon by Moran's watch they set the big oil flare burning, the one that Captain Harris had asked for. Its black column of smoke stood against the sky, higher than they could look without being blinded. For four days they would make the signal from twelve to one o'clock, so that Harris and Roberts would have a chance of finding their way back if they were lost. After four days, he had told them, they needn't bother.

The rest of the engine oil was being kept in reserve for burning when search planes were heard in the area. The night flares used very little.

The noon torpor had set in. It was the hour when they could no longer stand in the open sun, or touch metal, or stare at the horizons of the dunes, hoping to see aircraft; it was the hour when all they could think of was the shape of their water bottles, more beautiful than a woman's body. They sat in the glaring shade of the silk, waiting. Between moments of talking, the hot white silence of the sky pressed down. In this kind of silence one could hear how big the desert was.

Crow went quietly into the hull to talk to the German boy, but Kepel slept, with a shaft of sunlight striking from a hole in the roof where a stanchion had broken a panel away. The boy's head was gold in the light, his face too, where the sweat gleamed on the stubble; he looked like a sleeping god. Crow found some fabric and stuffed it into the hole, but Kepel's face still seemed lit with the last of life.

The monkey was awake but wouldn't drink.

"Bimbo," Crow said softly, "poor ole Bimbo, you're all right, mate."

He could see his own reflection in the small beast's eyes. What was it thinking? What sort of thoughts did a monkey have? The same as they all had, now. Thirst. But he couldn't make it drink. He came away and sat outside again.

Stringer had left them. Looking round the wreck again in the full sun, like a clot.

Tilney went to fetch another handful of dates. He'd been eating them like sweets for two days now.

Moran went off to urinate.

Loomis decided to take his second drink of the

day, one mouthful from the water bottle. He went out of sight to do it, because some of them had already drunk the whole of their day's ration, and the sight of his raised bottle would do them cruelty.

Bellamy sat propped against a parachute pack, his eyes shut against the glare. His sunglasses had been jerked from his head in the crash, and were broken too badly to use. He heard Crow saying, "We're lucky, you know."

Bellamy looked at him. "Lucky?"

"Bein' 'ere. Not out there."

He was thinking of Harris, and Rob. And poor Trucker.

"Yes. We are."

The great silence came back.

Sergeant Watson hummed a tune from the war, and after a while saw the others looking at him, and stopped.

"Your fags all gone, Dave?"

"Last night."

Tilney ate his last date and sat silent for a time. They could hear his breath trembling. "They'll have to find us," he said. "They'll have to. Won't they?"

No one answered him.

Poor little bleeder, Crow thought. He said to Bellamy, "You 'ear about the three tortoises?"

"What?" Bellamy kept his eyes closed.

"They was sittin' by a big rock on the seashore. Tom, Dick an' 'Arry. It was a stinkin' 'ot day, like we got 'ere, you might say, so they tossed up 'oo should go an' fetch some beer."

Loomis came back, stooping under the edge of the silk, and sat down quietly.

" 'Arry lost, so 'e started off, see. After 'e'd bin gone six months, Tom said to Dick, 'My cripes, ole 'Arry's bin gone 'ell of a time, 'asn't 'e?' Then they 'eard 'Arry's voice comin' from be'ind the big rock. 'Any more talk like that,' 'e says, 'an' I won't go at all.' "

Watson gave a barroom laugh, and the silence came down again. Crow sat biting his lip and cursing himself, but it was too late. He shouldn't have talked about beer.

They listened to Tilney breathing; it was the sound of fear itself.

The heat pressed at their faces. The column of oil smoke laid a shadow across the sand, a pathway ending nowhere.

Someone had come back under the canopy and Bellamy opened his eyes and saw Stringer. He stood there looking down at them all, until they wondered what he wanted. Against the glare of the sand they could see nothing of his face but the reflection across his glasses. When he spoke he was looking at Towns.

"I've been examining this plane." It was all he said.

Perhaps he wanted to know if anyone was listening before he went on.

"You have?" Towns said.

"Yes." He had a light, wary voice, like a nervous schoolboy's. "We've got all we need here to build a new one, and fly it out."

The seven men looked up at him in the silence. There was not much of him but a thin silhouette and the glint of his glasses.

Towns said, "Are you kidding?"

Stringer turned away. "I thought you'd say something like that." He left them, his shoulders in a sulk.

After a minute Crow said, "That wasn' a very good joke, was it?"

Bellamy said, "Better than the one about the tortoises."

The silence pressed in about them.

CHAPTER
6

HIS SHADOW LAY CURVED ACROSS THE BROKEN panels of the hull, motionless, and the fierce light of the sun shone through a lens of his glasses, throwing a jewel of colors beside the shadow of his face. The knots in the handkerchief on his head stuck out from the shadow like little horns, as if the god Pan had sired a freak, a beast with a curved back and a jewel for an eye.

He touched a metal spar to feel if it was broken at the hidden end but drew his hand back in pain. He would never learn, he thought. His hands were blistered on palms and fingertips after two days of poking about in the wreckage. You could fry an egg on this mainplane, as the saying was.

His mouth was parched; and this was the only reminder that he possessed a body that was shortly going to die. It didn't worry him; it was no good getting upset; but it would be a shame, certainly, to have to die when he had just created the beautiful problem. It looked like being the only problem he had never solved. He almost wished he had never thought of it.

A lot of the freight had come crashing through the hull at this point: the crated drilling bits had gone wild when the machine had spun; they had been hurled forward by the first deceleration phases, to smash across the rear seats until the machine had spun; then the centrifugal force had carried them through the side of the hull, and now they were tumbled on the sand, some of them with fragments of flesh adhering to them, the blood dried black. He had noticed it yesterday, and had wondered why there were no flies, until he realized that nothing could live here; not even a fly.

His mind juggled with numbers and the names of the things he loved: dimensions, weights, moment-arms and ratios, the estimated lift, drag and incidence of airfoil sections, the aspect and chord and camber of the thing that he loved above all others: the wing. He stood dreaming about them, a poet rummaging for rhymes among the wreckage of all these tumbled words.

The problem was beautiful, but not intricate. It was a pity to leave it unsolved. He had never turned his back on a problem in all his life, but there was no choice now. You could say that dying was a way of turning your back on everything.

A shadow was moving toward his own and he resented it at once. It was an hour since he had left them, and he still hated them for not agreeing with his idea.

"We haven't seen you before, on the oil runs."

He closed his eyes for a moment as if by shutting the man out of his sight he could stop him existing. The vast hot silence went on, the sweeter to him because it wouldn't last much longer.

"You a driller?"

"No," he said and turned to look at the man. It was the navigator. He didn't hate the navigator so much, because he had a technical mind, and thought in figures.

"You didn't come out here on a vacation," Moran said, and Stringer resented him again.

"Oddly enough, I did." People jumped to conclusions too easily. "My brother's an analytical geophysicist at the Jebel Sarra camp. I've been to visit him." He wouldn't mind if they talked about his brother; he was proud of Jack, who had a wonderful mind.

Moran stood with his hands on his hips. The sweat ran down his flanks and he wondered how in hell the kid could just stand here for hours in the full sun. There didn't even seem to be any sweat on him. But he had to be talked to, about what he'd told them a while back. If they were all going nuts they might as well go nuts this way.

"You in the same line?" he asked.

"Line?"

"Geophysics."

"No."

Moran waited but nothing happened. His feeling about the kid was right: you had to wind him up gently before he'd tick. It was like that with a lot of the back-room types. They weren't really with you.

"What line are you in, then?"

Stringer moved his feet in the sand, looking along the tilt of the mainplane as if he were searching the wreckage for the answer. Moran went on waiting.

"Aircraft design."

"That so? How long've you studied?"

Stringer's narrow face turned to look at Moran; his eyes blinked slowly. "Studied what?"

"Aircraft design."

"How old do you think I am?"

Head on one side Moran said, "Twenty, twenty-two."

"I'm over thirty. I've been chief of design at Kaycraft for two years."

Moran nodded, unsurprised, because you could never doubt anything this kid said, the way he said it.

"It's the clean shave that makes you look young."

"I never like going unshaven."

Moran nodded again. The remark was right in character: young Mr. Stringer liked to shave every day, as was decent. He'd brought along his shaver, into the Central Libyan Desert, and had plugged it in. Everybody had the right to go nuts the way he chose.

"You said," Moran told him, thinking how loud his voice sounded in the silence, "you'd been examining the plane. You said something about making it fly."

"I'm not prepared to discuss that." Stringer turned away and pretended to study the angle of the wrecked boom with concentration; and Moran thought, Christ, it's going to take hours, but I've got to find out.

With a show of disinterest, with casual questions, and with all the patience he could muster in the grilling heat of the long afternoon, he began stalking Stringer.

* * * * *

The day ended impossibly. It couldn't be true that the sun was setting again on silence.

They began standing up, as if to watch the dunes turn red and to admire the colors that crept across the sand as twilight closed in; but they were really rising to their feet in silent protest: their days were numbered, and here went another one without a sign that they weren't already forgotten by the world.

"Aren't we important, or something?" Bellamy

asked, and Crow looked at him with a swing of his sharp head. It wasn't like Bellamy to show his feelings.

"I don't get it," Towns told them. "I don't get it."

Tilney moved about as if going somewhere and remembering there was nowhere to go. "We should have gone with those two—we should have listened to Captain Harris. Oh, God—we can't stay here any more, can we? Can we?" But he was talking to himself or the darkening sky, standing with his back to them, already lost. Only two things existed for him: himself and the idea of dying.

For his sake Loomis said, "They'll show up to-morrow, large as life."

Crow felt for a cigarette, remembered he had none, and said, "Far as the search-an'-rescue organization goes in this bit o' the globe you can stuff it." There was a terrible relief in thumbing your nose at the only hope you'd got.

Loomis watched the last of the daylight leaving the sky, and thought, If anyone tells her I'm missing in a plane smash, she'll think of me as dead, and she'll stop fighting to live. We've sometimes said it aloud—if one of us dies, the other one won't want to go it alone; maybe a lot of people in love have said that, but I think we meant it. I think I mean it now. If I knew she was dead, now, I'd walk out there and these boys could have my water ration. She mustn't die, but most of all she mustn't die because she thinks she's alone now.

He talked to Jill across the shadows of the dunes and the miles beyond, facing the north as the stars appeared, because telepathy was a proven thing. He repeated silently the stilted phrases used in telegrams, saying that he was alive and well and that she must get better quickly.

Someone had lit the oil lamp and its smoke climbed in a dark vine to spread against the white silk canopy.

"Who's got a fag?" asked Watson. Their silence said, Not me.

"I got a bit for the *Mirror* when I get back," Crow said. " 'Ow I Stopped Smokin' in Three Days."

It was now that Moran, sitting down on the still-warm sand near Towns, said, "I've been hours with Stringer, and he's right. It's possible."

A light breeze was rising from the north, and the silk stirred above their heads.

"What is?"

"Given a month, we could fly out."

In this silence even a whisper carried; you never spoke to one man but to all. Tilney was looking at Moran and they could hear his tremulous breathing.

Towns' voice was like a shout: *"Okay, then we'll fly out!"* Moran's scalp crept. *"Start her up, why don't you!"*

Elleston Trevor

Loomis came away from the hull and sat down; their words had got in the way of his.

Bellamy looked round for Stringer but couldn't see him. The breeze moved the wick of Watson's lamp and their shadows danced along the hull, suddenly released.

"I was only just saying, Frank. Just for the laugh."

Towns got up and the silk billowed as his head touched it. "Here's me laughing my eyes out! Now we'll talk about something else, okay?"

"What you on about?" Crow demanded. Towns went to stand outside the canopy, his head up to watch the sky, by habit.

"It was just something to think about," said Moran, worried by the wildness of Towns' voice. "Stringer designs aircraft, and he's convinced me we could take this crate apart and build a smaller one from the bits. That's all." He didn't understand why he'd told Towns at all; it was pretty stupid and he wished to God he'd kept his trap shut. "It's nothing to get serious about. It's just a mental exercise."

Crow got up. "Then I 'ope you enjoy it, cock." He went into the hull to look at Bimbo.

Watson said, "Given a month, we could walk home, couldn't we?"

"Sure," Moran said. "Forget it."

"I don't see the point," said Bellamy.

"There isn't any point." Moran got up and left them, not going near Towns.

78

"I thought he meant it," Tilney said like a child. "I thought he meant we could fly out," like a child told that he couldn't go to the party. Bellamy moved away from him, unable to comfort him. At the oil camp he had never seen much of the kid: Tilney was a clerk with a bicycle and a sheaf of papers, a messenger; it had never been his face you looked at but the paper he brought for you. Here in the wan lamplight he looked only too human, with the shine of sweat on the soft stubble and the bright eyes escaping the moment you looked him back.

"We're here for keeps," said Watson, "don't worry." Bellamy wondered if he meant to frighten the kid on purpose. "Look at it this way—it's been three days now, and not a smell of 'em. If they was looking for us at all, they'll've packed it in by now. It's only sense."

"You ever heard of hope?" Bellamy asked him.

"I'm not a man to kid meself, that's all." He uncorked his water bottle. He had rationed himself with half the bottle for the night, next swig at sunup; but once his mouth was pressed to the cool metal neck he sucked until it was empty, feeling drunk and at peace because no one had hollered out "Sarnt Watson!" for twenty-four hours now, and no one was ever going to say it again.

Bellamy went into the hull to get away from the sound of the water bottle. Today his lips had started to crack. He took a look at Kepel, whose eyes were shut.

"All right, kid?" he murmured, but Kepel didn't open his eyes. His breathing was unsteady. Maybe Towns had given him another shot.

Bellamy thought, when the time comes, he'll be the only one who won't suffer, even if I have to give him the overdose myself. He shone the torch downward and saw that there was urine in the basin, so he took it outside and put the empty basin back. Crow was at the rear end of the hull, nursing the monkey.

"The stink's appalling," Bellamy said.

"Get yourself a clothes peg then." He caressed the small knob of hair.

"Has it drunk any water yet?"

" 'Ad 'alf my bleedin' ration for the day." He sounded proud of it.

"You're mad, then."

"That's me."

"Well, don't be a bloody fool, Albert. You know the odds. It's going to be your life or his."

"My ration, ain't it?"

"I'm buggered if I'm standing by while you go round the bend."

Crow swung his sharp nose up and said, "Little ole Albert does what 'e bleedin' likes in this life, mate."

"Then you won't have long to do it." He balanced the torch on the jumble of smashed seats and found his diary, aching not to have said that. He wrote:

The third day. No sign of search planes. Wonder if Rob and Harris are getting anywhere. Poor Trucker, can't get him out of my mind. Today the thirst's started, the real thing. Kepel still hanging on, almost wish he wouldn't. We're all feeling the strain now, me included, and Albert's giving his ration to the monkey. No cigs left, not that I could stomach one with a mouth like this.

For the first time and quite without thinking he began the last sentence with a phrase belying hope: *If anyone ever reads this, there's only one thing we want to ask. Why didn't anyone look for us?*

He closed the book. The smell of the animal was awful.

"Are you going to sleep outside with that thing tonight?" he asked Crow.

" 'E'd catch 'is death!"

Bellamy got up and put his jacket on, and with his knife began slitting at the fabric of the wrecked seats, bitterly enjoying the rip of the blade through the padded plastic, cutting and slashing until he had three or four panels. It had no warmth in it, but it would keep off the frost.

He shut his knife with a click and went out through the doorway into the clean air, saying nothing more, because it had been said.

*   *   *

81

The stars hung above him diamond-sharp. Every minute one of them and then another seemed to break free of the black stillness and race in a curve across the sky.

He had been trying to guess where the next meteor would strike, watching a part of the sky and then being fooled, time after time. He had to keep his mind off three things: the silence, the stillness, and thirst. At some time in the night he had slept, and the cold had waked him. A few minutes ago he had looked at his watch and seen that it would be dawn in an hour. The act of moving his arm had set him shivering, and there was the crackle of frost on the fabric. He could see the white of the frost along the ridge of the dunes where the starlight struck.

There'd been a bad time in the middle of the night when his thoughts had fastened on to Crow and his stinking monkey; he had lain pitying himself for having to freeze out here; he had lain loathing Crow for his selfishness, thinking back through all the years he had known him, to remember every mean act of Crow's that he could call to mind, reveling in his grudge until it bored him and he felt rid of it. Crow was Crow, take him or leave him. There were worse vices than loving animals.

His legs were cramped again and he moved them, hearing the dry crackle of the frost; and it was a minute or two before he realized his luck. Carefully, so as not to get sand on the fabric, he eased himself from under the panels and knelt down, and began licking them.

The pain in his tongue made him stop, every few seconds; then he licked again, crouched like a beast at a pool, while his mouth ached at the cold and the sweetness and his jaws grew numb. Sometimes he swung his head to the east to make sure it was not coming, the natural enemy of all desert animals, the sun. And then, sitting on his haunches with his mouth cool and moist, he looked across to the wreckage of the plane, appalled at how slowly his brain was working, at the criminal waste of time.

The cramp in his legs pitched him down once as he stumbled over the sand and as he ran the rim of the dunes burned red in the first rays of the sun. He ducked below the edge of the silk canopy that was drawn taut under its thick covering of frost and clambered into the hull, shaking them one after another:

"Gimme a hand outside! Come on—gimme a hand outside!"

CHAPTER
7

THEY RECKONED THERE WAS A FULL GALLON.

The sun was already warm on their bare arms and the sand was soft again, the frost all gone. Within this hour the scene had changed so completely that Bellamy wondered if it was really the same place: the great roof of stars, the black and silver of night and star and frost, the icy cold had all gone and here the sun lit the sand grain by grain with an intense light that hurt the eyes, and the heat rose everywhere. This hot gold world seemed here forever.

They stood round the pool and looked down at their faces. The morning was full of treasure. A full gallon.

By the time Bellamy had got them out of the hull the sun was above the dunes and the frost was already dew. They had taken down the white silk canopy without letting it drag in the sand, and they had wrung it out yard by yard over the wide dish they had made by creasing a metal panel three times toward the center. Now they looked down at the pool, intoning as if at a shrine:

"It's not dead clear."

"It's drinkable."

"It'll taste of the dope on the chute silk."

"We should worry."

"Must be a gallon."

"More."

"Christ, I've never seen s'much water. Who's for a swim?"

"Who'd've thought, though? All that much!"

"There's a lot of silk there, you know."

"Know how much a brick holds, when it's wet?"

"No."

"Pint."

"Christ, can anyone see any bricks?"

"Right," Towns said, "let's get it into the emergency tank before it evaporates."

They argued cheerfully about this: if they poured it into the tank the taste of the dope would taint what was left in it already. If they shared it out they might spill some, and anyway the measure couldn't be judged. Whatever they did, they had to get it out of the heat, and quick.

Like boys with a new puppy they didn't know what to do with it next. Towns won: it went into the tank; then they performed the solemn rite of filling their bottles turn by turn, a double ration for Kepel, who was conscious and asking questions. He had heard scraping, outside the hull, near where he lay.

"We were scraping the frost off," Moran said, crouching by the boy, half-naked and black-stubbled like a mariner pitching a yarn. "Didn't get much—about a mugful, but tomorrow we'll get it organized." His empty mug was still in his hand; there was a drop in the bottom and he tossed it down like a pearl, feeling so good that it irked him to talk to this smashed-up kid. It would take more than a mug of dirty water to put Kepel right. "How d'you feel, son?"

Kepel looked steadily at the stubbled face of the navigator, and knew that Moran would find an excuse in a minute to leave him. Kepel had passed the first day dreaming nightmares about his family and Inga, whose long fair hair had been on fire, because the morphia had unleashed dreadful things in his brain; he had passed the waking hours in thinking coolly of the house with the long low eaves and the carved shutters, and of his mother and father, and Inga, her skirts and her smile. The second day he had begun studying the faces that came to see him, and now he knew which ones would give him a dutiful few minutes and slowly hurry away, and which ones, despite their natural hate of a freak broken body, would stay for a long time, talking about their families in England, about anything they could think of except the crash and the heat and his legs. Moran was the only one—since Captain Harris had gone—who ever asked him about himself. The others were afraid he would tell them things that would sicken them: the pain, the imprisonment, the wish to weep.

"I feel quite well, thank you."

"It won't be long now. We've got plans. Tell you about it as soon as it's all worked out." He tossed the mug to his mouth again, pretending there was another drop, using the gesture as an aid to his escape, straightening up and saying, "Don't forget, if there's anything you want, just ask. Anything's yours, son, if we've got it."

He went off slowly as if reluctant to leave, thinking, When you're on top of the world, you'll promise anything to anyone. If it ever came to the push though, how much of his ration would he give to the kid, to keep him alive? You didn't have to think about things like that. Wait till they came at you, and face them then.

The others were still talking, on their feet, gesturing, arguing, even the quiet soldier, Watson, putting in a word or two. The canopy had been draped across the hull and boom again: it was meant to save your life, Moran thought, when you dropped out of a plane; but it was doing as good a job here, giving them water and shade.

Crow and Bellamy were sorting over one of the tool kits from the freight, trying to find a spanner that wasn't sprung, a file that wasn't broken off at the tang, a drill that wasn't burned blue. There were five boxes of the stuff, all of it in a bad way, because the Skytruck was shipping it out together with the big drilling bits for replacement at Sidi Raffa. Towns wasn't among the group and Moran found him talking to Stringer on the other side of the tail unit.

"Is it a go?" he asked Towns.

"How in hell can it be?"

Moran left them. It was up to Stringer. Stringer had convinced him yesterday; maybe he could convince Frankie today.

Loomis was carefully cutting off the legs of his slacks above the knee, and Moran said, "I'd value your opinion."

Loomis straightened up and looked down at him, the clefts set in his cheeks as he thought before speaking.

"I'm a geologist. I don't know a great deal about airplanes. I think Stringer does. I've listened to him and I know you have. Could be it's technically possible. Then there's the other thing: water." He turned his head and saw Tilney near them and said to Moran, "I'd like to show you something." He took him around the nose of the hull and hooked his arm through the curling tip of the starboard propeller blade, talking quietly. "I haven't said this to anyone—but that was a north wind that got up in the night, bringing water from the sea. It won't be like that every night. If we could reckon on a gallon a day, regular, fine. We can't. Then there's nourishment. You can't live for very long on just dried dates, even though we've crates full of them. We need greenstuff and we haven't any. In a week there isn't going to be a great deal of physical strength left in us, not for heavy work. If we were going to use our sense we'd trap all the water we could, and eke out the supplies, and lie still all day in the shade so we wouldn't sweat too much. We'd conserve our strength for the day when we had to get up and wave our arms at the first airplane we saw. I think that's pretty obvious."

He drew his long fingers round the curve of the twisted propeller blade, looking along the line of the tilted wing.

"But I think there's a chance, however small, of getting some of this junk off the ground again, and I believe in Stringer. So I'm ready to start. How about you?"

"It's as good a way of going nuts as any."

Loomis said very seriously, "If we're going to do this thing, that's an essential: to be nuts. It's like walking a tightrope. Never look down."

They couldn't persuade Towns.

Moran had known him three years but even in the intimacy of a flight deck you don't learn all there is to learn of a man in three years. He thought at first that Towns was digging his heels in because he knew there wasn't the spirit left in him to try the impossible. Towns so often stood looking across at the two mounds of sand where Loomis had stuck the cross. Then Moran thought he was testing them all, trying to find out how serious they were, trying to make them persuade him at all costs. He didn't see, for days, what Towns was up against.

But he listened to Stringer for an hour and Stringer gave him a complete breakdown on the work that would be necessary, even the timing of separate operations and the sequence in which they would have to be done. Sometimes, when he thought Towns wasn't listening, he stopped, and sulked in silence, until Moran got him to go on again. It was the kid's tone that gave a kind of weird feasibility to the whole idea: he spoke as if they were sitting in an aircraft hangar in England, with a mains-voltage supply and water in every tap.

"There's no component problem, you see. The Skytruck is a twin-boom design, and the port boom isn't damaged. There's been some rotational strain to the port engine shaft because the airscrew hit the sand, but not badly, because we were in a left-hand spin across the ground and it kept the port components high—airscrew, mainplane, boom and tail-plane. I think the shaft would stand more work. We would clear the carburetor of the sand that choked it in flight. The Coffman starter is undamaged, of course, so that we could start up the port engine without any difficulty. We have fuel in the port tank sufficient for a longer flight than we need. The coolant tanks are intact. We have enough oil if we don't use too much for lamps and the smoke signal for Captain Harris. The hydraulics have leaked most of the fluid away, but I have worked out direct rod controls. That is no problem."

He was drawing a five-barred gate on the sand as he talked, making five lines and crossing them out, smoothing the sand over and starting again squatting on his haunches, thin, dedicated to his every word, and looking, with his smooth-shaven face and rimless glasses, like a youthful Gandhi.

Towns leaned against the hull with his legs drawn up and his head tilted back. Moran couldn't see his eyes behind the dark-green sunglasses; they might be shut. He seemed to be listening.

"I've taken some rough measurements," the light toneless voice went on. "We have enough H-section bar in the cargo monorail and hull longerons to make up a skid cradle for take-off. I don't think we could repair the undercarriage. Would skids work on this sand?"

He looked up quickly at Towns, and Moran hoped he'd been listening because it sounded like a sudden catch question to find out. They looked like needing this kid badly and he was easy to scare off.

"They might," Towns said, not bothering to open his eyes.

Stringer licked his dry lips. "There is a problem with the wing root attachments because we shall have to fit the tapered bolts the wrong way round in the lugs. But we have room to mount a king post behind the engine cage and take rigging cables out to the wing. I see no problem with the tail unit because the port section is intact and we have enough left of the center section between the booms to provide the starboard area. We shall use two panels from the damaged boom to heighten the fin and give us increased keel surface, because we shall need it. I see no problem with—"

"You don't?" Towns' eyes had come open and his head was forward to stare at Stringer. The sweat coursed from his gray temples where the veins pulsed in the heat. "You don't see many problems, Mr. Stringer! Let me throw you a few!"

He stared at the narrow schoolboy face with its surprised brown eyes behind the spectacles. The tight straight mouth had come open, but at least the voice had stopped, that was something. You couldn't go on listening to that damned monotone forever—there was nothing human in it, no compromise. "There is a problem." "There is no problem." World without end. The kid had it all tied up.

"If I've got it right," he said heavily, "we just unship the starboard wing and stick it on the port boom?"

In the silence Moran kept a grip on hope. They would need Towns too.

"Well, yes," Stringer said. "As I say, the tapers would be the wrong way—"

"Hell with the tapers! You know how much that main-plane weighs?" He watched the lizard eyes blink slowly at him. "A ton. And there's just eight of us. Can you lift two and a half hundredweight, Mr. Stringer?"

There was still nothing in the kid's voice: no kind of emotion. "We use wedges and levers, Mr. Towns."

"Levers? On this sand?"

"There's no lack of flat metal sheering."

"You know how much physical strength we'll have in us a few days from now? On a diet of dates?"

Stringer rubbed out his five-barred gate as if wiping away the objection. "The wing would have to be moved first thing. Tonight."

"Tonight!" It brought the whole mad business horribly close.

"We would have to work at night, when it's cold, and sleep by day."

"Work with oil lamps? Build an aircraft out of a heap of scrap—by the light of oil lamps?" The tone of his voice broke and Moran thought he was going to give that terrible laugh of his.

"Okay, Frank, let's listen to the rest," said Moran. *He felt like a traitor,* backing this kid against Towns.

~~Stringer had stood up.~~ "I don't think Mr. Towns is interested." Moran said quickly:

"Certainly he's interested. Recap for me, will you, about the actual design factors? You convinced me, before."

Stringer looked across the expanse of sand like a kid looking through the school gate, wanting to be let out. Then he looked down at Moran, who said:

"Sit down. We're listening."

"If Mr. Towns is prepared to give me his attention—"

"We all are. Sit down."

Stringer swung one foot across the sand, leaving a crescent and studying it. "Not with oil lamps," he said stiffly. "I've worked out a simple winding gear for use with the starboard generator. It would keep the batteries charged, and we would be able to work with electric light."

"Fine," Moran said. He didn't look at Towns. The kid sat down uneasily.

"As far as the general design factors are concerned, there are no special problems. With the port engine mounted as it is, there'll be a nose-heavy moment, but we correct it by disposing the payload—that means ourselves, of course—well aft of the trailing edge. As soon as we balance the air-frame on the jacking points to find the C of G we can work out the weight distribution and arrange to dispose ourselves accordingly, each side of the boom—which will of course become the fuselage. The wing-loading will be about half that of the Skytruck, because we shall leave the entire hull, starboard boom, undercarriage and cargo on the ground—and that's an important point, because we have only one engine now. I estimate the new wing-loading at twenty-five pounds, and with only half the original thrust we shall still have a reserve of power. Of course there'll be excessive parasite drag because we shall have to lodge ourselves outside the boom, on outriggers made from the original tubular-metal seats; but the profile drag will be less, because we leave the hull behind."

Moran said, "There's a whole lot of sheet stuff to make fairings of." He dared to look at Towns, who was sitting as before, knees drawn up, head against the hull, eyes shut.

"We shall fair everything we can," said Stringer, "yes." He automatically drew a nacelle on the sand. "I estimate the lift-drag ratio at eight to one, even with the parasite drag as high as it will be. Remember how much weight we shall save, too—not only the hull, boom, starboard engine, undercarriage and cargo, but things like half the fuel, oil, coolant and hydraulic fluid." He looked steadily at Moran. "These are important points."

Moran asked deliberately, for Towns' sake, "And about flight handling?"

Stringer glanced across Towns' sunglasses, licking his lips. "I expect Mr. Towns will be working that out for himself."

Moran let the silence run five seconds. "You're the designer, kid. Tell us how she'll fly."

"Well, we shall lose the width of the hull and the two intermediate sections, and the boom is rather narrow, so the aspect ratio will be much higher. The plane won't be so maneuverable. But all we need is a machine to give us a path of straight and level flight for about two hundred miles and an absolute ceiling of a few hundred feet, with enough lateral control for avoiding plateaus. We simply fly on until we sight an oasis." Unconsciously he drew a palm tree on the sand.

Moran waited. Stringer said nothing more. He had finished. Here was his destination, a palm tree, and he was already there, because he saw no problem. And Moran knew suddenly what Loomis had meant: once they began work on this thing it would be like stepping onto a tightrope, and if once they looked down and saw how high they were and how nuts they'd gone, they'd fall. And the plane would never get built.

They must see no problem.

"Have you ever flown a plane?"

Moran looked up. Towns was staring at the

kid's face again, his head forward, the sunglasses throwing a sick green glow across his eyes. It hardly looked like Frankie any more. It was a blind man's face, old, stubbled with gray, the sweat of fever on it.

"No," Stringer answered.

Towns knew he was having to speak to this kid down the length of a thousand runways, across whole skies where he had never been. How much of the message could he hope to get across, that far away?

He said, "You've never flown a plane. I've flown them all. I'm not giving you the veteran-flyer recitation, Mr. Stringer, but I want you to know I haven't flown for the fringe operators all my life. I've captained the scheduled airline routes, years— Boeings, Stratoliners, a hundred tons a time, London-Tokyo, New York-Lisbon, trips like that. As well as the short-haul stuff—arctic helicopter, the jungle runs, all kinds. I'm not telling you how good a flyer I am." He looked across the sand at the torn-off undercarriage leg that lay in the track of the wreck. "You know how good I am. But—"

"You brought her down like a feather, Frank."

"Some feather." He looked at Stringer again. "But I'm telling you I've had a lot of experience. Okay, you know a heap more than I do about aerodynamics and drag coefficients and stress factors— your theory's fine. If you were going to fly what you want to build I'd say go ahead, you've got faith in yourself. But get this: that engine has a two thousand-pound thrust and once it got started up it'd pull your fancy bit of patched-up junk off the ground and shake it to hell before any of us had time to drop off and miss being cut to mincemeat by that prop. You really think you can just—"

Stringer was on his feet and his Sahara sandals blotted out the palm tree.

"Frank, you—"

"Keep it."

Stringer said in his monotonous voice, "I told Mr. Moran there was no problem about building the plane, but I said we might have difficulty finding a pilot." He walked away, his skinny bare arms held stiffly to his sides.

Moran wiped the sweat out of his eyes.

"Frank, there's—"

"Look, will you?" He kept his voice low and the words came out on grit. "I've killed two. There's Harris and Roberts and Cobb out there without a chance in hell. Kepel's on his way. Six. Six men, Lew. You want me to kill off another eight trying to get a death trap off the ground?"

Moran waited. Stringer was out of sight. The others were under the canopy, still talking, sorting the tools, ready to take the only chance there was.

"How many times have you broken flight rules and got away with it, Frank? Hundreds of times.

You've told me yourself the times you've put down a plane with excess fuel weight because it was safer than hanging around with the approach lanes jamming up with traffic—things like that. In the end it's the pilot who makes the decisions because he's up there with the plane and he's got to get it down somewhere, while the ground-control boys are safe on the deck with their arses in a chair and a cup of tea on the table."

Towns had shut his eyes again, but Moran knew he was listening. "I saw a flight of geese crossing our wake just before we hit the sandstorm, going west-east. You know what would've happened if we'd turned for El Aoussad and tried to lob down? It would've been shut, before even the damned geese got there. There wouldn't've been anywhere open to us. Christ, that storm wasn't just a local number! If you don't start setting your mind right on this crash, Frankie, you'll—"

"Okay, it wasn't my fault." The voice was old, like the face. "It's not going to be my fault either if that bright schoolboy builds a windmill and the rest of them climb on—because I'm not flying it. I'll take a chance with anyone, but murder is out."

Moran got up. The sand was sticking to the sweat on his legs and the sun struck across his back as he left the shadow of the tail unit. He said:

"You know we could go six months here, don't you, without being seen?"

"We can go just as long as the water lasts. It won't last thirty days."

Moran walked into the full heat, shutting his eyes against it, rounding the wreck and squinting at the big Thorpe and Crossley propeller that hung from the port engine. Two of the tips were damaged but Stringer said they would cut them short, all three, and lose no more than five percent of their reach. But he saw what Towns meant. Three metal blades, spinning with a 2,000-pound thrust, would make their own sandstorm and break up any structure that couldn't hold. A prop this big, let loose, would mow an army down.

A shadow passed against him.

"The tools aren't too bad," Bellamy told him.

"No?"

"They're lousy, but not too bad." He stood with his arms folded, confident, watching the navigator, deciding not to ask about how Towns felt, because they'd heard some of the argument and they knew Towns was against it.

"Do you trust Stringer?" Moran asked him. "I mean his capability?"

"Yes. Because he's barmy."

Moran knew what he meant because it was the truth that Loomis had voiced first. They were all of the same mind.

"I've met a few boffins like him," Bellamy said. "And the good ones are all barmy. Get an idea in their heads and you can't stop them. Stringer's like that."

Moran slapped the prop blade. It felt strong. He trusted Stringer, but he had faith in Towns too, in Towns' long experience. He felt his head being split in two by the need to decide. How much of Towns' pessimism was to do with the two mounds of sand over there, to do with his feeling of personal guilt? How much of Stringer's optimism was due to an obsession with technical problems that took no account of human things like thirst, hunger, the will to survive?

Never look down.

He said, "What's the voting, among the rest?"

"We're all ready to start, except for Watson and the Tilney kid. I don't know about the pilot."

"It's five out of eight."

"That's a majority."

"Then we start."

CHAPTER
8

AN ARAB GIRL, FOURTEEN OR SO, CAME WALK-ing across the sand, naked and dusky, little breasts jumping and the dark tuft dancing between her hips as she came; and Sergeant Watson waited for her, watching through half-closed eyes against the glare.

He'd never been a man to see mirages, except those he made up for himself. Christ, it must be three weeks now since he'd had anything. There wasn't a brothel at Jebel and it'd been near on a fortnight there with no one but bloody Harris—if you fancied him. How did the oil wallahs stand it? No women allowed in the camps, not even relatives, for they'd get raped soon as they'd set foot. No wonder the pay was high!

The girl's light shadow lay across him.

"Just for the record, we want to know if you're teaming up with us or not."

He squinted up at the navigator, cursed him quietly and said aloud, "I wouldn't have thought you was serious."

Moran looked down at the brick-red face; the

black eyebrows almost met above the meaty nose in a permanent frown. The sergeant lay with his legs stretched out in the shade of the canopy, his big feet bare. His whole attitude was off-duty, now the captain had gone.

"We're starting work tonight," Moran told him, and noticed that Tilney had opened his eyes not far away and was listening. "As soon as it's cooler."

Watson shifted his feet. "Well, I reckon that's up to you, i'n it?"

"So we'll count you out?"

"I wouldn' quite put it like that. But you know what's goin' to happen—you'll work your guts out day after day, an' before you've half finished you'll be dead o' thirst, never mind hunger. Stands t'reason, see. Now what we oughter do is lie quiet an' keep the sweat in, keep up our strength till they find us. A man can live twice as long in the desert if he don't go usin' up his energy, see."

Moran looked across at Tilney. "You feel the same way, kid?" He watched the boy mustering courage.

"I think he's right. I think we should all do what we think's best." He made it sound like a discovered truth, appealing to the sergeant for support. Moran left them, saying:

"We have to know who we can count on, that's all."

In the distance he saw the small figure of Towns on the ridge of the dunes. He had his back to the wreck, legs astride, head up, watching the sky.

There was nothing to do about it. The scared boy had a point: each of them had the right to choose his own way out of this. And the sergeant could be proved right, in the next few days. The five of them were going to use up energy by the ton. There'd been nothing he could say to those two; you can't force a man to his death.

It had been touch and go with Stringer. It had been like prising a giant clam out of its shell. He was badly upset that "Mr. Towns" didn't agree with the project: it seemed he had a lot of unexpressed respect for Towns and needed his vote.

"Could be he'll come in with us, kid, when things get started. You know what flyers are—they'll take up anything they can lay their hands on if there's a chance of it flying."

"He doesn't think it will fly." He drew patterns on the sand with his foot.

"You're the designer—you know better than he does about that." (Sorry, Frank, in his mind.)

Stringer wasn't worried about Watson and Tilney. He talked about their need of a good pilot, and the pointlessness of making the new plane if there was nobody to fly it; and Moran coaxed him back out of every blind alley he found as an escape. The kid was having a kind of first-night nerves: once they'd started work the main responsibility was his.

"I've sat next to the best flyer in the world,"

Moran told him, "for three years. If I have to, I'll take her off the deck myself."

It was an hour before sundown when he got them gathered together in front of the wreck. Watson and Tilney were still in the shade; Towns was still on the ridge. Kepel could not help them; Harris and Roberts and Cobb had gone. So they made five: Bellamy, Crow, Loomis, Stringer and himself. They had all cut their slacks short, as part of the master plan: not the building of the plane but the catching of dew each morning when the wind had been right. Pray it would be right tomorrow, when they took down the parachute silk and the seat fabric and the ends of their trouser legs and everything possible that would make a dew trap. There were long scrapers ready, bent into troughs; they would tap the hull and boom surfaces and the wing areas like a rubber tree.

The Jebel boys—Crow, Bellamy and Loomis— had laid the ten beaten-looking toolboxes in a line, the lids open and the tools arranged.

Their jackets were off and their arms were bare; they looked, despite their shipwreck stubble, like workmen.

Stringer had said to Moran, "Will you explain to them what has to be done? I'm no good at that kind of thing." He had repeated details to Moran, showing him the setup as they had walked round the wreck. There didn't seem anything he hadn't thought of; he'd even estimated their own combined strength in foot-pounds, in his head.

Moran stood with them on the quiet sand. They were all engineers of a kind—two drillers, a geologist versed in mechanics on the site, a navigator trained in calculation, and an aircraft designer. They had tools, however worn; and they would have, for a little while longer, most of their strength. But now that they stood on the threshold of their insane idea and waited to commit themselves to it, he had a sinking of the heart, and said:

"I've just listened to the setup again from Stringer, and frankly I don't see how we can fail. There's three main things to remember. We have to look after the tools all we can, especially drills and hacksaw blades because once they break we can't replace them. We have to get the main work over in the next two nights while we're fresh, and after that it's plain sailing. Third, we don't drive ourselves to the limit and squander energy. The motto is: Easy does it. Now Stringer wants me to recap the operation—and he doesn't fool me: he wants to know I understand it myself."

Loomis laughed gently on cue for him. Moran turned and looked at the wreckage with them. "You've heard the main scheme already. We've flown in with a twin-boom twin-engine machine and we fly out in a single-engine normal-fuselage plane. The port engine stays where it is at the forward end of the port boom, and the boom becomes the fuselage. The port area of the tail unit's also intact. We already have more than half our new plane. Tonight and tomorrow night we unship the starboard wing and disconnect the port boom from the hull. If it goes smoothly we'll have time to shift the wing ready for mounting on the boom. The third night we're through the worst. Then—"

"I said—" Stringer began but Moran spoke him down.

"Then we knock up the skid cradle, tail assembly and controls—that's light work and it shouldn't take long." He was ready to cut Stringer short again if he tried to correct him. Stringer had said three nights for the work on the wing, three for the hull and boom job. Almost a week, and it wouldn't bear thinking how they'd all be, a week from now.

He turned to look at their faces. "Now, Stringer has a very beautiful design worked out here, but he's agreed with me that the conditions are unusual. The main thing is to make an aircraft that'll fly a couple of hundred miles in safety, after which it doesn't matter if she just collapses where she lands." It had taken half an hour to persuade the kid about the "unusual" conditions. "So we work with the idea of strength and flyability, nothing more than that. This baby won't fetch any prize for looks."

"When we make a hole in a panel," Crow

wanted to get this quite straight, "we don't cut it, we bash it out."

"Right." He liked Crow's tone. The boy was ready to bash the whole plane apart and bash it together again. "But where there's any question, see Stringer. He's the boss."

He stood away a pace, folding his arms and looking down at Stringer's long thin shadow. After an awkward silence, Stringer said to no one especially:

"Who would like to fix up the generator? The light's important."

"I'm game," Bellamy said. It was the first time any of them had addressed Stringer.

"You understand mechanical things?" Stringer was walking on eggshells, scared by the word Mr. Moran had used: boss.

"Civil engineering degrees."

"Oh. I've made a rough sketch on the nacelle of the starboard engine, near the generator access panel. It's no problem—just two 15:1 ratio pulleys and a winding handle. There are suitable pulleys along the emergency-control lines to the tail unit—we shan't need them again. Use some of the covered-elastic light-freight cord for the cable—it's in the aft lockers in the hull. Set it all up somewhere near the batteries—I've disconnected them in case of shorting."

Bellamy nodded and left them.

Crow clicked his tongue. "That wing, mate. Must weigh a good ton."

"Yes. We'll use levers and cable for that. There's an H-section steel monorail and winch gear in the hull designed to lift three tons of cargo. I'll show you as we go along."

The silence set in again. The shadows of the west dunes were flowing across the sand toward them and the light was turning dull orange.

Moran said, "Right," and they began moving.

Just before the sun went down they saw the slow dark shapes crossing the sky and Moran walked to the ridge and said, "Did you see them?"

Towns swung round sharply: he hadn't heard Moran come up. "What?" His face was loose with worry.

"The vultures."

"Yep."

They had crossed the sky south-north, the way the three of them had gone, Harris, Roberts, Cobb.

"Frank . . . We can't hang on here much longer. And it's no use going out there." Northward the ocean of sand was purple and the first star gleamed. "Stringer's got the only answer and we need you in with us."

It was already dark when they came down from the dunes together, but among the black shapes of the wreck in the distance an electric lamp was shining, and they heard the ring of tools, and someone whistling.

CHAPTER
9

THE METAL SKIN OF THE BOOM WAS COLD AND
Bellamy stayed there a minute, leaning against it
on his hands, his tongue pressed to the metal to
drink the coldness; but the surface was dry. He had
felt the sagging silk of the canopy, and it was dry.
There was no white of hoarfrost on the dunes; the
sand was dry. The wind had not come.

Light lay along the east horizon. The bruise on his
arm throbbed. One of the makeshift trestles had collapsed under the wing when the bolts were knocked
clear, and its weight had knocked him down.

Crow was spread-eagled on the sand, eyes open
to the lightening sky. Bellamy lay down beside him.

"There's no dew, Albert."

"There wasn't no wind."

Crow's body ached and his mouth felt shriveled.
Twice in the night he had gone into the hull for his
water bottle and had stood with it in his hand,
shaking it, listening to the music inside; but he had
managed not to unscrew the cork. There'd been
only a drop or two, and he'd let them trickle into

his mouth, a few minutes ago. The share-out from the emergency tank would be at dawn. With the extra gallon they'd gathered yesterday there was still five days to go, a pint for each of them; but it was no good thinking about having a fling with to-morrow's ration thrown in, because if there was no more dew they'd see their lot. Five days on a pint, two more days on nothing, and that'd be it.

Stringer said the job would take thirty.

"You eaten any dates, Albert?"

"Camel crap's no use to me. Can't get it down."

The sergeant came round the wing-tip and fell on the sand. " 'Allo, Sunshine," Crow said. There was no answer.

Loomis stood near the tail unit watching the bar of light silver the horizon. Over the minutes it became tinged with smoking red, and color seeped into the dunes. The enemy was awake.

He saw Watson come to lie on the sand. Last night, before they had begun work on the wing, he had gone to Watson and said, "The thing is, we *all* have to try this chance, not only some of us. You're about the strongest man among us. I know it's not that you mind some heavy work—I understand that."

The sergeant had dug into the sand with his bare feet, thinking out what he had to say before he spoke.

"The only chance we've got is to keep doggo, and if that don't save us, nothing will. Listen. I'm in the Army, see, signed up for another ten years, don't ask me why I let meself in for it. I got a flat in Fenham East jus' by the gasworks an' it's the only place I can go because it's where the wife's mother lives, in fact the whole bleedin' lot of 'em—all her relatives. If I had a picture of the wife on me I wouldn' show it you because she's fifteen stone with 'air like a birch broom in a fit, never mind about her voice. I got no kids, thank Christ."

He looked once at Loomis, wondering how to make him see it. You could never talk personal and get out what you meant.

"I've been in the Army near on nineteen years, the war an' all, an' since then I've been pushed about the world by people like bloody Harris— you've heard 'im yourself—'*Sarnt Watson!*' all the bloody time—and him an' the rest o' them stuck-up bastards've been grindin' my nose in it till I'm sick down in me boots. Now I'll tell you somethin' you'll think soun's funny. I'm on 'oliday. Since we copped for this lot I've bin on leave, see? I'm out of the Army an' Harris has gone, an' there's nothin' to do but sit in the shade with me boots off all day long an' think about women an' the times I've 'ad. An' if no one finds us, and I get me lot, then I'll go 'appy—an' you want to know some-thin' else? I got near on fifty quid on me. Come in for a bit o' back pay, extra. An' this is the firs' time I've bin on leave without it's been Fenham East, where the whole pack of 'em's waitin' with their 'ands out. Fifty nicker . . . an' nothin' to spend it on, out 'ere. You think o' that!"

He let the sand trickle through his gnarled red toes. "I'm a millionaire, on 'oliday."

Loomis said in a moment, "If we build this plane, you'll be one of the passengers. Will you think about that?"

Watson had already thought. "My fare's paid, isn't it?"

It had been Moran who had found the way. They'd worked till past midnight, unshipping the monorail and winch, freeing the big 1½-inch nuts on the wing-root attachment, building the trestles from broken spars and the small rocks that had tripped the Skytruck when she'd landed; and their strength wasn't enough for hauling the wing root clear of the lugs. The monorail lever would damage the root strut, so they couldn't use it.

They were sweating, with the air below zero, and they gave it an hour before Moran went inside the hull and shook the sergeant awake, speaking quietly for Kepel's sake: "Come on, Watson, outside, quick!"

"What's on, then?"

"Come on—put a jerk in it!"

Tilney had been awakened, and followed them outside, watching the two men in the starlight. Moran said:

"You're signed up for this job. Both of you. My orders."

"Now look, I—"

"*Double up, Watson!*"

The others heard the crack of his voice echo from the dunes. The three of them came round to the group under the rigged lamp and Moran said sharply, "We've got two more men, now let's give it another go."

The trestle had collapsed but the wing was free by two in the morning and they'd begun the long struggle to winch and haul it across the sand, taking it a foot at a time and swinging it by the tip and swinging it back, spading the sand clear as it plowed up under the weight of the root, until Loomis had thought of bracing the monorail against the buckled undercarriage leg on the port side and winching from there; then they had taken turns at the gear with the steel cable bowstring-taut, hauling an inch at a time with each man resting when he'd had his turn, an inch at a time until the wing lay on the sand in the area that Stringer had marked out.

They had rested and eaten some dates; and those who had water left in their bottles drank some of it or all of it while the others tried to think about something else.

Moran had told himself, in the lonely unquiet of his mind, that you can't force a man to his death, but you must force him to live, if he can't work it out for himself. But his defense rang false; it was the dictator's oldest excuse: there was never a war fought except for the "good of the people," and he'd forced Watson into harness for the good of them all, because they needed his physical strength. And he'd played on the man's weakness: without direct orders from someone, Watson was adrift.

He'd worked as hard as any of them, all night, without a word. Now he lay on the sand exhausted.

The sun lifted, its warmth immediate on their skin.

"Put that bloody light out," Crow said, and closed his eyes. Bellamy watched the dunes take on substance, carved in crescents by the blood-red glow.

"My God," he said, "it's quiet." There was something dead about this kind of silence.

"After the drill," Crow grunted. The Jebel camp had been a mile from the derrick and mud pump, so that they could sleep; the drill never stopped except when the mud leaked or the drill jammed or there was a bit change. The Jebel drill was down to twelve thousand feet and still the rock was dry. They were going to abandon at thirteen thousand if they didn't meet oil. He wondered if he and Crow would ever see Jebel again.

He sat watching the dawn mirage: through the mouth of the dunes lay a sheet of bright water, reaching the horizon. There were no palm trees, thank God, or white-walled forts; the water was normal—light reflected at a wide angle from the glassy grains of sand; but when you started seeing other things you were on your way. He got up.

"Where you goin'?"

"Fetch my diary."

Crow went with him. Tilney was in the hull, just standing there.

"What's up, son?"

"Nothing. I was going to talk to him." He looked along the litter of smashed seats at Kepel.

"Leave 'im be." Crow had heard stories about the Tibbus of the Tibesti Mountains, how they could heal themselves of almost anything by sleep and fasting; there was nothing for that poor Jerry to do but sleep, and nothing for him to eat except for dates, and he'd touched none.

Crow sat with the monkey while Bellamy wrote in his book. Bimbo wasn't shivering so badly, but his little eyes were still funny, staring at you and then gradually shutting, then coming open with a click. Crow held him against his shoulder, and Bimbo hung on to a tuft of his hair. He could feel the beat of the miniature heart against his throat.

"Put down," he said to Bellamy, " 'ow it was very nice at the party till the booze run out an' Mabel fell down the stairs tryin' to be a fairy."

"Shut up."

"Proper bleedin' discourteous, eh, Bimbo?"

First night. We all worked the whole night, near enough forty-eight man-hours, not too bad. The mainplane's off and ready for mounting, but God knows how we'll do it. Can only trust in Stringer.

There was no dew, so the limit's still five days, if we can keep to the pint a day, but I don't see how we can, now that we're working. Last evening some vultures flew over, and we can only hope it wasn't because they'd seen anything out there.

He mentioned about Watson, and forgot to put anything about the trestle and his arm. He noticed that his writing was sloppy, a thing he had always tried to watch. This worried him.

When Towns and Moran came into the hull to share out the ration from the water tank, Kepel was conscious.

"How is our new airplane?" he asked, his eyes half closed. They told him it was coming on fine. "I would like to help. I could turn the handle of the generator. I have strong arms."

Towns filled his water bottle and brought it to him. It was still cold inside the hull but the boy's blond stubble shone with sweat, and his eyes were dull. "Keep on making progress, kid. It's the best way you can help us." If the new plane ever got built they would have to move him, without killing him. There was a last shot of morphia left in the medical kit, reserved for that day.

He asked for something to write on, and they gave him a batch of flying-report sheets. His zip-bag had been crushed under the seats, so Loomis lent him his pen. One by one they left him, their fingers itching on the caps of their water bottles as they pretended not to hurry. Each, knowing the others' need was urgent like his own, felt embarrassed, as if he should do this thing in private; lust of any kind wasn't a pretty thing to watch.

Loomis went forward into the control cabin, where the generator gear had been set up, so that the bulkhead door could be shut to save Kepel too much noise. Bellamy had done a good job, taking the wires through the ammeter on the instrument panel before linking with the batteries; a turn of the handle at barrel-organ speed gave a steady four amps. He had rigged loose panels over the windows to give shade and fitted four rough blades to the smaller pulley to provide a cooling fan for the operator. Loomis began turning, heard the cutout close and saw the ammeter needle swing over. The gear was light enough to turn; the difficulty was to believe that by doing this he might one day reach Paris, and in time.

His hour's spell was not yet up when Moran shouted to him from outside, beating on the hull: *"Stop the generator! Stop turning!"*

Other voices came.

He went through the length of the hull and dropped from the doorway. They were all outside the canopy, none of them talking now; they stared upward, shielding their eyes, listening to the high faint sound of the aircraft in the sky.

CHAPTER
10

BELLAMY WAS THE FIRST TO REACH THE PAN of oil-soaked rag and he struck match after match as they broke in his fingers before the rag caught and the black smoke climbed against the glare. His eyes streamed from looking up and he lurched back half-blinded.

Sergeant Watson had the signal gun and ran past but Towns called, "Hold on—don't fire!" Crow and Loomis were tilting the heliograph panel, crouching so that the sun's rays should strike its whole area; Tilney stood waving the semaphore they had made with a rod and a section of chute silk. Three of them stood still and did nothing: Stringer, Towns and Moran. They made tubes of their fingers and scanned the white glare, tears running down their faces.

The smoke climbed in a thick black rope, its sundial shadow at the acute angle of late morning. The sound of the aircraft whispered in the heights.

Towns and Moran stood with their shoulders touching.

"Four-jet."

"Ceiling high, north-south."

"Cairo-Durban."

The sound was east of them.

Tilney was calling something to the sky in a soft shrill gabble, swinging the semaphore until the silk fluttered. They heard Kepel's voice from inside the hull, wanting to know what was happening, but no one could answer him.

"No go, Frank."

"No."

They sat down on the hot sand, holding their faces and letting the tears stream, still blinded by the disks of light that were cut into their retinae.

"Save it," Towns called. "The deal's off."

They came into the shade.

"He didn't see us . . ." Tilney whispered. "He didn't see us . . ."

The sound was still up there and Towns listened to it for another minute until there came back by imperceptible degrees the great silence of the desert, and they were alone again.

"They wouldn't have seen us," he said slowly, "even if we'd set the whole wreck on fire." He wiped his hand over his beard. "She's up there thirty thousand feet. She's on course and on schedule and everything's going fine on the flight deck, though it's a little boring now she's reached her ceiling and there's nothing else to do. Any minute now they'll buzz the cabin staff and ask for coffee, to break up the boredom, and by this evening they'll be taking a shower at the new Hilton at Durban, before they go out on the town." He looked at the sky again through squeezed red eyelids. "Bless you, my friends . . . enjoy yourselves."

Bellamy was going across to the smoldering rag to put it out. Watson brought the signal gun back, unloading it.

"They didn't see us . . ." Tilney whispered.

"How the hell could they at thirty thousand feet?" Towns looked at the kid's shocked face, and finished more quietly. "From that height they wouldn't see us even if they were looking for us, and there's no windows in a flight-deck floor. Forget it."

Strangely, following the leap of hope and then its denial, they were not depressed; and it was Moran who put it into words as they lay in the shade and tried to sleep:

"It was nice, for a few minutes, to have company."

Mabel would worry.

The news would have been on the radio and there'd be a bit in the papers because it was a British company's plane. If there'd been a search at all, the Skytruck would have been presumed lost by now.

He didn't want Mabel to worry. But there wasn't anything to do, except get out of here as soon as they could.

Light grains of sand touched his face and fell away. The white silk rose like a huge bubble, and sagged again. The white looked green now, because he wore the sunglasses Bellamy had made. Bellamy couldn't sleep, couldn't rest, after the first hour or two; he'd knocked up three pairs of these sunglasses out of a broken colored-perspex panel in the roof of the hull. If they heard another plane go over they could have a chance of seeing it against the glare, cheer themselves up a bit.

The generator was turning. Watson's shift. It got on your nerves, moaning away in there.

The silk billowed like a sail and sand pattered against his bare arm; but the air wasn't any cooler. If you stood in the sun you could feel the heat sucking the moisture out of you; in a way you were bleeding to death.

He reached for his water bottle and tilted it to and fro, listening to the music. Half full. Four o'clock. Fifteen hours till the next share-out. Mouth like a lump of coke.

Sand blew against his face and he turned over, leaning on his elbow, looking around. Loomis, Towns, Moran, poor little Tilly—Christ, they all looked dead. This was how they'd all look when the last of the water . . . Shut up, Albert.

Bellamy came out of the hull with a drill in his hand and looked at the sky. There was no horizon in the south and the dunes smoked with rising sand. Stringer came round the wing, spindly legs and glinting glasses; he stood watching the south.

Crow got up as the silk began flapping; and the others stirred, brushing the sand from their faces.

"Dave!"

"What?"

"Breezin' up a bit." He felt for a cigarette and remembered reading in the *Digest* how it took three months before you could stop doing something you'd always done, because man was a creature of habit, it said.

Sand washed across his legs and Bellamy said, "Just our luck." Towns was up and Moran with him. They began taking down the spread of chute silk and Crow and Bellamy helped. Loomis shook Tilney awake and hauled him gently to his feet— and then the air went yellow and the ground smoked as the wind struck full across the dunes and flung sand in a steady wave against the dry shell of the wreck. They already had to shout to one another against the scouring gusts that sent the port mainplane lifting and dipping and the loose panels fluttering. They ran with what they could find in the hull—freight cord, seat fabric, spare shreds of parachute silk—and covered the port engine air intake, the winch gear, the exposed root end of the starboard wing, while Moran climbed the nacelle and slammed the access panels shut, his feet sliding on the sand-filmed metal skin of the wing.

The hot wind dragged at them as they worked half blinded by the sand; the pan of oily rag that was Harris' smoke signal went whirling and spilling past the wreck, and with it the sheets of torn metal they had laid out to spell the big SOS; the heliograph disc was caught and sent skating with a crash against the tail unit; and the sun went out slowly, to leave a world of dark ocher that had no horizon and no sky.

They ran, hunched and staggering, for the shelter of the hull, forcing the door shut against the wind, letting their eyes stream and trying, without saliva, to spit the grit from their mouths. Then they sat and waited, listening to the drum of the wind through the wreckage and to the surge of sand.

They waited for three hours, emerging from the heat of the hull to stand in starlight and silence. It was as if the dark had driven away the wind and brought the known world back: the faint curves of the dunes, the long arm of the mainplane with its sheen of light, the perspective of the boom.

"Look," said Loomis, and they turned. Low in the west sky was the bright curved needle of the new moon.

You got to wish, thought Crow, on a new moon. *Water,* he thought, *water*.

"Get started, do we?" he said.

Stringer led them to the work.

The second night. Everything went wrong, but we managed to do a bit more. This is being written at four a.m. I'm afraid I might forget to put things down, and it might interest people, if anyone ever reads this, to know how we tried, even if we fail.

He took great care with the writing and didn't mention the thirst. His diary must take it for granted now, that it was easier to write than speak, that in speaking you heard your words whistling and slurring from a swollen tongue and past brittle lips, your own voice unfamiliar.

It had taken an hour to clear the drifts of sand, and an hour to find and dig out the small rocks they had used for a trestle base last night and needed again. But after the day's shift work on the generator the batteries gave a good light and they rigged a stanchion and hung the bulb high, their shadows working with them on the sand.

Stringer had come to life again. Nothing, during the long and disturbing day, had moved him to speech; now he told Moran what he wanted, seeming to find it easier to talk to one man than to all of them.

"We have to shore up the port wing with two trestles so that it doesn't drop when we part the boom from the hull. I've already freed the inboard attachment bolts and there's no special problem."

It was for Moran to remember that they were human, with vulnerable bodies. "Watch it when she parts, and don't stand under the wing in case the trestles give." But even he forgot about Kepel, so that when the boom parted from the hull with a shiver of tearing metal as the weight came down, they heard him scream.

Crow was inside the hull first, already telling Kepel, "It's all right, son, it's all right," gripping the cold dry hand, keeping the torch beam low and seeing only the blur of the whitened face. "We meant to do that, it wasn't an accident, son—" *but we should've warned you first, Christ, we should've warned you.*

"I am all right. Yes." The words came out on a hissing breath of pain, the bright eyes flickering. Crow talked to him, and the others kept back, and Loomis dropped through the doorway and leaned with his back flat against the hull and his eyes to the stars, his long body shaking in self-disgust: because it had been obvious that when the boom parted from the hull, the hull would shear away and find its own level on the sand. He could hear Kepel talking, and the strength of his voice filled Loomis with an admiration that he had no right to enjoy.

"I was sleeping, yes. Therefore I did not know what had happened. If I make a shout, it was the nightmares. I have sometimes nightmares."

Too proud even to admit to the scream. They came away, not speaking to one another. They saw Stringer examining the exposed section of the boom and heard him say, "There's no damage," and Moran hated him.

They stood waiting for orders, but no one would ask outright for them. Stringer inspected the trestles, moving about as though they were not there; then he said in his soft monotonous tone:

"We have to swing the whole mainplane round, unless we can raise the starboard wing and rest it across the top of the hull."

No one answered, nor would he have heard. They watched him find a length of tube and climb on to the port wing, agile, absorbed and unconcerned by heat, cold, thirst or another's pain. The trestles settled into the sand under his weight.

They look dodgy, thought Crow. If one of 'em gives, he'll break his bloody neck and that'll be a shame.

Stringer leveled the tube, comparing the height of the hull roof and the base of the intermediate root where the starboard wing must be lugged home. He checked twice and came down. He looked at Moran.

"We can winch the mainplane up against this side of the hull, tip first, then swing up the root. I expect you see what I mean."

Moran surveyed the job in the white glare of the lamp.

"If the top of the hull stands the weight," he said.

"It might buckle, but it can't go far. It's better than having to swing the whole port wing and boom round."

"Fair enough. Everyone gets the idea?"

They began hauling the winch to the other side and Loomis went to tell Kepel, "There'll be a little banging and bumping, I guess, but the hull won't shift again."

Kepel was writing; he had filled a couple of the flying-report sheets, using the backs.

"I am all right, thank you. Do not worry about me."

His face was candle-white under the gold stubble and his eyes were dull in the light of the bulb that had been rigged up for him. Loomis felt he was intruding. It would be a long letter to his parents, probably. He left him.

They worked for two hours through the coldest part of the night, their hands numb from touching metal that in the daytime would raise burn-blisters. The winch cable fouled twice and they cleared it, raising the ton-weight of the starboard wing a foot from the sand before the cable slipped and the trestle gashed a hole in the wing panels. They worked almost without speaking, Stringer the most silent of all; they worked without resting. They used the steel monorail, trying to lever at the root end of the wing; but they lacked the strength and the root slid away a dozen times until Towns was cursing, with blood caking his arm from elbow to wrist because the torn hole in the panels had skinned it when the wing slid away.

Stringer gave orders and they winched the wing across the sand to the other side, taking the cables across the hull roof and hauling from there, root first; and the hull was smashed like an eggshell as the weight came on—but Stringer was right: it buckled only as far as the main ribs and then held.

By first light the wing was lodged aslant, tip down, root resting on the smashed control-cabin roof; and the winch would not move it further. They went on trying to shift it until Tilney staggered away and lay on his back in the churned sand, his body heaving for breath. Bellamy had pain on his face with a torn back muscle. The others were hunched over, hands on their knees, regaining their wind, the breath sawing in and out through dry lips.

Stringer said, "We have to make another trestle and lever up the tip end with the monorail, building the trestle higher as we go."

The light came up white from the horizon. Soon the sun would follow and bring the heat. There was no need for them to brush their hands along the boom as the new day began: if there had been dew there would be frost covering the sand; and there was no frost.

"We have to build a trestle," said Stringer tone-lessly.

Towns said nothing because he didn't think they could ever shift that wing without ripping it underneath from root to tip. And they hadn't the strength.

"Shall I explain in detail?" Stringer persisted.

It was Crow who said, for all of them, "No Stringy. Just piss off an' give us five minutes' peace, there's a good boy."

Loomis alone happened to be looking at Stringer's face and saw its expression change as Crow spoke; and he knew at once that something serious had happened to them all.

The spindly body went stiff and the hands hung down at the sides; the glasses made two spots of light against his shadowed face; and now he moved toward Crow, and stopped close to him, facing him, his light voice unsteady in its rage.

"My name is Stringer. Please remember. *Stringer*." He walked across to the hull and climbed through the doorway.

CHAPTER
11

THE CRICKET SANG. IT FLEW IN THE BLUE SKY, spinning and singing. When it fell he tried to catch it and eat it but his arm was pinned to the ground and the song clicked on beside him. The crickets battered themselves to death against the door screens and the Arab boys picked them up and took them to the cook and you could hear them roasting. They would eat anything. Fried locusts. Make you sick.

The cricket ticked and the white wall towered and then fell on him softly and rose again, and fell on him, so that he began shouting. He tried to run but his body was pinned by the heat and the white wall crashed across him in white silence, and he shouted at it.

"Dave," someone called.

That was Crow, on the other side of the wall. He shouted his name.

"Dave, pack it in!"

His bruised arm burned and the muscle in his back burned. The white wall dipped and lifted, a

131

breeze catching the silk above him. His eyes opened fully in the glare. His watch ticked against his ear; he straightened his arm and pain seared along the muscle.

Crow was sitting up beside him. "Midday," he said. He looked like a bird with red eyes and a bony beak.

"What?"

"Got to light the smoke, mate."

They looked around them at the others who were sleeping. Someone was working the generator, moaning away inside the hull. Towns, because he wasn't here.

"Come on, then." They gathered their legs and got up in the manner of drunks, finding a torn sheet of metal and tapping the starboard engine for more oil. For a wick they used somebody's trouser leg. The smoke rose at an angle toward the west; the breeze was not from the north, from the sea. They floundered back through the hot gold waves of air and sank in the shade of the tail unit. Bellamy said thickly:

"We'll have to ask Towns to increase the ration."

"Up to you. I can't ask 'im. I've been givin' some of mine to ole Bimbo."

"I wish to God you wouldn't. It's four days now." The ten minutes in the direct sun had brought sweat out badly. "If we all decide to increase the ration, it'll be down to three."

"I told Rob I'd look after Bimbo."

They could see Stringer doing something in the shade of the trestled wing, using a flat stone as a workbench. He was never seen sleeping.

" 'E's not 'uman," Crow said. He still didn't know what had happened this morning when Stringer had gone stalking off like that. He'd asked Bellamy:

"What was that about, then?"

"You called him Stringy."

"I did? What do I 'ave to call him, then, Lord Bleedin' Muck?"

"He's touchy," Bellamy said.

"Go on, is 'e really?"

But it couldn't be true. There must be more than that. He didn't even remember saying it. He was bent over trying to get some of his breath back and Stringer's voice had gone on and on, so he'd told him to piss off, that was all. Christ, he wanted to spend a couple of days at Jebel, where you got called all the names there was, except for bastard. Nobody liked that one. But this little sod hadn't got called a bastard. What was it that'd got on his tits, then?

He lay down again and tried to sleep, but couldn't manage. At one o'clock they went and pulled the wick out of the dish and smothered it, and the top part of the smoke went climbing on like a broken rope. The breeze had died and the white silk canopy was motionless again.

Bellamy said, "What about helping Stringer?"

"You daft?" Crow lay flat in the shade again. "If we don't keep the sweat in we've 'ad it. You know somethin'? Last time I 'ad a pee was yesterd'y mornin'. We're dryin' up, Dave. Bound to. Stringer's not 'uman."

The moan of the generator stopped and Towns came out of the hull, sweating, dropping onto the sand near Moran. He had fallen asleep winding the generator gear, lulled by the spinning pulleys. There was only just room to sit there now because the wing had flattened the top of the flight deck. The smell of the fuel had worried him: one of the tanks had been split in shifting the wing or the vents were working overtime in the heat of the sun. Fumes were always in the control cabin and there was always some sparking on the dynamo brushes; so that he'd sat there winding, thinking himself into nightmares—if the fumes were sparked off, the wing tank resting on the hull roof would go up and fire the whole wreck before they could get it under control with the extinguishers. Their last shelter would go; and there was Kepel, who couldn't be moved. Sergeant Watson had a gun. It would have to be that, before the flames got to him.

He ought to be moved anyway because of the work on the wing: a chance spark due to friction was a constant risk. Last night they'd heard the fuel slopping about in the wing tank and there'd been a lot of friction from the slipping winch cable. But they had nothing to drain the stuff into except the port wing tank, and that would double the fuel weight on one side; the trestles wouldn't stand it.

They ought to move the German kid; but it would kill him. The bleeding would start again and he'd lose both blood and moisture: loss of blood increased thirst automatically. Kepel was already on a pint and a half per day. So there was nothing to be done. Sit in there and wind the handle and breathe the fumes and leave it, if it had to be, to Watson's gun.

Moran said, "Who's turn, Frankie?"

"Bellamy's."

"I'll get him."

For the first two hours the light of the new moon was a help because the shadows cast by the lamp were less stark. They pivoted the monorail on the biggest rock and levered under the mid-section of the wing until by midnight the tip was man-high from the ground. Then they rested, not talking very much because talking was painful, the tongue bruising on the teeth and the lips moving clumsily.

They had begun work again when someone fell across the sand at the edge of the pool of light and Crow went to help him, and saw his face, and said, "*Christ!*"

The face was peeled raw and the dark tongue poked out between the husks of the lips; the body was sprawled with one hand forward, reaching into the circle of the light.

Bellamy came up. "Who is it?"

"Captain Harris."

* * * * *

They left him wedged across two of the seats in the hull, covered with their jackets; and Tilney, being the least strong among them, was told to watch over him. Towns had filled a bottle from the drinking tank, trickling it into the shriveled mouth until Harris' eyes came open and stared dully at them. Then his hand clawed at the bottle while a sound came from his throat, an animal sound that they were still trying to forget; some of the water was spilled and they had to force his hand away.

They had asked him only one thing: Where was Roberts? The one word had come hollow from the working mouth:

"Lost."

Leaving him, they took their thoughts with them, and with no comfort. In the desert, lost was another word for dead.

Working beside each other, neither Bellamy nor Crow spoke. They had known Robby a long time: nearly a year. A year was a long time in an oil camp. Nor could they forget the face of Captain

Harris, the way it had looked in the pool of light, the face of their own future.

Sitting inside the hull, Tilney looked up as the sergeant came through the doorway. In an odd voice Watson said, "Give a hand out there a minute, son."

When he was alone with his officer, he sat bent over him, watching the dry peeled face. He hadn't been able to keep away; he had to come and stare at this man, so that he could remember how he looked, and be able to think of him later, as he was now, not far off death, and helpless. He'd come back, but there was going to be a difference.

The voice seemed to be still coming out of him— *Sarnt Watson!*—as he lay wedged on the seats, his eyes shut and the lids raw. It wouldn't take much never to hear that voice again. The sergeant sat thinking on this, and remembering Harris and his kind; he'd have liked to talk to this face but the Jerry might be awake and he understood English, though he might not have heard of some of the words that Watson sat thinking on.

He talked in his mind to the face, minute after minute; and when he was done he left the hull and sent the kid back.

They worked at the mainplane until the sun shone red on the wreck. All night they had listened for a wind; and in the first light of the day they had looked across at the dunes, imagining they could see hoarfrost, but the surface of the wing was dry.

They found Captain Harris with his eyes open and intelligence in them. When he tried to speak, Loomis told him to wait a bit; their own speech would be difficult until the water was shared out.

When the bottles were filled and they had drunk a little, Bellamy told Towns, "The ration's not enough. Is it?"

They avoided looking at each other's face in the soft red light of the dawn. Their skin was peeling under the stubble of their beards and their mouths were puckered like old women's.

"It's got to be enough. There was no dew." He didn't add that their time here was shortened by Harris' coming back; they all realized that. He didn't add that there was less water left in the tank than there should be; it wouldn't be so easy to put into words. There was no type of lock he could put on the tap, but if Harris didn't lose consciousness again he could be given the duty of watching the tank.

They dropped onto the sand in the shade and sleep came down on them like a blow.

By noon Harris was talking in a painful whisper, falling silent and making a new effort time after time.

"It was the sandstorm—the sandstorm, yesterday. We'd gone a long way, north all the time, the first night . . . but he developed a sore foot—Roberts—a sore heel, was bleeding badly and slowed us. We de-

138

cided to march in the daytime but no good, too much sweat—then my bottle leaked, sand got under the cap, I thought the cap was down tight—nearly all gone, in the night. . . . We shared, after that—saw mirages, went three hours in the sun, thought we saw vegetation, certain of it—wasn't really there. Heat bad in the day, no shelter . . ."

As he talked they looked at their folded hands, at the scene through the window above his head, of dunes black and white in the glare; Tilney alone stared at him, with horror in his eyes, as he learned what it meant to be on foot and alone in the desert.

"We'd made a map . . . to cheer ourselves up—marked the plane and the nearest oasis group, far as we could tell, and the map blew away . . ." His gaunt face showed the surprise that he still felt, the inability to believe what had happened. "In the sandstorm the map blew away . . . and Roberts went chasing after it—I was trying to dig a hole in the sand, digging with my hands . . . incredible . . . incredible . . . going like that! When he didn't come back I shouted for a long time, went wandering to look for him but—you couldn't see more than a few yards . . . it was like thick smoke everywhere—stung your eyes. . . ." He leaned his head back and rocked it against the wall of the hull, unable to contain his regret, his tongue creeping to touch his lips as if to lick them, by habit. "He must—he must have come back, past me—would have heard my shouting, downwind, otherwise . . . I blame myself . . . blame myself. . . ."

They waited again. So a piece of paper had blown away, and that was all. That was the desert. The same with Joe Vickers, at Jebel—wandered five miles in a sandstorm and missed a 200-foot illuminated derrick and the camp as well.

It was the storm they'd had here two days ago, the same one, blowing for Roberts.

"It was dark when . . . the storm gave up, but I made a square-search, using the stars and counting my paces—then I knew he'd start back for the plane, once he knew he was lost . . . so I started back too—south by the stars, all night, hoping to catch him up. No sign. Saw your smoke-signal— thank you, thank you—just the top of it in the sky. No more water now, all gone—his own bottle was with him of course. . . . Mirages in the day, but held on—didn't let myself get fooled—and slept a long time. South by the stars—went off course a great deal, I think, head full of light, you know the feeling, when—your head fills—"

"Yes," Towns said.

Loomis too had heard of it. When your head fills up with light, you're not far off the end.

"I thought it was a mirage, the light . . . on the ground, brighter than a star—"

"Yes," Towns said again, trying to spare him.

"It—it was *your* light, you follow . . . the one

you had burning! It was the only mirage I let my-self—" He put his head back again and shut his eyes. After a minute Moran asked quietly:

"Did you ever see Cobb?"

"Cobb?" His eyes remained shut. "Yes. Yes, I see." His body began shaking. "So that was Cobb. Poor fellow." Quite beyond the task of softening the words—"He was picked clean. Skeleton. Thought it was someone been there a long time. Now I remember . . . saw vultures, second day." His eyes flickered open and stared at nothing. "Roberts didn't get back." Then pathetically he made it a question as if there were still hope. "Didn't get back?"

"Not yet," Loomis said. "We're waiting."

The captain's hand moved, stroking his legs, try-ing to stop the shivering; his eyes became intelli-gent again and he looked at their faces; and the mouth split into a grotesque smile. "Watson . . . well you're still with us, anyhow."

The sergeant didn't answer him but turned away; and the others, embarrassed by the sight of the captain's scaly mask of a face and his attempt to go on speaking, left him and went outside.

"I blame myself . . . about Roberts. . . . Keep a good lookout for him—for Roberts."

Even from outside they could hear the dry scuf-fling of his tongue. On a decision of his own, Towns came back and gave him a water bottle, half filled. Afraid that he might spill even one drop

141

he tried to hold it for him but Harris took it carefully in both hands, saying, "I can manage . . . I'm perfectly all right, you know."

Towns waited until he had emptied the bottle and began sucking at the neck, his eyes closed. The shaking of his legs had stopped.

Toward evening the birds crossed the sky again toward the north. Bellamy and Crow had lit the oil smoke when they had left Harris, in case by some chance Roberts was alive and within the area. When they saw the birds they sat with their backs to the north and tried not to think about the way the captain had described Cobb.

Loomis walked alone to the north ridge of the dunes and looked for a long time across the ocean of sand before he came back and sat down with them, saying nothing.

Toward sundown Crow went across to the pan of smoldering oil and doused it with sand; and for minutes the smoke stood like a red column against the sky, beautiful and meaningless.

They had not talked, all the afternoon, because, had there been anything to say, it would have been painful to say it; their withering tongues would make a poor job of communicating their dejection that was anyway better left unsaid. Stringer had been working underneath the mainplane for an hour before the dunes ran red and the first star showed; and after a time he came toward them, and said to them:

"We should be making a start."

No one moved. He stood with his hands hanging at his sides, looking at the ground.

Towns said for all of them, "There isn't any point."

Surprised, Stringer moved his hands that were suddenly emptied of all they had to do. "But we've been making progress."

Towns spoke quietly, too wearied even to feel anger at the man's stupidity. "We thought the water might last out. It won't."

CHAPTER
12

THE MOONLIGHT THREW THEIR SHADOWS AHEAD of them; they walked as far as the dunes. Beyond the dunes lay the vast silence, so deep as to be almost visible; they could see nothing over all those miles that was higher than a grain of sand. Behind them came the distant moaning of the generator that someone was turning. From here the wreck lost all semblance of an airplane; it might have been anything. A light burned inside the hull but the big working lamp on its stanchion was dark.

"We're goin' to pieces, Dave. The lot of us." They dropped on to the sand; it was still warm from the day. Not long ago they would have stood there, looking about them; now they had to sit, because their legs were weak.

"What did you expect?"

"It's bad. We ought to do something about it."

"Towns was right: there's no point in going on with the plane. We were barmy."

They were quiet for minutes, each with his thoughts. Bellamy had spent a little while talking to

Kepel, and listening to him, hearing about the house in Wünlich on the edge of the Black Forest, and about Inga and her long fair hair. Captain Harris had been in a coma and Loomis had been near him, taking drops of water from his bottle to moisten his forehead. Crow had held the monkey to him for a bit and given it a drink, the first since the dawn share-out. Bimbo belonged to him now and he'd saved his twenty quid; it was like one of those fairy stories in which greedy people made a wish that turned out all wrong for them when it was granted.

"Poor old Rob," he said without meaning to.

"He's only had a few days' start on the rest of us, Albert. We're next."

"For Chris' sake, stop talkin' like that, will you? That's what I mean—we're goin' to bloody pieces, an' it's got to bloody stop!"

"Look, Albert. I've never tried kidding myself, ever. The other night we had a freak dewfall that might not happen again for weeks—and it cheered us all up and we started building an airplane, of all things, just because Stringer sold us an idea that only a lunatic would think of. Now I've seen straight for the first time. How long d'you think Kepel's going to live? And Harris? And when they get near the end, are we going to watch them suffering without giving them half our ration to try keeping them alive? So where does that leave us? I'd sooner look at things as they are than kid myself."

He wanted to say more but he could hear the sound of his own voice coming through distorted lips; he sounded like an old man without dentures, comic and enfeebled. They were all old men, old in that they were nearing the end of life; he didn't want to talk any more; he wanted to lie down and sleep.

"Say what you like, Dave, but we got to do somethin'. I dunno what. But we can't jus' curl up an' bleedin' die."

Across the moonlit sand the drone of the generator stopped and the silence of the outer desert flooded through the dunes.

Only one figure moved, near the wreck; it was Stringer, restive and alone. Sometimes he made his way between the hull and the port boom, stopping to listen to the voices of the pilot and the navigator, because what they were saying was of tremendous importance to him.

Moran had thought deeply before tackling Towns, beginning:

"It's too early to give up."

"It's too late to do anything else."

"The kid was right, Frankie. We've been making progress."

Towns didn't reply for minutes. He'd wandered about the wreckage for a time, alone, keeping out of Stringer's way. The port wing was still up on trestles made of rocks and bits of longerons cut from the hull and the skeletons of smashed seats and the crates the freight was shipped in; the hull was down on the sand; the starboard wing was cocked at a crazy angle across the buckled control-cabin roof. Before they'd started work she'd looked like a plane that had crashed; now she looked a sight worse, like a plane that had never even flown and never would.

"Given a month, Lew, maybe three weeks, we might've had a chance; but I've told you—the water won't last. Tomorrow we'll be down to the dregs."

He had been watching them all, trying to fix on one of them, judging them before they'd even been accused. It wasn't Lew. Crow . . . Bellamy . . . no, unless Crow had been taking it for the monkey. Kepel couldn't move: the tank was high on the cabin bulkhead far out of his reach. Not Loomis. The sergeant maybe, out of revenge for being forced to work—a simple enough point of view with a man like him: he'd chosen to lie still and minimize sweating; they'd made him sweat; all right, he'd replace it for himself. Or Stringer? He was holding out better than any of them; but he had his obsession to keep him going, and he was slight-bodied, the type to survive longest in these conditions. Maybe the Tilney kid, scared to hell of having to die; his face didn't look so bad as the others', his lips hadn't even cracked yet; but he was younger, or it could be that the dates were helping him—he ate them the whole time, like sweets.

Kepel was asleep half the time and wouldn't be wakened by the sound of the tap and the water trickling into the mouth. Whose mouth?

It was an act of slow murder, and he was so appalled that he couldn't tell even Lew about it, couldn't put it into bare words. He had seen a man crash, once, on take-off, a man he'd known for years; and it had been terrible; but the shock had come three days afterward when he'd seen it in a newspaper, the name spelled out in cold print. Words had a finality about them, and there were these, now, that he didn't want to speak. *One of us has been stealing water from the tank.* It couldn't be said.

"If there's more dewfall," he heard Moran saying, and had to switch his mind back, "there's still a chance of flying out of this. We've got the wing off and almost ready for mounting—it's been the toughest part of the job. One more night— tonight—and there's a chance. If we don't do it soon we never will; we won't have even this much strength in us by tomorrow." He spoke very carefully, trying not to let his tongue block the sibilants against his stiffened lips: his argument against death by thirst was refuted by every word he said, in the saying of it. "This is the critical time, Frank. Get tonight over and the wing in position and the rest's in the bag, with Harris to give a hand and moonlight for the work." Maybe it sounded a little too easy. "If there's no dewfall, okay, so there's no more water, so we've had it. What can we lose?"

Towns was silent again and Moran was angry with him and got up and left him, going to talk to Stringer, saying:

"If I can round up the boys, do we work, kid?"

The young man's face looked pale and smooth in the moonlight; his eyes moved like quiet fish behind the glasses; and Moran was reminded of the novitiates of Rome in their robes and with their new-found cognizance of God. Stringer was in the thrall of what amounted to religious ecstasy, and the Skytruck was his angel.

"I'm working all the time, Mr. Moran." It sounded deliberate, the use of title and name; and Moran was warned again, and made a note of it. Mr. Stringer didn't like the "kid."

"It's just that they're worried about the water. We haven't much left."

"I don't let myself think about it. I haven't time."

Moran said, "You're dedicated to this job, of course. In a way I am too because I want to live." He went to find Loomis, who said:

"I'm ready, but can you persuade Frank Towns?"

"If I can't, we do without him."

"The trouble," said the Texan very softly, "is that we have no leader here. I expect you see that. Stringer's our key man, naturally—we're all in his hands; but he doesn't look like the leader of any-thing, does he? And he doesn't have very much in-terest in . . . the humanities. Towns is the one who can lead—he's the oldest among us and he's the captain of the aircraft. That's why we need him."

"I've done all I can but he's been badly broken up by this crash—he thinks it was his fault and that's partly right. He's killed people and he's dead scared of killing any more; and I can understand how he feels; whatever kind of aircraft we build in the end it's not likely to be a hundred percent air-worthy. And he's got to fly it."

Loomis shook his head slowly. "That's not what he's kicking against. But we'll get the others in. Maybe he'll follow; he did before."

Moran went into the hull and switched on the stanchion lamp and the shape of the wreck took on focus. Captain Harris was unconscious; Kepel was writing; he told Watson to get on his feet, and Tilney with him. They gathered round Stringer and he said: "Where are the others?"

Loomis could see two dark figures nearing the wreck from the dunes. "They're coming." Stringer waited.

"We 'avin' another bash?" asked Crow, coming up.

"Where is Mr. Towns?" Stringer demanded.

Moran said, "He'll be along."

"I am not starting with a man short," Stringer said. "It's important that we have him with us."

He spoke in petulant jerks. "It's his fault that we're here. He ought to realize that. I don't understand why he won't help. He ought to help more than anyone else—"

"I'll tell you why, Stringer." Towns stood with them, the light striking across his white hollowed face. "I've got no faith in your design, that's why."

He moved and stood facing Stringer, who looked at him with distaste, straightening his thin shoulders as if to make himself taller. With his smooth skin and his brushed hair, the polished glasses giving him the look of a student, he seemed very young, facing the heavier man with the gray stubble and the sunken eyes, the tousled hair, the bitter voice:

"You're dead right—it's my fault that we're here—it was a case of pilot error. I don't need telling. There's two men buried there under those mounds and there's two more out there somewhere in the sand without even a cross over them and there's two here in the wreck already dying—and there's us . . . there's us. And it was my fault. But it's not going to be my fault the next time, Stringer, it's going to be yours—your design. It hangs together in principle but that doesn't mean it'll hang together in the air. I've got no faith in it. But I'll do a deal with you: if you're prepared to take the risk of this thing smashing up I'll help build it and I'll fly it—but I'll fly it alone."

"I don't understand—"

"There's a hell of a lot you don't understand, Stringer, because you're too young."

And Moran felt the obvious hit him between the eyes: this was what Towns was up against. Youth. A kid like Stringer was taking over from a fifty-year-old veteran who failed, all along the line. It was a skirmish in the battle of the generations, with the older man already defeated by his own past.

Loomis had seen this. They must all have seen it.

"But it's simple enough," he heard Towns saying. "If the water lasts out and we build this thing I'll take-off alone and bring help back if I get through."

Stringer said, "We can't do that, of course. The disposition of crew weight is a critical factor in the design—she'll be nose-heavy because of the engine, and we have to add weight along the boom—"

"Then use ballast—use something that can't get killed when she smashes up."

"I've no intention of changing my design at this stage, Mr. Towns."

"Frank—"

"Then the deal's off."

"*Frank.*" Moran took his arm and swung him away, talking fast as soon as they were alone. "This is our one chance and we're wasting time because we're all ready to take it—except you. All you can think about is your own position—you're not worried that people might get killed, you're worried that it's going to be *your* fault if they do. To hell with that—it doesn't concern the rest of us—all we want to do is survive if we can, and if we can't we're not blaming anyone. Okay, say we don't build this crate, what happens? We sit here on our backsides and wait for the last of the water to run out and then we die—and that'll be your fault just the same, Frank, just the same; so if you want to make out a case against yourself it's too easy: Frank Towns crashes a Mark IV Skytruck and kills off fourteen men because he thought he was bigger than the risk he took—"

"Lew, for Christ's sake—"

"Let's get it said, good and said, the way you want it. Enjoy yourself—roll on the ground and cover yourself with ashes and rub your damn nose in the shit and have a real good time—but when you're through with it come and help us build our plane, because if there's one more drop of water left in this world we're flying out just as we flew in, and you're going to be the pilot."

He walked back to the wreck. "We start," he told Stringer.

"Providing Mr. Towns decides to help."

It would be good for the soul, Moran thought, to smash a fist into this prim little face and silence the twittering voice; it would also be a unique way of committing suicide.

"Mr. Towns," he said carefully, "will be joining us."

CHAPTER
13

BELLAMY WAS LEFT SICKENED AND SHAKING BY what he had seen, but he told no one. Writing in his diary soon after dawn, he made no note of it.

The work of the night had gone well; they had worked like robots, mechanical men, slaves of the machine they nursed. Through the dark hours they became in a certain way obsessed, as Stringer was, by the need to overcome problems and invent and improvise and somehow build the airplane; and Bellamy had been chilled by a strange thought: that they had to finish the work before they died; that once it was finished they could die in peace. For a moment he had forgotten that they had any reason for building the airplane: it simply had to be built, before they died.

He knew this was absurd; and he was therefore worried by it. There was no room for absurdities in this world of three elements: life, death, and the desert. *We're going to pieces,* Crow had said last night on the dunes. There was no comfort in the thought that the only one among them who would never go to pieces was Stringer—because he was already mad. The work obsessed him totally. You could believe that when the plane was finished and ready to fly he would stand back and look at it and say, Just as I predicted . . . there was no problem. And he'd fall down dead, satisfied.

You could see it by the way he worked. He never stopped, never hurried, never paused—as the rest of them did—to look up at the stars, to lie for minutes on the freezing sand exhausted, to ease his aching body before going on again. The stars weren't there, didn't exist: a star wasn't an aircraft component. His body didn't ache.

Crow said so many true things. *Stringer's not human.*

Through the dark hours they had become in a certain way like Stringer: a gang of quiet madmen in the lost world of night, building their own lunatic tomb. The air whispered the mumbo-jumbo words of the ritual—*still an inch this way, the lugs aren't mating . . . wedge up the leading edge to correct the tilt* . . . Mostly Stringer talking, King Stringer, call him Lord or even God but never Stringy or he'll down tools and we'll never leave here alive.

In this way Bellamy lost contact with much of what he was doing; but his hands worked and he obeyed orders; and the others worked with him, like automata, inhuman, like the tinny-voiced kid with glasses who saw no problem. And so by dawn

the mainplane was mounted, the bolts home and
the nuts locked; and they stood back to look at the
thing they had created; and Bellamy, still full of his
dreadful imaginings, prayed that Stringer would
not say, Just as I predicted, and fall down dead.

It was a long time before the first man spoke.
Moran.

"She looks like an airplane."

The rising light defined the new shape that had
been fashioned in the night, and they were awed by
its presence; because this machine might one day
be capable of ferrying them from this world to the
other: from this world of sand and thirst and death
to the world of green trees, streams, and loved
faces. This machine had the power of bestowing
on them another thirty, fifty years of life—they
could, a year from today, be represented by a heap
of bleached bones in this lost place, forgotten even
by the vultures that had fed on them; or they could
be found in the other world, watching a cricket
match under the shady chestnuts, a glass of beer in
their hands. This machine, alone, could cross the
only true frontier known to man and carry them
with it. In whatever way these thoughts came to
them individually, their meaning was the same.
Here was hope of life.

"She looks like an airplane," Moran said again.

Crow loosened his tongue from a parched
mouth.

"She does . . . Christ, she bloody does . . ."

The wing had been bolted home and winched level with the other, and a rigging wire was taut between the two, passing across the engine nacelle where the king post would go—and the shape was of an airplane: two spread wings and a three-bladed prop. They could see it as an entity, standing apart from the wrecked hull and starboard boom. Yesterday Towns had seen only a pile of wreckage made even more shapeless by the wing they had removed and hauled across the top of the hull; now there was the wreckage, and there was the airplane. He could not have put into words what he felt; it was the feeling that a pilot has in him when his plane is motionless at the beginning of the runway and the tower clears him for take-off. The heart is airborne before the airplane.

He had never needed the sky so badly.

Stringer stood apart from them, looking along the lines of the plane, already absorbed in the next operation: the mounting of the king post and flying wires that would hold the new wing against the strain of take-off. There shouldn't be any difficulty with that.

Bellamy said, "She looks as if she'd fly."

Towns moved toward the hull, his body heavy with fatigue. Drawing a hand along the wing as he went and looking at his dry fingers, he said, "It's a shame she never will."

They thought, for the first time this morning, of their situation. There had been no dew. They had petrol, oil, and an airplane; but they had no means of life.

Stringer moved away, saying nothing; and Moran thought, Did Frank do that on purpose? Probably. Because Stringer had won the night.

The sun came up; they felt its warmth; soon they would feel its heat. The night had been for nothing.

The ocean of sand was bloodied by the sun; the raw rump of the dunes lay humped against the sky; and Bellamy saw the three helicopters pass across the east horizon, flying in line, making no sound, passing across the sun's disk, three red shapes reflected in the water mirage that was always there at dawn.

"Albert," he said softly, the breath blocked in his chest.

"What's up?"

Making no sound, keeping their formation, sliding across the water that wasn't there—three of them, oh, Christ alive, why *three,* why not one, or a dozen, or a hundred of the bloody things—what did it matter? Now they had gone. They hadn't been lost to sight behind the dunes; they had simply gone.

"Nothing," he told Crow.

So this was how it felt, to be like Trucker Cobb. Not too bad at first—you longed to see rescue planes, so you saw them, and even while you watched them you could keep hold of yourself and know it was only a mirage. But next time he'd say to Crow, Look. Can't you see them, for God's sake? Over there! And Crow would look at him sideways, and purse his lips. You lost your grip, slowly, like poor Trucker; and in the end you knew the helicopters were real and that everyone else was mad, because they couldn't see them.

He followed Towns into the hull.

"What happens," he asked him, "if we step it up to a pint and a half today?" His voice sounded quite steady though his mouth lisped and fretted the few words out.

Towns was filling Captain Harris' bottle from the tank. The water trickled musically in the close confines and Bellamy wanted to knock the bottle away just to stop the sound it made.

"It'd bring things a bit nearer," Towns said. "You in a special hurry?"

Bellamy thought, You look dead already, damn you. The pilot's face was hollowed and shriveled looking, bits of dead skin hanging from the stubble, the mouth a gash in a mask, a hole in torn paper.

"I can wait," Bellamy said. The others came in, bringing their water bottles, lining up; and Loomis took water to the German boy and the captain. Harris pulled himself upright, one hand gripping the seat-back until white bone showed under the skin.

"How . . ." his mouth sounded numbed, "getting on . . . the good work?" A bright smile in the eyes, the rest of the face a grimace.

"We did well," said Loomis. "When you feel like it, come out and we'll show you."

"Capi-thal—capi-thal!" The bottle shook in his hand and he saw Loomis watching him and steadied it against his chest, waiting until they had gone, because he knew that he might spill some of the water and they would want to run and catch the falling jewels and not be able to.

"There y'are, Bimbo," said Crow, and watched the monkey drink, the whole of its skeleton-body quivering, its brown eyes closed in ecstasy; and Bellamy said:

"You could do with that yourself. I could do with that much—any of us could." The ugly words were no prettier from a cracked tongue. He hadn't meant to say it: they were just thoughts stuttering out of him through his mouth; in the same way he had "seen" the helicopters.

Crow did not look at him. "It's not your business, nor mine either. 'E belongs to Rob."

When Bellamy wrote his diary he made no mention of the three helicopters, or of Crow. Crow was dying, and keeping faith with the dead. You had to laugh, or cry; but you couldn't put it down in any diary. It was hard enough to keep the writing straight, so he just put:

Kepel still alive. Harris looks better. We got the wing on. No dew. Sleep now.

* * * * *

Moran rolled over and struggled to get up, fighting for consciousness, already conscious enough to know that he had been sleeping and had been awakened by a sound that could mean only that he had gone mad in his sleep—the sky glared in his eyes and the heat crackled in the sand as his hands scattered it; he heard his own breathing like an animal's grunts; he knew that if he didn't wake fully the mad sound would go on. It was a woman singing.

Hanging like a dog on hands and knees, he swung his head and saw the blue and white reeling sky and the liquid gold off the ground, both circling around him as he shut his eyes and listened because he had to listen, because he couldn't shut his ears. The woman sang:

L'altra notte in fondo al mare . . .

He hung on the ground cursing the sound of the beautiful voice of the woman from the dream; he clenched his eyes, afraid that if he opened them he would see her there, singing. Her song rang bell-pure, echoing from the dunes, trapping him—he was awake, aware of the sand where his bunched hands dug, of the heat on his back, of the pain in his muscles: but her voice sang on in his sleep.

A man called out and someone moved past him—in the glare he recognized Loomis staggering to the door of the hull; and others were waking. Then the voice stopped. He dropped onto the sand, released of nightmare.

"Let's 'ave some more," called Crow, and Moran moved his head and opened his eyes. How nuts could you go?

A man was speaking in Arabic. *National referendum . . . the duty of the people . . . committee of advisers to convene . . .* The voice grew faint suddenly.

Moran got to his feet and lurched for the hull doorway where the others were clustered.

"Let's have Callas back," said Crow.

Sleeping for an hour, Towns had awakened to sick thoughts, of wanting to kill Stringer, of wanting to rouse the lot of them and shout at them, *Which one of you bastards is taking water from the tank?* He had gone into the hull stealthily, hoping to catch them; but there was only Kepel and Harris. A duffel bag had fallen across the gangway and he picked it up, realizing it was Cobb's. The drawstring was loose and the chrome face of the dial showed through the opening; he took out the transistor: if it still worked they could get the news from Cairo and Rome.

Rome had the Callas record on, part of *Mefistofele*; he couldn't turn the dial for a minute because it was a voice from the world outside and they were no longer alone.

The political broadcast must be from Beida, the new capital of Yemen. He spun the dial back to Rome. Now they listened, all of them, to the voice of Callas; they dropped to the sand and leaned on their elbows, listening to her voice, saying not a word until the record ended.

"Where'd you find it?" Crow asked.

"It's Cobb's."

After deliberation: " 'E won't mind if we use it."

"We can get the news," Watson said.

" 'Ell with the news, let's 'ave some music, mate."

As it had been when they had wrung the gallon of water from the silk, so it was now: they didn't know what to do next with the treasure. Towns brought it outside so that the noise wouldn't worry Kepel; and Captain Harris followed him shakily on to the sand, leaving the hull for the first time since they had carried him in there. Seeing him, Crow said:

"She's a girl, she is. She gets 'em on their feet." He didn't know how the poor bloke found the strength, he looked like death. "Come on an' sit along of me, Cap—I got the tickets—what you want to 'ear next?"

They tried all the stations and in the middle of the day they heard the news in English from GLR Cyprus. There was nothing about a freight-transport plane missing since a week ago. Beyond the far rim of the desert the world went whistling on its way.

*   *   *

Somewhere in the middle of the afternoon Tilney began cracking up.

Loomis had been watching him playing with his water bottle, shaking it, resting its flat side against his face, unscrewing the cap and sucking at the neck as if it were not empty; and Loomis had told him there'd be another share-out first thing in the morning, not long now, not long, while the kid had looked at him with dazed eyes, his dried-up mouth opening and shutting, idiot-fashion.

Bellamy thought, That's not an act. He went to Towns when he couldn't stand it any more. "A drop or two now might save him."

"For what? Tomorrow? And what happens to-morrow?"

"I'm just asking you to give him a few drops now."

"Look." Set deep in the peeling face the blood-shot eyes were perfectly steady. "We've got half a pint each still in the tank. When that's gone, that's it. You with me? So it doesn't matter very much when we have it. It's just a question of time." He had wondered, all today, who would be the first to opt for a bullet. "The kid can have his share now—you too if you want it. But either he chooses for himself or it's your responsibility if you choose for him. Up to you. I'll tell you, though, that I wouldn't ever take that much responsibility myself."

Bellamy went away and sat where he couldn't

see Tilney. It was right: it didn't matter when they finished the water. Give some to the kid now and he'd last the night, but he'd be the first to go, tomorrow or the next day. He must shut his mind to things, hold on to sanity. Don't look at Tilney, don't watch Crow giving the monkey water, don't look at the horizon too long—or he'd see those three things again. And tomorrow write a short letter home, saying they didn't suffer in the end, all that kind of thing; because you were obliged to do that; and there was a chance of the letter's being found, one day, one fine day.

Toward evening Captain Harris made his way to Towns, standing pathetically upright. "How much coolant is there in the tanks?"

"Fifty liters. Ten gallons. Ten gallons of glycerine and additive. In our condition, call it strychnine."

Harris swayed, steadying before Towns could put out a hand.

"What's the water content?"

"About half."

"Yes. I see." He drew himself up and turned away, taking great care, as a drunk does when he knows he mustn't show anything.

Bellamy and Moran and the captain were working on the idea before night fell, draining the coolant into a jerrican, finding a curved metal tube from the wrecked seats, making a step joint and fitting the tube to the can, setting the can on a grid of crossed metal and stones. Beneath it they lit a burner filled with mixed oil and petrol, and below the end of the tube they put a water bottle. The others watched but no one talked about it. Towns had told them: "The closest I'd sit to that thing is ten yards. You've got a small outlet, and if that stuff ever boils, you've got boiling glycerine."

"We shall take good care," said Captain Harris, and remained where he was, to watch over the makeshift retort.

During the night none of them worked except Stringer. They had all been told that each had a half-pint left, and that he could have it when he liked. Tilney and Sergeant Watson had asked for their share immediately and had drunk half. The others would wait until dawn. Although Stringer was working on his king post, no one asked him what they could do to help; and he asked for none. The lamp on the stanchion was dimmer than last night because no one had volunteered to wind the generator for the last twelve hours.

There was the feeling among them, quite unspoken, that they had done their best and now must stop. Their limbs ached as with the ague; their eyes were sores in their faces; it was difficult to think coherently; and speech was painful and terrible to hear. Those luckiest were those with an obsession, because they need think of nothing else—not of thirst nor of death. Stringer, his mind among machinery; Harris, sitting before the shrine of the little flame; Bellamy and Moran, his disciples, beside him.

Loomis knew what was soon going to happen to him because he felt closer to Jill than ever before in his life. Kepel had complained of pain at nightfall; and Towns, knowing that only unbearable pain would be admitted by the boy, gave him morphia, the last there was. Crow sat watching the first stars appear; he had turned on the transistor but the others had told him to switch it off or take it across to the dunes. Again unspeaking, they had agreed that the memories of the outside world—of rain and home and friends—would be brought to them too clearly by the sound of the little radio. Crow switched it off, and held the monkey against him, and made quiet noises to it, hardly words, that the others wouldn't have to hear.

Sergeant Watson sat apart from them in case Harris called to him and ordered him to do something. Not knowing any other way of flouting an order, the sergeant knew that he would kill the captain; the itch had been in him since the bastard had crawled back here. All he could hear was the Tilney kid, praying; and Watson listened, not troubled by it, although most of it was gibberish and sobbing.

Towns had looked often at Kepel, dreading the time when he would come to, because the only answer to pain now was the gun; he walked in the first light of the moon as far as the dunes, because he didn't want to hear the madman, Stringer, working on his plane. There'd be wings here soon enough.

Not long before midnight the moon sank behind the dunes. The air was winter-cold. The flame below the jerrican burned too feebly and the coolant had still not boiled. The shadow of the dunes, on the going down of the moon, drew over them.

CHAPTER
14

SOON AFTER DAWN THEY MADE A GRAVE BESIDE
the other two and carried him to it. Their shadows
were long across the sand.

Most of the night Bellamy and Moran had lain
half-sleeping but Captain Harris had remained
awake, sitting cross-legged by the yellow flame, feed-
ing it with oil when it burned low. Sometimes the
other two opened their eyes and watched him; he sat
like a yogi, the light of the flame playing on, his
gaunt and dying face; only the occasional movement
of his eyelids showed that he was awake and alive.

They found him, when the sun rose, in the same
posture, his limbs locked in it. Moran heard the
bubbling of the coolant over the flame and for a
moment he couldn't remember what the jerrican
was for; then he spoke to Harris, despairing at the
idiot sound of his shriveled tongue.

"How much have we got?"

The captain didn't seem to have heard, but
turned his head when Moran sat up, saying again,
"How much have we got?"

Harris took the water bottle from beneath the tubing and held it out to him, putting another one in its place, making it firm in the sand.

"Half." He could barely pronounce the word, but his crusted mouth was in a smile and his eyes were bright. Moran weighed the bottle, hearing the sound of the water.

"Good," he said, "good, Cap." Normal speech was now an effort; you found yourself choosing short words so that you could grunt them out like an Indian. He thought, It's been burning all night long; twelve hours to get half a pint; we need a pint each for a day and there's eight of us, that means eight days' boiling to give us enough for one day—what do we use for the other seven days? He felt a pain shaking out of his chest and heard that it was a kind of laughter that now turned to coughing.

Captain Harris watched him with a smile.

When the coughing was over, his throat burned and the pain became permanent; but he said, "Wha' we do with it?" He shook the bottle.

"Give it to Ke'el." He forced his lips together. "Kepel."

Moran got up and swayed, shutting his eyes against the huge red sun, hearing Harris calling to him through the mists of red: "Don' drop bottle! *Don' drop—*"

It struck his foot and he lurched over, scrambling in the sand for it, opening his eyes and seeing the dark stain on the sand. Harris was trying to say something. He gripped the bottle, sobered by terror, and held it upright. About half the water had spilled. Whispering came from his mouth:

"*Sorry . . . sorry . . . sorry . . .*"

"Accident," Harris said, "accident."

Six hours, Moran thought in pain, six hours to make what he'd spilled. He gripped the bottle in both hands, walking away with it, trying to show Harris by his careful walk that he would not spill any more. His legs ached already; his calves were sore from the heat cramp that had set in yesterday. The new sun burned against his face.

There was only Kepel in the hull. The night had been cold and they had stayed outside, drawn by the flame that Harris watched. He kept the bottle rigidly upright in one hand, supporting himself on the wreckage of the seats in case the gash in the metal floor tripped him. If he dropped the bottle again he would never be able to tell the captain; he would have to say, "He drank every drop." It would be hell, having to say that.

He reached Kepel, whose eyes were closed and whose face had the color of tallow even in the glow of the sun that filled the hull. He stood looking down at the boy, holding the bottle upright, the thought in his mind: Now we'll have to give it to Tilney. Somehow Kepel had managed, sometime in the long night, to move the canvas bowl until it was below his arm; and now his arm hung down, the white hand zebra-streaked with blood, the fingers touching the surface in the bowl. The pocketknife was still in his other hand, folded on his chest.

The report sheets were neatly piled on the opposite seat that had served him as a table for his things: cigarette lighter, some keys, a few coins, the pen that Loomis had lent him. On the blank back of the topmost sheet Moran read:

I hope that my water ration will be of use. Please post the letter. I wish very much to thank you for attending to me so kindly. Otto Gerhard Kepel.

It was very quiet in the hull.

Moran came away, taking care with the bottle; even so, it was jolted as he made his way over the torn flooring, and the sound of the water hurried him, so that he could reach Tilney before the terrible urge to jam the neck of the bottle into the husk of his mouth overcame him.

He told them, and they agreed that they must see to the burial while they had the strength left. After the boy had been taken from the hull Captain Harris tidied the seats, retrieving some papers that had fallen. One sheet was folded intricately, forming its own envelope. *Vater, Mutter, und Inga.* The Wünlich address was below.

Harris would have expected him to have written: *Herr & Frau Kepel,* their proper names. Perhaps, in the final hour, these were the names he most dearly knew them by, and therefore the most proper.

Almost half the batch of flying-report sheets had been filled with writing, and Harris wondered if they too were to be sent home by whatever angel chanced by. The first sheet bore a title: *The White Bird.*

Once long ago, there lived three people in the depths of a forest far greater than the Black Forest or any other in all the world. Their house was of larch wood with eaves that sloped down upon each side . . .

The captain was aware that his foot was sliding degree by degree on the blood that had spilled from the bowl; and he changed his stance to the other foot as he read on.

Two of the people had sadly lost their son, long ago; and the third, who was the most beautiful maiden in all the great forest, grieved for her lover . . . so sad was she that she cut off her long fair hair; yet it grew again, as if her lover had not wished it so; again she cut it, yet again it grew, to shine so beautifully. . . .

On the third sheet the writing became disjointed and the nib had been pressed harder as if in an effort to continue.

There was a white castle, and an old woman in a cave who made spells and gave a magic promise to the three people of the larch-wood house, telling them to wait.

. . . The day came when they saw a great white bird flying above the heights of the forest trees; and on the back of the bird was mounted a youth appareled in golden armor, whose form they seemed to recognize. Three times the white bird circled, lowering towards a nearby clearing; and the three people began running in that direction, with the long fair hair of the maiden flying out as she ran between the giant trees, while the—

Sounds came from the hull doorway.

"That's it then, Cap."

Crow stood there with some rag in his hand and Harris rolled the sheets together, tucking them into the net rack above the seats.

"Got to clean up a bit," said Crow, and went to his knees with the rag, and the captain left the hull, wishing to stand for a minute by the new grave; he knew the prayer from memory, for he had been required sometimes to assist the padre, along the road to Benghazi.

Five.

The white silk hung motionless, blued by the sky beyond. The sky and the sand and the silence burned about him, burning his face and eyes.

Sammy, Lloyd, Roberts, Cobb, Kepel.

You said it, Lew. Frank Towns crashes a Mark IV Skytruck and kills off fourteen men because he thought he was bigger than the risk he took.

The glare gouged at his eyes and maybe if he ever tried to open them again he'd know he was blind, that would be okay, he didn't want to see anything any more.

Five. Nine to go. Getting there slowly. You're going to be right, Lew. I hope it makes you feel good.

The heat raked at him.

The gun was in its holster on his belt. He liked having it with him. If you wanted to get through this world you had to have one of two things that made you bigger than the rest: money or a gun. It was all anyone thought about; kids pinched it and played with it—Gi-us a shillin', *bang* an' you're dead! It was all the bloody taxes were for—money for guns.

Sign on, Watty, another ten years' hard. If you're lucky we'll get you another luvverly war.

Whores' arses, they could stuff it. He was king of the bleeding lot, a millionaire on holiday, with a gun.

Since noon he'd been watching bloody Harris. Bloody Harris sat by his little chemistry set, giving it oil. It'd been funny to watch him. He never took any notice of the other people except when they spoke to him. You'd think his life depended on it, that little pocket cookhouse he'd got there. The most it could ever do was to give you enough to spit with, but he couldn't realize. He sat upright just as if he was on parade. Watson knew that kind: carry on as if there was nothing wrong and suddenly they fell over stiff as a corpse.

The sergeant was in pain and was lying almost flat in a hollow he had made in the sand, the nearest thing to a bed, the nearest thing to a grave, if you like. His mouth felt as if he'd had all his teeth out and his tongue cut off and somebody'd stuffed it full of bayonets. He kept seeing a waterfall right in front of him, spray bouncing off it, all the bright rocks shining, green ferns, everything; but he didn't take any notice because he was watching Harris.

The captain sat with his back to his sergeant, with bits of skin flaking off his neck. Watson couldn't see him very clearly because of the glare and his sore eyes. Sometimes Harris changed color and swayed about, disappearing and coming back; but Watson concentrated as best he could; and he couldn't remember actually pulling the gun out of its holster; all he knew now was that it was in his hand. It was black and heavy in his hand.

Sarnt Watson!

Sir? Don't move, sir. Don't move. Keep just like that.

Sarnt Watson!

Sir? Can I be of service, sir? Ten years' fucking service, sir? Don't move then. Six rounds. One in the neck, one in the mouth, two in your luvverly eyes, sir, two in your bleeding ears.

Try it now, sir. You know my name. Title, sergeant. Let's hear you shout it out again, you nasty little bastard.

It was black and heavy in his hand. Too good to be true, fit to beat the band. A millionaire on holiday, a loaded gun, and Captain Harris' neck at a five-yard range—and no questions asked . . . ever in this life. What a glorious end to a fine sergeant's career! Clover, this was, plush and clover. Roll in it, Watty, roll.

The moaning from inside the hull was getting on Crow's nerves. It had gone on for an hour now, enough to drive you barmy.

The light ebbed and flowed against his closed eyes and his legs were on fire. In another minute he'd get up and take a turn again because if he didn't he'd finish up lying here on his back. He'd been to talk to Bellamy but he was writing a letter home. He'd wanted to tell Bellamy they couldn't just curl up and die without doing something about it; but he didn't want to interrupt what Bellamy was writing.

Poor little Tilly looked bad, over there. All he could think about was God. The kid had rattled his mouth at him—

"I's not too late, i's not too late to think about God, we mus' call 'pon the Lord an' 'seech him to save us if we don't phray now to God to save us no hophe if we don' phray—" On and on like that, gave you the creeps. If the Lord couldn't see for himself what a fix they were in, it was no use bloody squawking to him.

The heat flared against the cinders of his eyes. Soon he got up, you could call it that, legs all over the place, hit his head on the tail unit but got up, and went inside the hull, the monkey clinging on, poor old Bimbo. The hull was like an oven, all the seats empty now, miss old Otto, never mind, he was happy now. The moaning got on your tits.

Stringer looked up at him and stopped turning the generator, and the moaning died away.

"Come to take over," said Crow.

"Why?" The pale school-kid face was shining, quite a surprise to think of Mr. Stringer actually being so proper highly indecent as to sweat, like a human being.

"Why?" repeated Crow. "Well, we got to do somethin', we can't jus' curl up an' die. Shift over."

Then an amazing thing happened to Stringer's face. Crow stared at it, finding it hard to believe. Stringer was smiling. It hadn't ever happened before. Crow had known him eight days now, half a lifetime, here; and this was the first time such a thing had happened. Stringer's face looked entirely different. Human.

"I'm glad to hear that," Stringer said. "If we all stopped thinking about dying we'd get more work done." He moved past Crow. "I shall be needing some proper light out there tonight," he explained. "I'm going to fit the king post." He made his way carefully down the hull.

Crow put the monkey on the locker above the winding gear and began turning the handle, looking up at Bimbo and forcing his parched mouth to produce sound:

There's . . . a long long trail . . . a-winding,
Into the land of . . . my dreams . . .

Loomis leaned over him.

"My stomach . . ." Tilney kept saying.

"It's heat cramp, son. Nothing bad." His own stomach was knotted, and his legs felt on fire. There was so little water in their bodies now that the bloodstream was slowing, unable to carry the heat to the skin fast enough. "It'll be night soon, another hour, that's all; it'll be cooler soon."

Towns sat with his head on his folded arms; when Moran spoke to him he raised it and leaned it against the side of the hull, his red eyes half open in the glare.

"I didn't mean to say it, Frank. You know. Last night."

"Was true."

"No. Did all you knew, brought her down like a feather—"

"Pilot error."

"Bad luck and a bum weather report, and no one looked for us. . . . Anyway . . . forget I ever said it, will you?"

They went on talking in spasmodic grunts, each

trying to clear his own conscience while there was time left.

Bellamy sat near Captain Harris watching the flame; soot was on their faces from the oil smoke. They had shaded the water bottle and the tubing, leaving the jerrican in the sun to help the condensation, moving the torn metal panel every fifteen minutes to keep pace with the sun. Bellamy reckoned that by nightfall there would be enough water in the bottle to share out between all nine of them, two or three drops on the tongue for each.

Captain Harris had moved only twice since noon: when Bellamy had brought him a couple of dried dates and when some unknown force had persuaded him to turn his head and look behind him. Watson was staring at him, his revolver in his hand, by some chance aimed in his direction. He tried to call to the man—*"Sarn"*—but his mouth was locked, and nothing came. He turned his head away. Watson was a good soldier, never fool with a gun, and the safety catch would surely be on.

He noticed Bellamy's suffering; his eyes were rolling upward under their crusted lids and his dark tongue poked from his mouth. He must rally the poor fellow.

"Shlow work," he said, forcing his face into a smile. "Shlow work."

The liquid bubbled in the can.

*   *   *

THE FLIGHT OF THE PHOENIX

The shadows of the dunes were black-cut by the moon; the stars were huge and blue. Toward midnight the silk canopy was lifted, and fell inert, and was lifted again by the breeze that rose softly from the north, from the sea.

CHAPTER
15

NINTH DAY. *WRITING THIS AT THREE IN THE*
afternoon. Very hot. It was a miracle. I felt the wind
getting up about midnight but didn't believe it. North
wind. First thing this morning we really worked at it,
squeezed the chute silk dry, wrung out everything
there was. Even the legs of our slacks we'd cut off
gave a few pints. Moran found the scrapers we'd
made, and skinned the frost off the whole plane. Har-
ris even fitted the chute silk with cakes of frost and
sand, then we waited till it melted, and squeezed the
silk a second time. The stuffs muddy, but it's water—
WATER—near enough six whole beautiful gallons in
the tank! So we're alive alive-o, and we're not damn
well giving it up. All resting now, saving our sweat for
tonight. Can't believe it, can't believe it.

They looked the same, like dead men, with gaunt
faces and the skin peeling from them, with eyes
like wounds and lips like peanut shells; they lay
without moving, without talking, waiting for night
to come. But life shone in them now.

Nothing had been said but they knew that tonight they would work like blacks on Stringer's angel. They would work tonight and tomorrow night and all the nights it took to finish the plane and get it airborne and out of here.

Even Stringer had sat for an hour in the shade doing nothing, conserving his strength, until he couldn't bear the inactivity; then he put his knotted handkerchief back on his fair quiffed hair and went back to work, squatting under the new mainplane with a toolbox, knocking up brackets that he needed. They watched him from between their encrusted lids, and none of them thought ill of him any more. He had the ace now and if he won they'd win with him.

Towns lay near the door of the hull so that if anyone went in there he would know. They had started taking turns again to spin the generator so that they could work with a brighter light; as each of them went into the hull, Towns listened to his movements, so that if one of them stopped even for a couple of seconds near the drinking tank he would hear. He was conscious of his change of mood: yesterday he'd gone quietly into the hull hoping to catch someone at it; today, listening to their movements, he hoped he would hear no one stop on the way to the generator. Tonight he was going to tell them what had been happening, because it mattered now. They'd proved that, given a north breeze, they could reap a harvest of life itself, using even the sand that trapped them here. It mattered very much that no one went to that tank again in secret.

He lay listening until the sun touched the dunes in the west. They all began moving, as if in answer to a signal. Even Sergeant Watson got up. He had spent the day thinking, and he'd come to a simple conclusion: there wasn't much future for a dead millionaire, for all his money and his gun.

The sand was still hot enough to burn their feet and they put on their Sahara sandals, trudging toward Stringer through the long shadows of the sundown. The moan of the generator stopped and before Loomis came out of the hull Stringer called to him:

"The light on, please."

The scene leaped into clarity. All around the ring of light the moon's quarter threw its glow across the sand.

"Before we start," Towns said, "I'm going to tell you something."

Moran was immediately worried. There'd been a showdown between Towns and Stringer about the design of the plane; now Towns was going to make a claim as boss and beat the younger man to it.

Even now, with the hope of life in him, Towns found it hard to say: "In the past three days someone's been helping himself from the drinking tank."

The night was made ugly. The white light accused. Crow thought, *Watson*. Loomis thought, *Tilney*. They all looked at the ground. Moran was no longer worried; he was shocked. If the dew hadn't come they would have started dying; and the first man to die would have made this a murder charge. There could be only one thing worse: that Towns was wrong.

"Sure about that, Frank?"

"I kept on checking." Towns looked at their faces in the cold white light. "Yep. I'm sure about it. The thing is, it wasn't so important before. Now it is. We've got close on six gallons and it won't last us long because we'll be working right through every night and maybe even in the day. We might have to try finishing this job before the next dewfall—which could come again tonight or in a month from now. We stand a chance of getting out of here alive." He looked at no one now. "So I'm just telling you this. If it happens again and I see who's doing it, I'll kill him with my two hands."

He turned away and Stringer said, "I won't do it again."

The words seemed to echo about their heads, repeating themselves monotonously. Stringer was looking straight into Towns' blank face, his mild brown eyes blinking slowly.

Towns said, "It was you?"

"Yes."

"I didn't ask who it was."

"No."

"You didn't have to admit it."

"No."

Towns found his right hand bunched and he could see blood on Stringer's face even before he hit it—yet there was no blow, no blood. His hand fell loose. He heard himself asking, "Then why?"

Stringer looked impatient and a shrillness sounded in the otherwise toneless voice: "Of course you don't understand, Mr. Towns, do you? I was thirsty. I have been working every night and almost every day, much harder than anyone else. You seem to expect me to build this machine without even water to drink! I do wish you would try to see things like this for yourself."

He turned away but Towns grabbed his arm and swung him back, the rage threatening to choke him. "So I don't see it for myself—so you tell me—if you don't think you've done anything criminal, why did you do it by stealth? I'm in charge of the rationing— why didn't you come to me and ask for extra water?"

"Because you wouldn't have given me any."

Towns took his hand from Stringer's arm and for a moment had to shut his eyes, not to see the kid's brazen face. People said in the dock, *I don't know what happened. Something came over me, and the next thing I knew he was dead.* It would be his own defense, if it happened.

His body shook. A far voice said, "Easy, Frank."

Stringer was talking. "You wouldn't have given me any, because you don't understand these things. You keep giving up—you all do! And that's not just because you were thirstier than me; I took an extra bottleful for those three days, but I lost it in perspiration, working in the heat while you lay about doing nothing." The more he talked the more impatient he became. The naked bulb, reflected from his glasses, sent two spots of light swinging across their faces. His voice broke on a note of indignation: "How do you expect me to build this machine if I'm dying of thirst, and without any proper cooperation?"

The silence drew out.

"Easy, Frank."

"Shuddup." Towns shook his arm free and turned away from Stringer, standing with his back to him, staring up at the unbelievable sanity of the stars.

The voice went on.

"But I don't intend taking extra water again, as I have already told you, because I expect you *all* to work as hard as I do, and that means we shall *all* need an increased ration. Now, is that quite clear?"

He was looking at Towns' hunched back, and no one spoke. Three, four seconds, five—

"Quite clear," Moran said, impatient with Towns, with Stringer, with himself, with all of them—they stood here squabbling like spoiled kids just because there'd been some water to drink and they could brush up their sensitive egos again. Here was a plane half built and it could save their lives; but they stood bickering. This was the desert, out to kill in one of its countless ways: reducing a man in its heat, shriveling him and taking away his dignity, giving him water again to send him in search of what he had lost: his pride. Towns had nearly smashed a fist into Stringer's face—Christ, it would have meant their death!

Crow asked levelly, "What's the job then, Stringer?"

The knotted handkerchief was removed from the school-kid haircut and put carefully into a pocket; the bright glasses were adjusted; the brown eyes leapt in love of what was said:

"At this stage the prop-tips can be cut. Nine inches precisely—I have measured the extent of the distortion. While I carry on with the king post mounting I want ring brackets bolted to the mid-section rib of each mainplane. The brackets are in that toolbox ready for you. The rigging cable will run from one mid-section rib, through the top of the king post, and down to the other wing. We fit the cable later—it will have to be taken from the winch gear and we need the winch for the next few nights."

Moran noticed Towns moving, getting ready to

work. So the second round had gone to Stringer, like the first. Pray God there wouldn't be a third.

"I want the port engine carburetor dismantled and the sand cleared out of the jets and ducts, and this must be done carefully, because we're working in sand as it is, and we don't want to put as much back as we take out." Stringer paused, making sure he had their attention; then he told Bellamy: "You said you have engineering degrees. I want you to do the more technical work, and also advise and supervise the others as necessary."

Twitters like a bleeding bird, thought Sergeant Watson, just like a bleeding little bird. If it wasn't the Old Boy touch it was bloody engineering degrees—thank Christ for three good stripes, just wait till he found a corporal back at base, just wait.

They moved about in the bulb's glare. There came the clink of tools. Loomis stalked off with a spanner to find bolts from the wreckage to use for the ring brackets.

"When there's time," Bellamy said, "I'd like to knock up a bigger distillery for the rest of that coolant."

"When you have time," Stringer told him, "but don't rob the port tank—we shall need it for the flight."

"Cut them tips square?" asked Crow.

"Dead square, and chamfer them. Mr. Bellamy—"

"I'm here."

"I want to show you the tail unit and explain what we have to set up."

The two of them passed out of the circle of light.

Towns unbuttoned the carb-access cowling and started work on the control rods and flanges. Crow called:

"Tilly! Give 'and 'ere, mate."

Watson rummaged for a hacksaw.

"Frank, I'll clean out a panel to put the bits in."

Captain Harris told Moran, "Leave that job to me—I'm no engineer and you can be better employed." The naked bulb lit his bright smile. "Organization. Works wonders."

A saw blade began rasping at a prop-tip. Stringer's voice sounded monotonously, detailing the tail unit setup for Bellamy. The tools rang musically. Crow began whistling.

Above them the moon rode high.

CHAPTER
16

WITH THE COMING OF THE FULL MOON THEY saw the mirage. Used to the desert, they knew that a mirage is never seen after sundown; but when the full moon rose the mirage was there. It was a sandstorm; yet there was no breath of wind.

At the day's end Bellamy had written:

Twentieth Day. Work still going well, but water very low. Struck a lot of snags. Hunger bad now; not hungry for food, just weakness and stomach pains.

In the past week of nights they had suffered three setbacks; raising the whole new machine by supporting the jacking points and knocking the wing trestles out from under, Stringer located the center of gravity by balance. He had to have the C of G to work out crew disposition and the center of lift; and no one, not even Towns, had dissuaded him from this very dodgy operation. One of the supports keened over and it took two whole nights to reerect the trestles.

Moran had dropped a carburetor jet into the sand, took an hour to search for it, failed to find it, and spent the rest of the night digging under the starboard engine to get at the spare carb and remove the jet. He had carried it like a priceless pearl in the warm dawnlight; it was no bigger than a hazel nut but Crow told him: "Lose that one, cock, an' that's our lot." The new machine would fly—if it could fly at all—with half a hundredweight of monorail skid added on or chopped off; it could not ever fly without this tiny jet.

Watson had broken five hacksaw blades and Tilney three; and a half-round bastard file had to be used to cut through the last of the toughened-steel monorail when they made the skids. Blisters broke on their hands and turned septic. They worked on.

With these three setbacks, a score of minor ones. Stringer guided them, contemptuous of any clumsiness, impatient with lack of grasp; but he never lost his temper as Towns did, as Sergeant Watson did. They worked on, sometimes through the grilling heat of day, once through an electric storm that left their nerves in rags, and always against pain: the pain of the glare that burned the eyes, of the heat that felled them, of the cramps that gripped the stomach and paralyzed the legs—pain in the muscles, pain in the mouth, in bruises and in broken skin, and in the thought: We might not make it.

Work still going well.

Dew had fallen two nights ago, giving them some three gallons of water brackish with the taint of the chute dope and unfilterable mud; they sipped at it as one sips champagne. The rest of the starboard-engine coolant was now distilled. With it, and with the dew, there had been two pints per day per man for almost a week; it was hunger that nagged at them now. How long could a man survive on a diet of dates? Nobody asked. As long as he must, until the *Phoenix* was finished.

It was Loomis who, one night, had scraped dope from the identification markings below the wings, melted it, and painted the name on the boom that had now become the fuselage.

The Phoenix.

It took time to paint it neatly; but he didn't hurry. The thing they were building had already lost the look of wreckage; now it had a name and they were proud of it. Watson alone had doubts:

"The on'y pictures of phoenixes I've seen've been on fire."

Crow had patience with him. "Well, that's the point, see? This bird catches alight, then it goes an' lays an egg, an' another bird 'atches out an' flies off, an' Bob's y'r uncle. That's what we're goin' to do."

"So long as I know," said Watson.

Some of them, when the others weren't looking, came to stand for a minute gazing up at the name. In the days that followed they conceived a kind of love for the name of this machine and for the man who had devoted himself to making it. Hate they had for him already; now they bore him love, seeing in his cold lizard-eyed face an aspect of godship. Stringer was an ugly wizard in whose wand there lay the power of life over death. They obeyed him in everything.

"Turn the engine. The pistons want freeing off."

They earthed the magneto and swung the three-bladed prop by hand; those who were not engaged in this stood back and observed the miracle, half expecting a gust of exhaust gas from the pipes as the engine fired and spun the propeller into a haze of blades. It did not happen; but it would happen one day; and life would begin again.

"Strengthen that skid cage with cross-brackets. Use the existing holes to save drilling. You can supervise, Mr. Bellamy."

They reached for their tools. The new wing no longer rested across the crushed top of the hull; it was spread out level with the other, held by the heavy rigging cable from the three-ton winch. The *Phoenix* no longer sagged on the makeshift trestles but stood on her own legs that were made from sections of the monorail, sawn, hacked, and filed to the correct length by worn and broken tools and bleeding hands.

"Get those control rods free on their stops, Mr. Towns—they're fouling somewhere."

Nobody questioned, not even Towns.

Until the twentieth day, nothing happened except that they worked, and that Jill died.

It had been two nights ago when Loomis was standing alone and apart from the others, talking to her with the starlight against his eyes; the moment had come without warning, and the news from nowhere; and already the quiet words were sounding in his soul—*Good-by, Jill—Good-by, my darling Jill—I will see you there. Good-by.* His eyes on the high stars and his mind far from here, he knew with sudden and numbing certainty that she had this minute died. He knew a loneliness unimaginably deep, and all known things were now lost to him, and it didn't matter, because now that she had gone all else could go. So it was over.

The next morning he had wandered through the mouth of the dunes and they had brought him back, Towns and Moran; and he couldn't remember his own name. They said it was a heat stroke and gave him water. Now he was all right again, and worked with them through the night, a dead man working with the living.

The work progressed; but the water was very low; they tried to eat the dates and sometimes managed, swallowing them unsalivated and waiting for the stomach pains that would follow. The work on the plane, with its successive problems—most of them caused by the lack of good tools and the need for improvisation—enabled them by a little to ignore the heat, the hunger, and the thirst;

only when they took a few minutes' rest did they doubt that they could ever get going again.

The sun went down on the twentieth day and the working lamp came on; and in two hours the moon rose, and the mirage appeared.

Bellamy saw it first and said nothing, being afraid, remembering the three helicopters; but he couldn't look away from the strange cloud of sand that rose and hung against the disk of the moon. The air was unmoving; he turned his face but could feel no breeze against his cheek. The sandstorm was driving northward, an isolated veil, smoke-dark across the moon; and there came voices, thinned by distance. He turned away so that he would see nothing; but couldn't shut his ears.

Crow came down the length of the fuselage to borrow a drill, and turned back, and stopped dead, listening.

"Dave." The far voices troubled the night. "You 'ear anythin'?"

Bellamy went up to him. "Yes."

"Christ! Sand risin'—look!" He called to the others. "Shut up a minute! Listen!"

The voices were still there beyond the east ridge of the dunes; the sand was thinning and drifting in the cold light of the moon. Work had stopped; they all stood watching the east; then Captain Harris said:

"Arabs."

"Eh?"

"Bedous. Making a halt."

Crow was almost angry with him for saying it so calmly. "Then for Chris' sake!" How to put it? Couldn't just say *We're saved*. Like telling someone he'd just won the pools, the lot, the jackpot. Didn't mean anything till you could get your mind round it. "Then fer Jesus Chris' *sake*!"

A figure broke from among them and began running—Tilney—running like a rag doll across the sand with Harris after him, catching up, swinging him round, bringing him back.

"They'll give us water—they'll save us, they'll save us, won't they, won't they?" The captain cut him short:

"No talking. Sarnt Watson, switch that light out, quick, man!"

They stood in the gloom.

The voices came eerily as if from the sky, because of the bulwark of the dunes.

"Yes," Harris said. "Arabic. Dialect. Zollurgh." He fell to listening again, standing bolt upright.

In a minute Towns said, "Add it up for me, Cap. Where do we go from here?"

"What? I don't know."

Stringer said, "I require the light."

Moran looked at his pale face in the moonlight and knew just how nuts this kid had gone. As if to enjoy the proximity of true madness—like scratching an itch—he said to him very simply as to a child, "A bunch of camelmen have just made a halt over there. If they've got spare camels they can take us along, or we could ride two to a beast. Or they could send a rescue team tomorrow." He waited, scratching the itch till it bled, because he knew what Stringer would say.

"I can't work without a light."

There must be a dozen fancy names for this type of mental derangement among various psychiatric schools, Moran thought, but one simple word would do: obsession. The kid was obsessed by the dream of his machine that he must finish and make to fly. If the rest of them rode back to the living world on camels, this kid would stay here with his phoenix, and die in the flames of his obsession.

"We mustn't put the light on," said Captain Harris, also speaking as if to a child. "They didn't notice it because of the dunes, but they might wander, looking for a water point. You see, we don't know who they are yet, and they might be a *razzia*—that's to say a band of raiders. Mr. Towns, do you carry a gun on board your aircraft?"

"No."

Harris puckered his mouth. "Sergeant Watson and I have one each. Those chaps may well have a dozen rifles. Slim odds. We'd better parley."

Tilney's voice was a whisper of bewilderment. "But why won't they save us? Why won't they?"

"They may." Harris spoke gently; the night was

full of children. "But we are Christians, you understand, and some of the Arabs are fanatical in their religion. Allah is their only god and they'd murder a Christian—an unbeliever—on principle. Like stepping on a fly. Correct, Watson?"

"Yes, sir." The "sir" was habitual.

Tilney began saying on his breath, "Oh, God . . . oh, God . . ."

"Don't go an' bloody advertise it," snapped Crow, his nerves near the edge, "you're in the wrong mob, you 'eard what the captain said!"

Harris murmured, "We mustn't speak too loudly, and it's most important that nobody makes a sound with a tool or anything." A man of action, he relaxed his shoulders, as if donning an old favorite coat that he felt easy in. "Now we have to get things organized all round."

He told them his plan quietly, seldom asking advice but seeming grateful when one of them interrupted.

"I'm taking my sergeant with me. No need for more than two of us. The uniform might help." He was already checking his revolver and rounds. "We shall climb the dunes west of here and make a full-circle detour and come up on them from the east so that if they decide to look for the rest of you they'll search in the opposite direction. For your own sakes don't show a light or make a noise until we can signal you they're friendly."

Moran was looking at Stringer, mounting guard on him. If Stringer tried to switch on the light, someone else had to get there first. Death was so easy in the desert: hit the wrong man in the face because you couldn't stand him; drop a jet in the sand; throw a switch; so easy.

"Approaching them from the east, we shall say we dropped by parachute. Engine trouble—don't know where the plane came down—somewhere east, we were flying east. You'll be perfectly safe here providing you don't reveal your presence. Now, re parleying. I shall want to take all the loose cash we can muster. I doubt if it's worth offering them pickings from the wreck—they wouldn't know where to sell aircraft instruments, things of that sort, but they might go for the dates, depends what shape they're in. I'll have to decide on the spot. Well, I think that's about all."

Towns said, "No one here's got any goolie chits?" In this area the murder of stranded air crews wasn't common; but it happened. The drilling crews working for three companies—Newport Mining, Ausonia Mineraria and Franco-Wyoming—were always provided with goolie chits in five major Arabic dialects: *The safe return of the bearer will be rewarded by the cash payment of 100 Libyan pounds.* The sum varied, but even ten pounds would provoke a raiding party into fighting among its own members for the prize of a live Christian they would otherwise murder out of hand.

Nobody answered Towns. There were no goolie chits.

"We'll do without them," Harris said. He fetched his cap from the hull. Between them all they mustered a hundred and thirty pounds, Watson chipping in with close on fifty back pay. The captain rolled the notes into one bundle and thrust it into his pocket. "Easy money for them, they ought to see that. If they don't, I'll persuade 'em." His tone had the briskness of forced confidence. "Just in case there's any trouble, stay here and lie doggo—if you hear any shooting, that sort of thing, don't make any attempt to help us or you'll upset our little campaign." He looked at the moon. "Light's pretty good, won't need a torch. Sarnt Watson!"

He moved along the fuselage, one-two, one-two, and the sergeant watched him go, standing automatically to attention in the presence of a superior; not, in this case, a superior officer, but his own emotion: fear. It was the only thing he had to beat: the fear of giving best to the enemy. He knew this and was ready.

The figure of the captain appeared again by the tail unit. Softly, sharply, "Watson!"

Hold your ground, Watty. Hold.

Captain Harris approached him, his eyes wide in the moonlight. "What's the trouble?"

"No trouble, sir." He tried to bite the last word

off but it was too late, it was said. Habit. Got a man down, in the end. "I'm not going, that's all."

They faced each other and unconsciously the rest of them stood back, as a small crowd does when a fight starts.

It's not possible, Moran thought. This is the British Army.

"I've ordered you, Sergeant." No anger, just surprise. "Come along—look sharp now!"

"I'm not going."

The faint voices came drifting across the dunes from the silence of the outer desert, meaningless.

"You refuse my order?"

"That's right." He looked at the officer. Cap dead square on his head like he always had it— "Harris-fashion," they called it at base. Face was thin and covered in skin and stubble, looked different in this light; might have been a stranger instead of the one man he hated most in all this world.

"Sergeant, we've soldiered together quite a time. I'm giving you a chance. We'll forget what's just been said and we'll start again. Give it a minute's thought for your own sake." He straightened his Sam Browne unnecessarily, checked the holster clip, stood for a moment with his shoulders drawn back, and said easily, "Sarnt Watson, forward march!"

Hold, Watty. Hold.

But it wasn't so simple. When you'd had years of

it, all those years of it, you didn't just chuck it up with a word. You'd got to hack away at a kind of chain that'd got wound round your feet, all those years. Wasn't easy. Hold.

"I'm not going."

Towns and Moran moved away, unnoticed. This was going to be embarrassing. A man, custodian of an ancient law, was being stripped of his authority.

"So you refuse the order to support your officer in circumstances of imminent danger to life."

Go on, you bleeder, throw the lot at me, Queen's Regs and all. Get it over with. You just love the sound of your own bleeding voice.

But Sergeant Watson stood trembling and was aware of it. He had no fear of the man in front of him; they had a gun each, if it came to that; he could flatten the bastard in unarmed combat with a couple of stone to spare. He had fear of the great big all-powerful It. The Army. The Army had your soul, once you'd been in it all those years—there were things you couldn't shake off so easy, because they'd gone deep into you, and it was painful when they came out, because of the roots they'd grown, right deep down in your guts.

Name and number? Watson, 606. Smarten up there, Private Watson! You're a soldier now, you know, not a bloody jellyfish! Get that salute right, private! Sir! Sir! Sir! Corporal, what's your unit? Corporal Watson, dress that man! You in charge of

*this rabble, Corp'l Watson? Sir! Report to my
quarters, Sarnt Watson, oh six hundred hours! You
should know better than that, Sergeant—now get
those men in order! Sir! Sir! Sir!*

Hold, Watty. Now you can say what's on your
mind, just let it rip, the lot, give him the fucking
lot. Watch his face the first time you call him a bastard, after all those years.

"That's it. I refuse." He said no more than that.

There'd be no joy in it, somehow. It was enough
to win, without any song and dance. Keep it decent,
like.

"You realize you'll face a court-martial for this?"

"I do."

Bellamy had moved into the shadows. This was
nothing to do with him. Sorry for old Harris,
though; but he'd have it all his own way, later. You'd
get a case like this in the papers, once in a while; two
blokes arguing the toss in the middle of a jungle or a
desert or at sea, and long afterward there'd be their
names in the *Mirror*, and pictures of them. Sipping
your tea, you'd nothing more to go on than their pictures, and you could usually make up your mind:
that one doesn't look a bad bloke, but this one looks
a right bastard. Now who's playing Brum this week?

The moonlight cast the captain's shadow against
the fuselage; it was very erect.

"Very well, Sergeant. I am placing you under
open arrest. Give me your revolver."

He held out his hand.

"No."

"Give me your arms, Sergeant."

Silence.

"You refuse?"

"Yes."

Captain Harris stepped back one pace, smartly.

"Very well." He turned about, and Loomis said:

"I guess I'll go along with you, Cap." He came out of the shadows. "Needs two."

Briskly: "The protection of civilian life and property is a concern of the armed services in peacetime as in war. I thank you, but I prefer to go alone."

"It needs two, Cap. Just let's get moving."

As they reached the tail unit Sergeant Watson snapped open his holster flap and drew the gun.

"Loomis . . . You better have this."

The Texan looked back at him. Harris waited.

"I don't need it. I'm with the Captain."

They moved off again, turning toward the west dunes; in half a minute they were two small figures pushing their shadows across the moonlit sand.

Sergeant Watson stood watching them, shaking all over. It was the end of all those years; but he wasn't free; he was lost.

CHAPTER
17

SHOOTING STARS WENT CURVING ACROSS THE
night, following one upon another so fast that the
sky was never still. The moon, smaller now and of
a pure white, hung at its zenith.

"How long are you going to wait?"

Moran said again, "Till daybreak."

"But we're losing precious time!" He had been
saying it since midnight, and none of them would
listen. He took off his glasses and rubbed them
nervously, putting them on and blinking at the
navigator. "I need the light, to work with."

Moran had tried argument; it was like arguing
with a speak-your-weight machine: it spoke only
what it was designed to speak. There was something almost sinister about Stringer; he was a robot
out of a horror story.

"If you try to put that light on I'm going to knock
you out cold. Get it?" He was sick of argument, sick
of having to talk to this kid as if he'd break if you
threw a wrong word. Now he'd thrown it.

"I'm not afraid of you, Mr. Moran. I know you

could hit me if you want, but if you do, I shall simply set fire to the plane. *Then* see where you—"

Moran turned away before his fist went out and wrecked everything. He told Tilney and Watson, "Keep watch on that nut while I'm gone. He could kill the lot of us. Watch him."

He crossed the pale sand toward the east dunes, his shoe kicking sometimes against stones and small meteorites. The dunes shone in the moonlight; the three figures lay prone below the ridge. He came up quietly.

"Anything new, Frankie?"

"Nope."

Moran eased himself up on his stomach to lie between Towns and Bellamy. Crow said, "They're too quiet, for my likin'."

Moran watched the glow of the fire two miles east, a red eye watchful in the night. It had been lit before midnight. Straining the eyes, you could see—or imagine—movement around the fire; the line of dark humps to the left would be the camels, sleeping; the other group would be the men, and sometimes there seemed to be movement among them. Their voices were no longer heard. They had been last heard about an hour after Captain Harris and Loomis had left—there'd been a sudden outbreak of tongues, and the moon, at that time lower, had shown the movement of the men. Now the sands were silent.

"We ought to go and see, Lew."

"I told you before, there's no point—"

"I can't just stick here doing—"

"You just stick, Frank. Trust Harris; he's no nut. If he told them there was only the two of them, and the situation's touch and go, he can't suddenly up and say there's seven more of us. And he can't get a message to us without making it look like he's just wandering off into the desert. He's got to play it safe."

They fell silent for minutes. No one had talked about tomorrow. Tomorrow, Harris and Loomis would either ride off on camelback and send in a rescue team as soon as they could raise one; or they'd be left stranded, to make their way back here when the caravan was over the horizon. No one had talked about the third alternative. Towns had a thought of his own and had left it unsaid: If the Bedouins wanted to, they could follow Harris' tracks in the sand, coming full circle and finding the plane. But Harris might have spent time covering the tracks; he was a man to think of that.

"I still can't understand," Moran said, "why Loomis sat up and begged like that. Remember I told you he'd got a cable at Jebel—something urgent? It was why he was on board. I don't get it."

Towns said, "Loomis is that kind of saint. He couldn't stand seeing the Cap walk off alone after what happened. He did it to save the man embarrassment."

Silence again. Someone looked at his watch. Dawn in an hour; then they would know. It would be the longest hour of this night. They lay with their elbows dug into the sand, their chins propped on their hands, gazing at the line of dark shapes and the smudge of the fire. That was their future over there; it could go either way.

"Stringer'll do 'is nut," said Crow quietly. "If we're in luck, an' go ridin' off on them camels, 'e'll bust a gut."

"Who cares?" Bellamy answered. A day, two days' ride, and there'd be palms, and water, and the world. To hell with Stringer; he was a convenience; better to believe Towns, who said there was only a fifty-fifty chance of taking off in that thing without a smash-up. Two days' easy ride, with men who were born here, who knew the way. Harris had to pull it off; and he was the man to do it, spoke their lingo, had a hundred and thirty quid as a present for them; he couldn't miss.

From behind them metal rang and Moran cursed and slid back down the dune and went at a jog trot across the basin of sand. If Stringer had made that noise he'd beat hell out of him.

Crow shifted his elbows and pain shot through his arms. His face was so close to the sand that his breath blew dust from it. "What's the time, Dave?"

"Three, just gone."

"Christ, I'll be glad when this lot's over." His tongue was beginning to dry up again; today they'd cut the ration down to a pint, with two days' water left in the tank. All night the air had been calm; no wind; no frost; no dew.

"Be dawn soon," Bellamy said, and let his face fall onto his hands, shutting his eyes; the red glow had begun to hypnotize him and sleep was dulling the edge of pain.

They were still there when the sun broke from the rim of the earth.

"Dave."

Bellamy jerked his head up still half in sleep; and the pain came back. "Wha'?"

"It's mornin'."

He opened his eyes and looked at the face of the sun. In the Sahara day there are two moments—at dawn and sundown—when distance can be judged by the eye, with the horizon defined by the low sun's disk. It was easy at these moments to believe that the desert went on forever, that these were the sands of eternity.

Between the dunes and the reddened edge of the world the line of men and camels lay like a black reef of rock; and soon it began moving, changing shape, breaking and joining again. Voices came on the wastes of silence, sharp as the first bird notes from a wood.

Moran joined the others, crawling on his stomach to the top of the ridge.

"See anything?"

"They've woke up."

"Can you make out our two boys?"

"Some 'opes. It's two mile or more."

The black shapes were turning red as the sun lit the scene; within minutes there was only white and brown: burnoose and camel hide with moving shadows darkening the sand. The voices became more urgent; the long necks of the beasts swung about.

"They're mounting," Towns said.

"There's one white camel."

"That's for me," said Crow.

The line of shapes became gapped, a chain of brown and white slackening and tightening, now joining and slowly moving against the glare of the sun, moving toward the north. Heat haze was forming and the dust from the top sand rose in a long smudge behind the caravan.

Bellamy made binoculars of his hands, watching the moving dust. The voices of the Bedous were no longer audible; they had become a cloud on the sand toward the northeast.

"Come again," Crow muttered, "any time." The white one was not for him.

It was a while before anyone spoke again, because they had waited for twelve hours; and to-

gether with their fears for Harris and Loomis there
had been hope for them all.

Towns was the first to get to his feet. Sand ran
from him in rivulets. "I'll go and make sure they
took our boys along."

The others got up. "We better be quick," Crow
said. The sun's warmth was already on their faces.

"We don't all go," Towns said. "Just me."

Crow looked at Bellamy. It was sense; sweat was
precious. They ought to draw lots but you could
see there'd be no arguing with Towns. He started
down the east slope of the dunes. Moran told the
other two:

"In a couple of hours make some smoke, will
you?" In the blinding light and with eyes already
uncertain, the sunward side of these dunes could
be invisible at two miles. He let himself fall down
the slope, digging his feet in to keep upright.

"Lew, go back."

"I need a walk." He couldn't trust Towns any
more. Their nerves were drawn pretty tight by now
and Towns was on this guilt kick of his. Moran
had seen a shape, a blob of substance left behind
by the Bedous; it floated in the water mirage; it
was probably a camel, lamed and abandoned; but
if it wasn't, Towns might go right off the handle,
start right out into the wilderness on some damn
pilgrimage of atonement, because the score would
be seven, and he'd make eight.

They walked for forty minutes, keeping their eyes shut to slits between the crusted lids. The blob of substance hadn't been a mirage; it was a camel. It must have been kneeling in sleep when it had died, because the forelegs were splayed out under the weight of its body.

They passed it, going on toward the other two shapes that had been too small to be seen from the dunes.

"Take it easy, Frank."

They made their way through the churned sand past the ashes of the fire.

"We expected this," Moran said. "You'd be a liar if you said any different."

Towns stood still and didn't answer.

Their shoes had been taken; their shoes, wrist-watches, the Sam Browne, and the revolver. They lay with their faces to the sky.

Moran looked at Towns and away again. "It was their decision, not yours." He began scooping at the sand.

They were there for nearly an hour and the sweat was on them, the little they had. Towns hadn't spoken in all that time. When they had finished they came back past the camel, and Moran stopped.

"Even if they'd taken them along, they wouldn't have got far. Those bastards were lost." The hump of the camel was shrunken; ridden too hard, it had used up its store of fat. The neck veins had been cut in four places: in the last resort an Arab, becoming mad, will drink the salt blood from his own beast, hoping to stave off thirst. The taking of the shoes and watches and gun had been habitual, the traditional trophies of murder seized even when there was no hope of selling them.

"Let's have your bottle, Frank."

Towns turned away and began walking, head down; and Moran had to take the water bottle from him. With a pocketknife it would be slow work on the camel and there was the danger of vomiting and losing liquid in bile, so he kept on repeating the thought: *This means life for two men for one day.* The blade hacked at the stomach wall and twice he had to stop and just whisper *"life, life, life,"* until the nausea passed and he could work on again, with most of the greenish fluid oozing over the bottles and his hands; and when they were filled he screwed the caps tight and burrowed in the sand to clean them. No more fluid had come from the gash in the hide; a camel's stomach can hold fifty gallons but this beast had been on its last reserves when exhaustion had finished it off. The Bedous couldn't have known it hadn't got up and followed them, or they would have tapped it for the fluid. They too were on their last reserves; the thought consoled him.

He wiped the bottles against the beast's hide and started after Towns, who was making straight back along their tracks. A stem of oil smoke stood from the basin of dunes. In twenty minutes he caught up and gave Towns his water bottle:

"It stinks but it's drinkable."

"I'll put it in the tank. Dilute it." He stopped and turned a blank face to Moran. "I should've helped."

"Only needed one." He wished Towns would break up and yell or run or something, anything better than his awful blank face and toneless voice. "You know why I expected this would happen, Frank? Because Harris was an honest man. He didn't have a chance. He thought hard cash was just as good as a goolie chit. With a goolie you've got to deliver the goods to get the cash, but give 'em the cash and why should they make any delivery?"

Towns was silent. The soft sand coughed beneath their feet. Sweat came under their left armpit and down their left leg as they kept up their pace toward the west.

"They'd make the delivery," Moran answered his own question, "because they'd been paid. How the hell could we have made a man like Harris look at it any other way? He meant to go. He—"

"*All right he meant to go, he meant to go, and now he's gone and so's Loomis, don't you think I know?*" It all came seething and hissing out of him through his cracked lips and his whole body shook with the effort to get it said; and Moran listened to this and to more until Towns was silent again but for the soft screech of his breath as his lungs gaped for it and dragged the dry air in. It was terrible to hear rage coming out of so enfeebled a man; but Moran was glad he'd got it done with.

The column of smoke was now above their heads; they climbed the flank of sand and topped the ridge, going down into the basin and seeing a man in front of them. Sergeant Watson. For a second or two he looked at their faces and asked nothing; his eyes were wide even in the glare. From what he saw he knew. But he must give himself the treat:

"Dead, isn't he?"

They looked at his brutish face, unable to believe such a light in any man's eye, such triumph.

"Yes," Moran said, and a sound of laughter came jerking out of the sergeant's mouth in spasms: the sound, ugly and unsharable, of pretended joy. It went on until Towns' fist smashed the man down.

CHAPTER
18

MORAN HAD KNOWN THERE'D BE TROUBLE BY the way Stringer behaved. Most of the day he'd lain in the shade like the others, though he hadn't slept: his eyes watched them in secret, glancing away when anyone went near him. He couldn't have made it plainer: he was on strike.

"How long," Moran asked him, sometime in the afternoon, "is it going to take us now?"

The thin shaved face was turned away, as when a child is offered a sweet to coax it out of a tantrum. Moran waited, sitting with his head cupped in his hands; he'd slept for two hours but was groggy with the need for more.

"How long, Stringer?"

"I am no longer interested, Mr. Moran."

The silence burned about them. Not far away, Towns sat with his back to the hull, awake; he'd not spoken since they had come back this morning. Tilney was moaning in his sleep. Crow was nursing his monkey, talking quietly to it; beside him Bellamy was writing in his book. In the shade of the tail unit lay Sergeant Watson with his nose broken and his beard black with dried blood. All he had said to Towns when he had regained consciousness and lurched back to the shelter was: "I don't expect you to understand. I don't expect you to. It's not your business. It's mine." From the clotted mess of his face his eyes had looked out, still with triumph shining in them. Then he had lain down under the tail to dream of it all.

Moran told Stringer, "Okay, you're no longer interested. I am. And I'd say ten days."

There must have been a figure in the kid's mind but the bait wasn't taken. "I should explain my reasons for giving up the project. There is no co-operation."

"We'll cooperate. We have before—"

"But you keep stopping work! Last night we lost twelve whole hours!" He sat up, clasping his knees, one shoulder turned to Moran.

"Last night we lost two lives."

"Well, it was their own fault, wasn't it? *I* didn't ask them to go out there! It was—"

"Skip it." The effort of patience was bringing sweat. "Skip it. The thing is we're going to finish the plane now, just as you plan—"

"With two men short! Twenty-four man-hours lost, every night we work. Last night alone cost us eighty-four man-hours because none of you worked at all, and now—"

Moran got up and moved away, sickened. They had both been left in the same position, their heads almost severed by the long curved knives; their eyes had been open, staring up, still surprised. Harris, who had always been ashamed to show a sign of weakness in front of them, who must have known what he was going into: "Slim odds," he'd said; and Loomis, who had lent them all his strength in subtle ways, taking his bottle out of sight to drink from it so that they weren't reminded that theirs were empty. Twenty-four man-hours, buried in the sand without a cross.

But they needed Stringer. It didn't have to matter that he'd been born without a heart; not his fault; maybe there had been one in him, once, but it had been shriveled by lack of love in his infant years; maybe, if he could tell you, he felt the loss. That's what Loomis would have said. Loomis had said of Tilney, "Try to feel something for that kid. He's dying all the deaths there are—how would you like to be him? Have pity."

Moran went back to talk to Stringer, not fooling himself that he was learning the compassion of a Loomis: he had to talk to Stringer to save his own skin.

"I don't have to tell you," he said, "I've got a lot of faith in your machine. I think it'll fly. We all do."

Because this was what needled the kid. He'd heard Towns say last night when Harris and Loomis had

gone, "They may have a chance. I'd sooner ride out
of here on a camel than climb aboard that coffin."

You shouldn't say things like that in front of
Stringer.

"I know what you think of my design. You think
it'll crash and kill us all. Mr. Towns said—"

"Listen, you ought to see it his way. He feels
badly about getting us in this fix, and he's afraid he
might make an error of judgment, when he's flying
your machine—and it'll be his fault again. You
ought to see that. It's a big responsibility for him."

He went on wheedling, hating himself for having to use this way of fighting for his life; but there
wasn't any other. Stringer kept going back to his
loss of man-hours, and this time Moran stuck it,
and tried not to listen.

"It was obvious that Mr. Harris was doing a stupid thing—certainly it was obvious to *me*. This
place where we are is right in the middle of the
desert; it's not on the way to anywhere. I could have
told you there was no point in asking those natives
for help—they must have been lost themselves!"

"We never thought of that." Play it cool; never
mind what was said; it would be forgotten. Just get
airborne while there was still life in them. "We're
in your hands, Stringer."

"Of course!" He deigned to look the navigator
full in the eyes at last. "The trouble is that *I* am in
your hands, as well. If I'd had the strength of ten

men I'd have had the machine finished by now; but I have to rely on you people—and you're unreliable. If we start work again, you'd only stop again on some excuse; and I can't work like that, because the whole of this design is in my head, and you can lose track of what you're doing, very easily. I wish you could understand that, Mr. Moran."

They spoke quietly, but the others must be listening. It didn't have to matter.

"I understand that. I can't speak for the others, but I'm telling you this: you can count on me from now on, until we're through." The kid, anyway, was talking sense: there was a sight more to building an airplane than simple mechanics. The pure theory that Stringer had at his command had been long forgotten by pilots like Towns, if they'd ever learned it. He asked again, "How long? Roughly?"

He couldn't tell if Stringer was still sulking or really having to work it out; the silence lasted a long time.

"We are two men short."

Moran didn't remind him of the whole truth: that of the fourteen men who had been on board the Skytruck seven were left alive.

"With two men short—how long?"

"I would need to make an estimate, Mr. Moran."

"Give me a rough idea."

Stringer sat with his knees clasped, doodling in

the sand with his toe until Moran got up again and left him, standing in the sun by the trailing edge of the port mainplane, his eyes screwed up against the glare, reading: *The Phoenix*. One more of the subtle ways in which Loomis had lent them his strength: with his own hand he had named their hope of life. In a minute or two he went back.

Stringer hadn't moved. Moran looked down at him.

"How long?"

"A week."

Twenty-first Day. We start work again tonight. I couldn't believe it when Stringer said we could finish the plane in one more week. We were all so shocked by what happened to Harris and Loomis that we lost hope altogether, I think. Fly out of here in one more week! I'm cheered up, immensely!

Sergeant Watson sat in the heat of the control cabin winding away at the generator; he'd volunteered as soon as he heard the news. His head throbbed and his nose was giving him a lot of pain; the dried blood had cracked and fissured on his beard, looking like a patched black mask; but he felt no grudge against the pilot or against anyone in the world. Harris was dead. If they ever got out of here there'd be no rap to take, whereas a couple of days ago he'd come close to shooting that bastard, and that would've been murder. Must have been half-mad; it was the thirst, of course.

Another thing. If they got out of here, none of these blokes would bother with telling anyone about his little one-man mutiny. Wasn't their business. So if they ever got out of here it was going to be roses all the way. No bloody Harris.

Sarnt Watson!

Stuff it. Tell it to the bleedin' angels.

The generator moaned.

Under the canopy Crow and Bellamy waited for the sun to near the dunes. They had everything ready: the jerrican, two more containers they'd made by bending scrap panels, and the Arab knife that Bellamy had seen in a market and had bought to take home.

There'd been a conference, everyone except Stringer, who was making up control-rod linkage. They'd worked it out that there'd have to be one more dewfall if they were to stay alive for a week. There were two days' rations in the tank plus a couple of pints of fluid from the dead camel; there was nothing else; the port coolant tank couldn't be touched. Today, by Bellamy's diary, was a Monday. They'd be all right until Thursday morning, when the tank would be dry and there'd be no share-out. After that, they might go a day, two days at most, without water; but there'd be no work done on Thursday night: they'd be beyond it.

Friday would see the end, without a dewfall.

"There'll be one," Crow said. "Got to be, ain't there? Well, then."

It was the feeling they all had since Stringer had said, "A week." Nothing could stop them now. Loomis and the captain had gone; there was no point in thinking about it; they had to think about themselves.

"I like your faith in Providence," Bellamy had said, "but it won't help us. We've got to assume there'll be no dew for a week—it's happened before." He had led Crow out of earshot of the others and had told him what they had to do. Now they waited for the sun to near the dunes.

The birds came sailing in from the south, some ten or twelve of them, lowering and circling beyond the east ridge of sand.

Crow saw them and said nothing; but when the full heat went from the sun and they were ready he found Watson and asked, "Can you give us your gun for a couple of hours? Just on loan, you'll get it back."

In the dreadful mess of the sergeant's face the eyes looked alarmed. "What's come up, then?"

"Nothin'. Just a precaution, see."

"What d'you want it for?"

"Shoot them bleedin' birds."

Watson had seen the vultures. He handed over the gun.

It was two hours before sundown when Crow and Bellamy left base. They told Moran, "If we're not back by about seven, make a light on the dunes, give us a guide."

Crossing the ridge and trudging into the wastes beyond, they stopped every five minutes and kicked hollows in the sand; with a week to go they were taking no chances.

By Crow's watch it took them fifty minutes to reach the spot, with two spells of rest; the jerrican and the two containers, even though empty, were a burden, reminding them of their weakness. They had not talked; their dried-up mouths made talking difficult and there was nothing they wanted to say, or needed to.

They got within fifty yards of the camel before the vultures took notice of them, croaking and beating upward, falling again on the carcass, some of them rising to make a feint attack on the two men, wheeling away, returning, their naked heads and necks outstretched, their bloodied beaks cackling in rage.

The jerrican rang like a bell as Crow beat on it with the long knife and the birds flew up in a cloud of wings, keeping together, their cries sounding above the ringing of the can, their legs hanging with the talons spread in the attitude of attack. Bellamy had seen vultures before at close quarters—the oil-camp mascot at Jebel was a desert fox and one day it had wandered—but he had never had to compete with them for carrion; and it was this intellectual aspect that sickened him: he and Crow were reduced totally to animal dimension, not even of the lion but of the pariah dog.

Crow was shouting at the birds, banging the can above his head; they circled fifty feet above the camel, prepared to attack if there was a chance, their instinct, informed by the memory of their species, measuring the enemy: they had seen men before, in isolated places, too weak to lift a hand; and the feast was on before the blood was cold.

Guano dropped from them, splashing whitely across the camel, and Crow flung down the can and loosed off with the gun, firing into the middle of the maze of wings, still shouting, cursing, dragging at the trigger until two birds dropped like black rags from the air—and Bellamy chose the nearer one, slashing down with the knife at the bald white neck, seizing the hateful body and thrusting it across the top of a container, leaving it to drain while he fetched the other one, his hands in a frenzy with the knife because if he stopped to think this thing out he'd throw up and run blindly for the dunes.

There was a week to go and they had to have water and there might not be a dew—there was water in blood, and here was blood, camel or vulture, it made no difference, slash away and hack away and think of nothing, nothing, except that this thing had to be done.

When the two dead birds had drained he took them by the legs and flung them as far as he could, their weight tearing at the muscles of his arm—and the flock came down, fighting for the carrion while he and Crow worked on the camel's carcass whose hide was already ripped red by the razor beaks.

They never knew how long it took to fill the three containers because time had become a nightmare, timeless, and only the blade and the blood had any meaning for them. Crow was hissing a string of words as he worked, half aware that he must feed his anger and keep it fed because in anger a man can do things that would otherwise be beyond him.

A vulture, beaten back by the rest that fought for the headless birds, swept low across the sand for the camel, the sweetness of blood already in its beak, its courage increased by the need for more—it came in a long low swoop, wings spread flat, head forward, talons wide, a cackle of rage sounding out from the reddened beak—and Crow sprang for it with his hands hooking and his feet slipping on the bloodied camel hide as the hate that possessed him carried him on and drove his bare hands at the bird while the bald head swung and the talons met him like grappling hooks before he caught one wing and dragged on it and found the naked neck and wrung it; and the screech was silenced. Swinging the body above his head, once, twice, he flung it across the sand, shouting his joy at its death because these were the things that had sailed through the sundown when hope for Robby had gone. The gun had been too good for this; he'd done it with his hands.

Bellamy had glimpsed his face, and had seen it for a stranger's: this was the meaning of the phrase you never thought much about: a man possessed.

"Albert, we're done!" The knife was red to the hilt, his hand red to the wrist.

They lifted the containers, moving away from the camel, hearing the flock bear down again. Crow stopped, the whole scene swinging against his eyes; he shut them and stood for a minute fighting off the nausea and the urge to drop onto the sand and sleep and forget. When he opened his eyes he found himself looking at the two mounds that Moran and Towns must have made. Their sides were smooth and the low sun cast their shadows softly.

"Come on, Albert."

"Yeh."

They had not bargained for the weight of the full containers. By the time they reached the dunes a flame was burning there for them, as they had asked.

CHAPTER
19

ON THURSDAY THEY MADE A SEESAW.

The night had gone well, but since Monday they had weakened physically and some of the operations took twice as long as Stringer had planned: he had again failed to take the human element into account. Working against cold, pain and thirst they had finished the tail unit in the last two days; and four control rods ran forward from the stern post to the "flight deck," which was nothing more than a seat cradle and a frame for the levers.

Stringer for the first time showed fatigue; but he did not rest; he was another example of a man possessed. He made the seesaw not long after dawn, using a longeron from the hull with a rock for the pivot and a second rock—hauled from the sand some fifty feet away—for the weight. They sat on the other end, one at a time, while Stringer weighed each man, adding and subtracting the units of smaller stones. Towns had said:

"I think we're wasting time."

Stringer recorded the figures with a stick on the sand. Moran: five units; Crow: three; Watson: four.

"The leverage," Towns said, "isn't more than a couple of feet. It's not as if we were going to ride on the wing-tips."

Stringer calculated in silence. Moran said:

"It won't take long, Frank." He said it slowly, as a warning.

"In this heat, a minute's too long."

Stringer held the end of the balance. "Mr. Towns, you're next."

Towns stood in the shade of the canopy, pilot's cap on the back of his head, eyes screwed against the red of the lifting sun. "I think you're wasting time," he said; but he moved across to the seesaw; and Moran relaxed, his clenched hands loosening.

When they had all been weighed they dropped to the sand; while they slept, Stringer worked; and when he saw Moran's eyes open he said, "I'd like you to understand how we have to dispose ourselves, Mr. Moran." He waited until the navigator was on his feet. "Mr. Towns will sit at the controls on the left side of the fuselage behind a fairing scooped at the top to flare the slipstream over his head. Behind him will be Bellamy and Watson, as they're the heaviest. I shall be sitting upright on the other side, parallel with the pilot, using a similar fairing to balance the drag. From that position I can call any necessary instructions to the pilot during the flight. Behind me will be yourself, Crow and Tilney—the three heaviest on the port side, the four lightest on the starboard. Apart from the pilot and myself, the others will have to lie flat on their stomachs, using a handgrip formed by the forward rib of the cradle. There should be no difficulty in hanging on."

He detailed the setup to Moran, assigning them to their positions along the fuselage with the care of a rowing coach. Towns, lying in the shade, listened to the light drone of the kid's voice and heard Moran put questions so respectful in their tone as to be sickening.

"I have marked the fuselage, Mr. Moran, to show where the cradles have to be fixed. I expect you understand all this; it's quite simple."

"I get the hang." It was easy, once you realized that Stringer, not Allah, was the only god in this earthly hell, to choose your words and adopt the tone of worship. Stringer might not even have meant it that way—so simple, Mr. Moran, that even you can understand—but whether he meant it or not, there was only one way to answer. In the last two days the kid had worked in a kind of fever, and his face—even his schoolboy face—had aged; for food and water his body was drawing on his nerves. One wrong word from Towns and he'd blow up and the *Phoenix* would never fly.

"Tonight we shall rig the cradles," Stringer said. "I shall spend today checking over the controls."

He took off his glasses and let them dangle from his hand, where blood from a gash had dried. Shutting his eyes he leaned his head back against the fuselage and Moran saw the lines of the face relax; he was reminded of a monk withdrawing into meditation.

Quietly he asked, "We can still reckon to fly out on Sunday?"

"I see no problem that would stop us."

The 24th Day. The last of the water has gone. This morning there was no share-out. Plane's getting on, but we're all too weak to be excited. Just have to hang on somehow.

There didn't seem much more to put. Usually mentioned Albert but there was nothing to put about him today. Three days ago he had tried to describe Albert the way he had seen him, out there; but he wasn't a writer, and the diary was meant only to record things; but he'd never forget Albert with his long bony nose and the terrible shout coming out of his mouth, dragging that vulture clean out of the air and killing it with his bare hands, whirling the black mass of feathers round his head, still yelling his war cry, his face utterly unlike Albert's face had ever been, just for this minute. It was like watching something symbolic, George and the dragon, or something like that, good struggling with evil, man combating the black angels of death. But you couldn't put it like that, in a diary; it'd sound barmy.

There was something else he hadn't put in the diary: the way poor old Albert's face had looked when the blood had been "distilling" for six hours. A bit of steam had come out of the tube, enough for a thimbleful of water, then it had stopped. Albert had taken the tube off and dipped a stick into the jerrican, bringing it out covered in what looked like black treacle.

"It's no go, Dave. It's no bleedin' go."

The stuff had just congealed. They'd had to talk Stringer into giving them a third of the coolant in the port side tank, leaving a minimum for the engine's needs. It was distilling now, and Watson had polished up some Dural panels from the wreck, to focus the sun's rays onto one side of the jerrican, like a solar oven. It had been on the boil since Monday night and had so far given four bottles of water fit to drink—little enough, but something.

So it had been no go, that little trip. They couldn't even use the camel flesh, half starving though they were: one mouthful of cooked meat and their thirst would've got ten times worse. Never mind. It was all you could say. Sunday, with any luck, they'd be out of here.

With any luck. It was beyond thinking about. When you wanted something very badly you were certain it wouldn't come off. Anything could wreck them before Sunday; the engine might not start; Towns could finish up too weak to handle the controls; Stringer could make a mistake. That was beyond thinking about too. You didn't have to think; just lie doggo in the day and pretend you couldn't feel the moisture being sucked out of you even in the shade; and work your best in the night, keep faith in Stringer.

He looked down at Albert, in a dead sleep on the sand beside him. The beaky nose stuck up from the matted and peeling face like a conning tower. Poor old Albert; he'd nearly broken his heart today, trying to tell the monkey there wasn't any more water.

In the shade of the tailplane Watson woke from a nightmare full of shiny brown snakes with gold heads that had turned into Sam Brownes. He must have stopped breathing for a second or two and it had woken him up; he drew at the hot dry air with his lungs working like bellows too heavy to move; blood had seeped again inside his broken nose, half blocking it; but it was too painful to touch.

Since yesterday the doubts had started to get at him. If he ever got out of here it wasn't going to be so rosy after all.

So there were two occasions when Captain Harris left the base without you?

Yes, sir.

The first time, you had to remain behind be-

*cause you had sprained your ankle. The second
time, you say that Captain Harris ordered you to
stay at base to safeguard the civilians in case he
failed to return from his mission.*

Yes, sir.

*Why, then, on the first occasion, didn't he order
you to stay at base to safeguard the civilians, as he
did on the second occasion? From your evidence,
there was a great risk of his not returning from the
earlier mission also. In order to satisfy ourselves on
the true circumstances of this officer's death, we shall
have to ask you to suggest why he didn't order you
to remain at base on both occasions, or on neither
occasion, since the risk of his not returning would
seem similarly great. Further, the civilians were all
men—there were no women or children there—and
they were men used to the desert conditions. We thus
question the fact—as presented in your testimony—
that Captain Harris ordered you to stay at base. Can
you help us with this point, Sergeant?*

It wasn't for me to question orders, was it, sir?

*Not verbally, of course. But didn't you ask your-
self, in your own mind, why Captain Harris ordered you to go with him the first time, yet ordered
you to stay behind on the second?*

I can't rightly say, sir. I can't remember.

They'd never take that for an answer. He'd remembered plenty of other things. They'd go on at
him over that. And they'd know the names of all

these other blokes, especially Towns. It'd be all over the papers, this lot—How We Survived in the Desert—all that lot, in the *Sunday Pic*. They'd ask Towns about it—and why should he want to help him? Already broken his nose for him.

It didn't look so rosy.

Sarnt Watson!

He'd hear that voice again.

In the evening there happened the thing that Moran had been dreading for three days, ever since they'd been given the hope of flying out in a week.

At sundown the generator stopped moaning, and Tilney came out of the hull with sweat on his soft fair stubble, his legs giving way as he came across the sand; but he picked himself up and reported to Stringer with the rest of them. The working lamp was switched on. The moon had not yet risen and the light enclosed them in the vastness of the desert night. They were aware of the desert, and its size, and its silence, more acutely than ever, tonight. There had been nothing to dismay them since their hopes of riding out of here on camelback had become a cloud of dust on the north horizon; Stringer still said that by Sunday the plane should be ready for take-off, and tomorrow was Friday. They were even, tonight, about to make the cradles for the crew, the last major job before

Stringer checked the whole machine and gave his verdict; certainly the drinking tank was now dry and a dewfall couldn't be relied on, but the coolant bubbled in the jerrican hour by hour, filling the little bottle. The process was slow, too slow: they knew that even with a thousand gallons of coolant available, thirst would race production and they would die of it within a given time, to leave the stuff still boiling; but the fact that water *was* being produced continuously was a psychological weapon against despair.

The despair that was falling upon them tonight stemmed from the fear that the *Phoenix* wouldn't fly; or if it flew, would crash. Now that they were getting near their goal it was taking on the aspect of a mirage. Only one of them seemed unaffected:

"I've explained to Mr. Moran what we're doing tonight. There's no problem, but ask him about anything you don't grasp for yourselves." He observed them coolly, and Moran remembered the time when he'd had to do all the talking for Stringer, who wasn't "much good at it."

Bellamy said, "There's a full bottle ready."

Moran nodded. "Then we'll kick off with a drink—all right with you, Stringer?"

There was no objection. Towns measured the share-out as fairly as he could and they held the water in their mouths, letting their dry tongues swim in it; there was a little over a mouthful for each.

After a minute Towns asked Stringer, "Are we testing the engine tonight?"

He'd asked him before, earlier in the day; but Stringer hadn't answered. He didn't answer now. Towns put his water bottle in the hull and came back into the white circle of light.

"It's time we tested the engine." He stood right up close to the kid, so that he had to answer.

"I think you can leave things to me, Mr. Towns."

Moran was some way off, cutting the skin of the wrecked starboard boom and chopping rivets to remove the longerons they would use for the cradles. He heard Towns and Stringer talking, but didn't catch many of the words because of his chisel on the rivets.

Towns said slowly, "I'm not forgetting, Stringer—you're the designer. But I've got to fly this thing."

Crow, drilling holes in the after-section of the fuselage, muttered to no one, "Turn it up, fer Chris' sake."

Tilney came up with a handful of bolts he'd taken from the hull seat brackets. "Do we put washers on, Mr. Stringer?" There was no reply. Stringer had straightened up from the toolbox and was facing Towns.

"This 'thing' has a name, Mr. Towns. It is called an airplane. I expect a pilot of your experience to have respect for the machine he flies." His brown eyes blinked slowly behind the glasses; there was no expression in them; it was like staring out a reptile, Towns thought. He said:

"All right, it's an airplane." Maybe Moran had the right idea: you had to play this kid along, then he'd eat out of your hand. "But I'd have a heap more respect for it if I knew the engine ran."

Stringer was getting taller. It had happened before, when he'd had the showdown with the pilot, insisting that Towns should work on the plane like the rest. He was drawing himself up; and now his shoulders touched the trailing edge of the wing.

"The engine was running perfectly, Mr. Towns, until the sand blocked the jets in flight. I understand you've had the carburetor dismantled and cleaned out. There is therefore no reason why the engine shouldn't run as it did before—unless you think you haven't cleaned the jets properly, in which case you will have to do them again. I should see to it now."

From the far side of the hull Moran's hammer made the sound of a slow machine gun. Nearer, Crow was whistling through cracked lips, managing no more than a tuneless hiss; but it stopped his having to listen to those two bloody schoolgirls over there.

Tilney went away with his handful of bolts to ask Moran about the washers. He was rather afraid of Stringer, though he couldn't think why.

In the jerrican the coolant bubbled all the time and the flame threw shadows leaping against the plane where the light of the electric bulb didn't reach. The hammering stopped as Moran listened to Tilney's question; and for a time the silence came back, flooding in from the dark. In the silence the shadows danced, witches at a black mass.

The mud-brown eyes regarded Towns.

"Stringer, the jets are clear. I cleared them myself. But that engine hasn't been run for three weeks. There might be oil condensation on the plugs by now in this kind of heat, condensation on the mag points—the fuel flow could have got an air-lock by now—there could be a short in the Coffman circuit—or don't you know about these things? If we try to test-run the engine tonight and it doesn't fire, we've got time and strength to find out why and put it right—there's a spare engine we can strip for parts if we have to." He tried to play it like Moran but it was no good. "If I'm going to fly this machine, I'm going to test-run the engine tonight."

He felt sweat creeping on him and knew that anger was dangerous—anything that brought out sweat was dangerous, but this damned little freak didn't know *everything*. This was Moran's fault, treating him like a damned tin god until he thought he was all-powerful—Christ, he'd never even taken a crate off the ground!

Along the fuselage Albert Crow had stopped work with his drill. Whistling was no good. He went round the tail unit to the other side where Bellamy was bolting seat tubing to make the aft cradle.

"Dave. They're playin' silly-buggers again."

"I can hear them."

"Gets on yer tits." His beaky face was puckered with worry.

Bellamy dropped a bolt and dived for it, sifting the sand; it had gone forever and he'd have to find another one from the wreckage: ten minutes' time lost.

"Gets on yer tits," Crow muttered again.

"All right—it gets on your tits! Mine too—but it's not my fault!"

Crow gave him one straight look and said nothing. He could hear Towns and Stringer still at it.

"If we test the engine," the high monotonous voice came clearly, "the sand's going to blow up against the tail unit and smother the control linkage. The vibration's going to strain the whole structure needlessly. We're going to waste cartridges, and there are only seven in the Coffman. It might take four or five to start up, leaving only two or three for Sunday. I imagine you understand, Mr. Towns, that once we've used all seven cartridges, we'll have no other means of turning the engine." The tone became shrill. "You want us to risk dying of thirst here when there's an airplane standing ready to fly without any means of starting it up?"

Towns felt the sweat crawling on his neck, and his hands were bunched; vaguely he was aware that he wasn't listening to Stringer word by word but could hear only his voice; and when it stopped he had to think back over the words before they made any sense. The pale face of the freak swam in front of him, the glasses gleaming in the light of the naked bulb.

In thirty years Towns' authority as a pilot had never been challenged, when the matter concerned the aircraft he was to fly. *Sorry, but I'm not taking her up with a hundred mag drop: try a new set of plugs. I'm not satisfied with the boost, have to get Thompson onto it. If you can't fix that cowling button, change it—you've got fifteen minutes.*

Yes, sir. Okay, Mr. Towns.

He heard his own voice speaking to Stringer. While his conscious mind concerned itself with outrage, his unconscious reasoned for him. "That is precisely my point. If there's any doubt about this engine starting, now is the time to get it right." His voice sounded unsteady. "You will please prepare the machine for a test run."

From the other side of the hull Moran heard what he first thought must be the screech of a bird; then something smashed the electric bulb and the shape of the *Phoenix* vanished into the dark.

CHAPTER
20

IN THE COLD OF THE NIGHT, IN THE HEAT OF the day, he lay as if dead. No one had gone near him except Moran, once.

Moran had looked down at him. The schoolboy face was pinched, and the eyes, without the glasses on, seemed to have shrunk. They had been staring for hours at the ceiling of the hull; now they looked at Moran, who said:

"I've talked to him." He crouched so that he could look at the kid closely, worried by the feverish face. "Now we all want to know if the flight's still on." There was another way he could have put it: we want to know if you've decided whether we're going to live or die.

Stringer's eyes had intelligence in them. He said nothing. He must have heard. He said nothing.

"Last night we finished most of the cradles, and I'm ready to start on the control grouping. I think I could do it but I'd like you to supervise. After the immense amount of work you've done, I'd hate to spoil it. Quite apart from what it would mean, if I did."

The mud-brown eyes blinked slowly, and Moran prepared himself for the long strain of keeping patience. He said, "You know that I've gone right along with you from the start—it was me who took you up on your idea and got the others interested. There's no reason why we two can't make a success of this thing, to hell with everyone else. If your machine flies us out, you'll have saved the lives of seven men; and I'm ready to respect a man who can do a thing as big as that."

The words fell quietly from him, the sibilants lisping through shriveled lips, the consonants difficult for his tongue; but it was the tone that mattered. "We're going to work again tonight, too. We'd be able to work better if we knew we could count on you."

From outside, the sun's glare hit the sand and bounced into the hull, shining on bared metal, dappling the curve of the ceiling. When he stopped speaking he could hear the steady sound of the kid's breathing. He went on again, and got no answer, and went on again, pretending that he didn't mind that there was no answer, because pride was dangerous, a killer.

After a time Stringer's eyes closed, and he looked dead. It was a kind of answer; and Moran left him, going to sit in the shade of the wing, where Crow and Bellamy were on their backs, sleepless.

"What's 'e say?"

"Nothing."

In a while he would go back and try again. He wondered where Towns was. Twice in the heat of this day he'd lost sight of Towns and believed he'd simply walked out into the desert.

"Where's Towns?" he asked them.

"Tailplane."

Moran hoped he was asleep, conserving his remaining strength, because tonight Towns was going to work like a black.

It had been a pair of metal shears in Stringer's hand that had smashed the light. Nobody knew or would ever know if they'd been aimed at Towns' face or at the bulb or just nowhere, when that inhuman screech of rage had come. By the time Moran was on the scene Stringer was walking into the hull and Towns was climbing the mainplane.

"Frank. What happened?"

Moran looked round at the others but none of them spoke.

"I'm going to test-run the engine."

"Now? Tonight?"

"We have to know if she'll run."

Crow told Moran, "They were arguin' the toss again, that's what 'appened. Christ, I can't bleedin' concentrate on what I'm doin', with this lot on!"

Moran made for the hull. "Stringer?" Silence, except for the shivering of breath. Yellow light flickered through the hull doorway from the oil flame outside and he could make out the white of Stringer's face.

The kid was shivering in a fever and couldn't answer Moran; he left him and went back to the wing.

"Tilney! Take a torch and get a new light bulb from the hull—there's two more in the roof of the freight section. Frank! Does Stringer agree we test-run the engine?"

Towns was trying to unbutton the top cowling, fumbling in the dark. "Pilot's orders," he called, his tone strident.

Moran had to keep a grip on himself. So this was it—the thing he'd been dreading—the third round. There'd be no talking Frank out of this one. He stood shaking, shutting his eyes, praying for miracles. Tilney came out with a new bulb and Watson helped him lower the stanchion and fit it; the scene was suddenly there again, etched with acid light and shadow, and there was Towns up there, working quite steadily, not fumbling now there was light; if he was in a rage he didn't show it; maybe the rage was dying out because he'd won; the first two rounds had gone to Stringer; this was his.

They stood in an awkward group: Crow, Bellamy, Watson, Tilney, watching the man on the mainplane. Moran took a long breath: "Whose idea was it to test-run?"

"His," Bellamy said.

"And Stringer said no?"

"That's it."

Crow was letting out a string of quiet and calculated obscenities in an almost conversational tone as if killing time the only way he knew, until Bellamy told him to shut up. They stood in the harsh light, each of them dependent on the others for his life, yet among them none was a friend of another. Their spirit had broken at last.

Moran stood trying to get his reason back. Nothing new had happened: a few men had got stranded in the desert and they were in the last stages of thirst, and now they were going mad.

Stringer had stayed too sane for too long: for three weeks he'd flogged his brain with a pressure of work that would have taxed a man with a home to go to and water to drink and food to eat. Now he'd cracked. In a different way Towns had cracked, finding in Stringer's youth and ability an accuser, a finger pointing to the succession of failures that made up Towns' career. A first-class pilot had gone on flying, failing his conversion tests and turning his back on the big main-schedule routes, accepting short-haul work because he had to live in the air; he'd gone on flying, making himself believe that jungle and desert and ice floe gave him a better chance to show that anyone could fly the big stuff with their automatic control whereas it took a born flyer to take up a Beaver from a swamped strip or put a Skytruck through a sandstorm and live. Towns had gone on flying until his skill went rotten on him and he had to brave it out— *What's the risk? We're bigger* . . . Gone on flying, with forty thousand hours in his book, until the final hour had come and he'd flown himself into the ground.

All the things he'd shrugged away—the failures and the humiliations, even the fact that as a flyer he was growing old—had crashed in on him, not when the Skytruck had hit the sand, not when he had seen there were twelve men still alive, but when he'd had to fetch the spade and dig a grave with his own hands.

There'd had to be someone he could hate, a kicking boy he could use to express the hate he had for himself; and Stringer was there—young, confident, an aircraft designer at the age of thirty-odd, brilliant, on his way up. But the kid refused to be kicked. It was no good thinking what appalling luck it was that these two should meet at a time like this when life itself depended on good relations—the "time like this" was caused by the crash: by Towns; and life itself depended on their building an escape plane: on Stringer's terms.

Towns had shown that he was ready to work with them—he had worked harder than some; and he was prepared to fly them out. But his bruised and bleeding ego was at war. His career was finished, but for one last flight; and he was not going to suffer the final humiliation of flying under orders from a kid.

Moran looked up at him; the cowling was nearly off. It was probable that he didn't realize himself why he was so adamant about the test run; his ego, the black tulip that is within all men, was flowering strongly in the suitable conditions of hunger, thirst, guilt, and the threat of death. Sometimes Moran himself had done something on impulse, inexplicably; and afterward he had asked himself, Now why the hell did I do that? It happened to everyone. *Ye know not what ye do.* It was happening to Frank Towns now; and it was going to kill them all.

Crow was saying beside him, "You'll 'ave to stop 'im, Lew. It's one thing revvin' up for take-off, an' another thing doin' it with chocks an' brakes on. She'll shake to pieces like Stringer told 'im."

Bellamy asked, "Is she ready for starting? Primers and Coffman all set up?" He'd been working on the tailplane the last two nights.

"She's ready," Moran said. "He did the job himself."

For two nights Towns had worked steadily, unconscious of the fact that the terrible forces within him intended that he should wreck this machine before it could ever fly. If you told him, he'd say you were nuts.

And if he couldn't shake it to pieces on the ground, he'd make a mistake with it in the air and prove that he was right: the thing wasn't airworthy, and Stringer was to blame. The fourth round would go to Towns and he'd die the winner.

"Tell you one thing," Watson said. "I'm not goin' to 'elp 'im start it up."

"No one is," Bellamy said.

"You'll 'ave to stop 'im, Lew."

On the mainplane Towns checked the primers and began putting the cowling back. After the business with Stringer just now he felt tired and couldn't remember whether he'd screwed the unions tight last night; but they were checked now and she'd start first go, with any luck. She had to start with a will, and run sweetly; he would watch the prop swinging and listen to the note, rev her until the front skids began shifting, keep her under control; then he would switch off and go and tell Stringer, "I'm satisfied." Then they'd know where they stood. This aircraft had a captain.

It was necessary to demonstrate this. No one could do it but himself. Moran thought the best way to treat Stringer was by sucking up to him; the others had been obeying the kid's orders from the beginning without question. They were all wrong: Stringer had become a dictator because of it. Now he would stop the rot.

These thoughts and other thoughts flickered through his mind as he worked on the cowling, his hands quite steady. Nerve lights went jazzing across his eyes but that was just because he was in bad shape physically: his brain was okay and he was in command of it; soon he would be in command of them all. This needed doing.

"This needs doing." He was surprised by the mutter that came from his own mouth. You knew what they said about people who talked to themselves; but he was just giving his thoughts emphasis, that was all. Once he slipped on the smooth metal skin of the wing and felt a muscle twinge in his groin. He was tired, would have to watch it; he was in the limelight now. They were down there on the ground, the small men, watching the captain of aircraft preparing to test-run his machine. They were safe in his hands; he wouldn't let them down.

He primed the cylinders with the Ki-gas pump, and heard the stuff squirting in.

"Frank." Lew's face was down there, a blur against the glare of the bulb. "You're going it alone, you know that?"

"It suits me."

He climbed onto the forward cradle and set the throttle open a quarter, putting the mixture to rich and checking that the switches were dead. It was all coming back to him, the wonderful routine business of the start-up, doing it all for himself as he'd done it a thousand times in the bush or on a mud strip where there were no mechanics he could trust. Cocks on; primed; mixture set; switches off.

It felt to be a long drop from the mainplane but the sand was soft and he staggered upright, someone's hand grabbing his arm.

"Frank, you won't have the strength—"

"*Who me?*" Now he was angry. Lew was a fool, trying to show him up in front of the others. He shook his arm free and went round the wing-tip;

the sand was surprisingly soft, tripping him at every step; he straightened himself. The prop was in the one-up position and he reached for a blade, gripping with both hands and hanging from it until his weight moved the pistons. Throbbing began in his head and white flashes burst in his eyes; he stood for a minute shaking the pain away. The prop was one-down now and he put his shoulder against the blade; but it didn't budge. Lew was right; he was in bad shape, though he shouldn't have said it in front of the others. He tried again with the prop, gripping the blade and trying to drag it this time; but the muscles in his back flared up and he had to stop. He waited another minute, didn't want to let them see how he was panting. Hell with the sucking in—the first cartridge would have to do that; there were seven, it was plenty.

The lamp dipped and swung as he walked back round the wing-tip and something crashed into his shoulder, must have bumped his shoulder on the leading edge, sand was too soft and it tripped you.

No one spoke. Lew had gone. Fool.

He clambered up the trailing edge, slipped and fell and got up and climbed again, grabbing the pilot's cradle, one leg over; Christ sake, don't let go now. Sweat on his flanks, lot of effort but nobody'd help him, bastards. See who's captain aircraft now, show 'em. Switches down. Two more squirts for luck. Contact.

They stood in a group on the sand, their stark

shadows lined along the wing. They looked up in silence at the man hitting at the Coffman button, hitting it again and again and getting no result.

"Frank, listen. The Coffman's empty. No cartridges."

Towns sounded drunk, trying to shout with his dried-up mouth: "Course got cart'idges, got sheven cart'idges!"

Went on hitting the damn button.

"Listen to me, Frank. Try to understand. We took the cartridges out while you were at the prop. It's no go."

Towns' hands stopped moving. He understood. He understood what they had done to him. Captain of aircraft. They had left him sitting up here like a monkey in a trap.

He jerked out of the cradle and landed on the wing and stared down at Moran's white blurred face.

"You—did—what?"

From below he looked big, hunched against the stars, thick legs bent and arms out ready to spring.

He was mad. Moran had known it and had asked Watson for his gun.

"Watch it, Frank."

The red eyes stared from the gray matted beard, the head jerking down an inch to look at the revolver, jerking up again to look at Moran's face. For a moment he swayed, got his balance, and sprang as the gun banged and he hit the sand and lay still.

CHAPTER
21

THE MOON WAS FULL, ITS LOWER EDGE BAL-
anced on the black back of the dunes. It was long
after midnight. Moran looked at it sometimes as
he listened to Towns; and sometimes he said a
word to let Towns know he was listening, and understood.

Moran had given the gun back to Watson and
helped Towns to his feet; Crow had taken his other
arm and they had walked him away from the light;
there was no moisture in him for tears but his
breath shuddered in and out of him and his body
was shaking.

"Okay," Moran told Crow. "I'll look after
him." He put his jacket under Towns' head. Crow
went back to the others and they began work, not
talking to one another. After a long time Towns
said in a whisper:

"I didn't think you'd do it. Didn't think you'd fire."

"I shot to miss."

Towns opened his eyes and looked at the high
white stars.

"I didn't think I was that bad, Lew."

"You're not bad."

"I didn't think I was that far gone." He blinked at the stars as if surprised to see them up there. "I was trying to start the engine, wasn't I?"

"Yes."

"Why did I want to do that, Lew?"

"To show you were boss."

"Was that why? Dear Christ."

Moran could still feel the recoil of the gun. They'd been lucky. With Towns flying at him like that it had been difficult to miss. The thing was, the shot had gone home, metaphorically: even in his crazed state Towns had realized that his best friend had fired a gun at him; when he'd dropped to the sand he must have thought he was dead. It amounted to shock treatment. He was speaking quite normally and his eyes were quiet.

He said, "They're working on the plane." He could hear the tools.

"Yes."

"Go and help them, Lew."

Moran couldn't detect any false note in the tone, any slyness of the mad. "You be okay now, Frankie?"

"Yep. Just want to think about things."

Moran got up and left him, joining the others under the cold light.

" 'Ow is 'e?"

"He'll be okay."

"Thought you'd killed 'im."

"So did he." He climbed the wing and checked the controls in the pilot's cradle, switching off the mags and fuel cocks, screwing the Ki-gas home. He'd told Bellamy to hide the seven cartridges; they could stay hidden until Sunday or whatever day it would be when they tried to fly out, if ever the day came. The designer and the pilot were both flat on their backs recovering from brainstorms; the chances didn't look so hot.

Many times, working on the crew slings, he stopped and took a close look at Towns. His eyes were shut; maybe he was sleeping. It was long after midnight and the big moon was up before Towns opened his eyes.

"That you, Lew?"

"It's me."

"How's the work going?"

"Okay."

Towns got up onto one elbow and looked at him full in the eyes. "Lew, I went loco, didn't I?"

"You did."

Towns looked away. "I knew it'd happen. Days ago. It got so bad that whenever I saw his face I wanted to smash it up; I didn't know anything except that I hated him. Now I've had time to think. I'll tell you something: it was because he's young, and he's here to pull my chestnuts out of the fire . . ."

Sometimes as Moran listened he looked at the enormous moon; he listened to things about Towns that he'd never known, and to things that even Towns had never known until now, when it all came out. It was the confessional.

"And there's this, Lew. In a small way I've always had authority—a pilot's only a bus driver but on board his aircraft he's king. And you can see that kid's never known authority, till now, and it's gone to his head. So there isn't room for the two of us here. That's the whole thing, isn't it?"

"It is."

"So what's the answer, Lew?"

"You accept his authority."

"Yep. That's how I see it."

Moran said something more but there was no answer; Towns had rid himself of torment, and sleep had swamped him. Moran covered him with what he could find and went away.

There had been no dew. Each had rinsed his mouth with his share of the water that had been distilling in the night, and Moran had taken some to Stringer, who had accepted it without speaking. There had been no sweat on him but his eyes were fever-bright. Later Moran had talked to him for a long time, asking him if they could count on him; but the kid had said nothing, though he had listened.

Now Moran sat in the shade of the mainplane,

with Crow and Bellamy. Every fifteen minutes he moved the jerrican and burner to keep the sun's direct light on the can, with the bottle in the shade.

Bellamy had written: *The 25th Day, Friday. I think this is going to be it. Towns and Stringer are still out cold, and neither of them worked last night. I don't think I can do any more work, either. Very ragged and no strength. Coolant still distilling but not nearly enough. If no dew in the morning, that will be it. Almost glad. Want to sleep.*

Crow asked Moran, "Why can't we make some kind of a bleedin' blow-lamp for that thing? Can't we use the Ki-gas from the other engine an' blow bleedin' petrol through it or somethin'?"

Moran was adjusting the solar reflector again. "The stuff's boiling," he said. "If it boils any harder it'll shoot up the spout, and contaminate the water."

The silence came in again. Watson and Tilney lay under the white silk canopy, spread-eagled. Nobody had thought of turning the generator today because even lifting a hand was an effort.

Across the east dunes the vultures still fought over the camel's remains; and some time before noon a flock of them had begun circling directly over the plane, sighting prone men. Watson had fired three rounds into them without a hit; but they had scattered and gone.

Moran got up again and walked across to the

hull, with the sun scorching on his shoulders and head; it was difficult to see clearly today: shapes had lost their outline and bars of dark and light swam against his half-closed eyes.

Stringer wasn't asleep. He looked at Moran with recognition. Moran chose short words and phrases because his tongue was like a lump of dry wood. The sounds came rustling out of him.

"Stringer, you want to die?"

"No." It was the first time Stringer had spoken since that terrible screech.

"You're going to die."

"I expect so." He didn't look at Moran.

"Today's Friday. Got a chance, if you'll help. Tell you again. Listen. Towns says he accepts your authority. All you want, isn't it?"

"Leave me alone." He closed his eyes.

"Tonight I'm going to finish the controls myself. In the morning, going to try take-off."

"You'll crash." The eyelids flickered, the tone was impatient.

"Maybe will. Rather do that than die of thirst. Won't be your fault, Stringer. Design's good, just never finished. Listen, if—"

"Leave me alone."

"If you'll help—"

"Leave me alone."

Moran went outside and dropped onto the sand under the canopy. Done all he could. Sleep.

There was no movement anywhere except that of the slow shadow on the sand. The sun was lowering toward evening. Below the tip of the wing the jerrican was now in shade and the metal reflector shone uselessly. The oil in the burner was running out and a thick scarf of smoke dragged on the air; in the can the coolant was no more than simmering.

The bird's slow shadow wheeled on the sand, becoming darker as it circled lower, the long neck curved and the head down, watching for movement, seeing none.

The canopy hung limp. The silence was total: the birds, sated, had left the camel and winged heavily westward to the mountain, leaving this one. It had perhaps fed less than the others or its instinct was stronger: the instinct to note the presence of death among things on the earth that normally moved.

It came lower still, the tips of the black wings splayed to support the turns, the bald head moving on the neck to keep the prey observed. The shadow was now as black as the bird and as silent.

The shot ripped feathers away and the bird squawked, flapping awkwardly across the dunes; the feathers floated down and lay curved on the sand.

The sergeant watched it go. He'd meant to let the thing come closer before he fired but the sight of the beak and the eyes in the bald white head had turned his stomach and he'd fired early.

"Christ, 'oo done that?"

"Watson."

"Ye'?"

"What was it?"

"Vulture."

"Get it?"

"Winged it."

They dragged themselves upright and memory came back, thoughts worse than vultures. Some of them sat down again. Albert Crow lurched to the can of oil-and-petrol mixture and fed the burner, spilling some, throwing sand over the pool of flame. His hands shook; the shot had sounded in his dream where Moran was killing Towns.

They listened to the silence consciously, forgetting that it was the moan of the generator that was missing.

" 'Allo . . ." said Crow.

Stringer was standing in the doorway of the hull. Bellamy hadn't seen him. "What?" he asked Crow.

" 'Ckin' lordship's woke up."

Stringer didn't move. He was standing right in the middle of the doorway, hands by his sides, not leaning on anything. He looked at them, turning his narrow head in jerks. They sat watching him. When he saw that they had all noticed him he called shrilly:

"I want to talk to you!"

The sun was above the west dunes, and this side

of the plane and the wreckage was in shadow. Not for anyone, not even for Stringer, would Moran have walked into the sun; he was prepared to walk in the shadow. The sand burned under his feet. He walked until he stood facing the man in the doorway. No one else moved.

"All of you!"

The echo came piping from the dunes. The bright sand reflected in the glasses made him look like a science-fiction character from another planet, with huge gold eyes that could burn whole cities with a glance.

Crow muttered, "Christ. Look."

Towns had got to his feet and was walking toward the doorway in the hull. Of all people, Towns. He was standing beside Moran, facing Stringer.

Sergeant Watson was moving. Tilney.

"Come on, Albert . . ."

Stringer waited. They stood in a half-circle looking up at him. Their own reflection darkened the rimless glasses and they could see his eyes; they were very bright. He said nothing, but watched them, his head jerking by inches until he had observed them all. The low sun slanting through the windows of the hull on the far side framed his head in an aureole of light.

"Mr. Towns."

"Yes?"

"Who is in authority here?"

The voice was tinny, rattling out the words. No one turned to look at Towns. They all looked up at Stringer. He seemed to be drawing himself up, standing very erect even though the doorway made him feet taller than anyone. He looked down directly at Towns.

Moran listened to his own breath sawing in and out of his parched throat. He thought: Life or death, one or the other, life or death.

The silence was over.

"You are."

Life.

CHAPTER
22

MORAN CLOSED HIS EYES. HE FELT WEARINESS, as if he'd come a long way to this place. He stood listening to the tinny monotone.

"Very well. I am in authority here. I want to tell you that I have decided to finish the airplane and try to make it fly. You will have to understand certain things. We are running short of water. Tomorrow it will be worse. But there is a lot of hard work to do, and the first one of you who gives up—as you've given up before—will put an end to all our plans, because I am not going to use up all my energies for people who don't cooperate. Now, is that clear?"

The glasses swung across their faces.

"Clear." Bellamy.

"Another thing. When I tell any one of you to do something, it isn't a request." The glasses shone upon Towns. "It is an order. I want no disobedience from anyone. Most of you have worked very well. Now we are *all* going to work very well, until the airplane is finished. When it is finished I think it will fly. I want you to concentrate on that thought, instead of thinking about dying. I will tell you something—I haven't got time to die!"

He looked at each of their faces.

"Mr. Towns, I want you to turn the generator. Give it an hour."

He swung down from the doorway and walked the length of the fuselage toward the mainplane, where the toolboxes were gathered. His walk was stiff, the thin arms swinging, the back straight; but there was no self-consciousness in it; now that he had finished talking to them they had ceased to exist.

They broke up, but no one made any comment. They moved through the purpling shadows as the sun lowered to the dunes; and in a few minutes the generator began droning. In half an hour the working lamp went on.

In the morning the white silk canopy was dry; there had been no wind from the sea or from anywhere; the sun lifted from the rim of the wastelands, a clear disk in a dry sky. A little afterward the miniature tornadoes began, one of them spinning along the ridge of the dunes, dancing like a rope. Only one of them was awake: Bellamy. He saw the little tornado and for a time watched it; when he saw the whole south sky turning yellow he roused the others but the wind was on them even as they dragged themselves to their feet. It came as it had come before, sweeping the dunes until they smoked with sand.

Towns was at the engine, covering the air intake, the flying sand already blasting the skin of his bare legs. Someone was shouting above the hail sound of the sand against the fuselage and figures were running half seen through the murk. Stringer was climbing to the aft cradle on the windward side with a bunch of fabric in his hand but he lost his grip and fell and the fabric went swirling away on the storm. A flare of orange light unfolded below the main-plane as the distillery burner was overturned; the oil pan took fire and was whipped by the wind, the flames tumbling beneath the wing tank and flutter-ing out of sight toward the dunes; and Crow dived for the jerrican—coolant was spilling from the spout and he righted it, saving most.

The sky had darkened to ocher and the *Phoenix* was a shadow, the port wing lifting and dropping as the gusts hit the underside. Somewhere a rigging wire twanged in the wind. They made for the hull and climbed in, bracing the door shut and stacking crates against it. Their eyes burned but couldn't water; sand was in their mouths but they had no saliva.

The storm tore at the gaps in the metal skin of the hull and sent puffs of sand exploding in the gloom. Moran, crouched at a window, could see the port wing lifting and dropping, flexing from tip to mid-section; above it the rigging cable sagged and tautened, twanging like a great guitar string. He came away from the window and called to Stringer, "Is there anything we can do out there?"

The eyes were calm in the pinched white face.

"Nothing."

The *Phoenix* stood wing-on to the wind, taking the strain from the worst angle. They couldn't swing her round; she must stand as she was and try to weather it. Moran thought, Stringer's dream. He didn't know how he estimated Stringer even now: maybe there was a heart inside him somewhere; or maybe he was just an empty tin can with a brain, or an ascetic inspired by mechanical things, or a man on the edge of madness—but whatever he was he had his dream and it was out there being battered by the storm and he could do nothing.

Crow was hunched on the floor, holding the monkey against him, scratching its miniature head and talking to it. Sergeant Watson asked Bellamy:

"This lot going to break her up?"

"It might."

"I'm sorry for 'im, you know." He was looking at Stringer.

"Yes."

Sand blew in through the gaps. Papers left by Otto Kepel fluttered about the floor and Bellamy collected them, and saw the title on one of the sheets—*The White Bird*—and tried to read on, but his German wasn't good enough, and he rolled up the sheets and stuck them into the join of the seat where they couldn't move.

The light was mustard colored in the hull; their faces were yellow. Some of them looked now and then from a window and saw the wing lifting and dropping, and came away, looking at no one.

The big guitar string twanged.

"I know what you want, my ole Bimbo." The sand roared against the hull, drowning his voice. "What you want is a nice green tree t' swing in, an' a great big coconut full of lovely milk, don't you, eh? An' a lot of other little Bimbos t'play with, lark about like, up among the leaves. There'd be a stream there, wouldn', there, full of lovely water, an' you'd sit an' watch it till the blee—till the cows come 'ome."

He always made a point never to swear when he talked to Bimbo, because he was such a little 'un.

"That's what you want, i'n'it? An' all Uncle Albert c'n do is give you a good scratch. Ne' mind."

The hull shuddered, hit by the wind—and a new sound came: the starboard wing was lifting and falling with the other one, buffeting the roof of the control cabin. They listened to it, counting the seconds between thuds and willing each next one never to come. The sound went on.

The 26th Day. Saturday. Worked all through night. No dew this morning. Thirst very bad. Now sandstorm, bashing the plane all over. Writing this in storm, all of us sheltering in hull. God, how Albert's monkey stinks! But I see what he means. It belonged to Rob, and I wouldn't like to see it die before we do.

The dreadful thudding had stopped. Stringer had been into the control cabin with bits of broken crates and the rest of the seat cushions to wedge the wing.

Bellamy shut the diary and went forward through the dim tunnel of the hull and began turning the generator. It whined like a lost soul in the rushing of the storm.

Trapped in the oven heat of the hull, some of them slept, stupefied. Tilney sat with his back to the freight bulkhead, his eyes shut and his face drawn, his lips moving involuntarily. The sergeant cleaned his revolver for the third time. Stringer leaned against the curved wall, arms folded, watching the dip and flutter of the mainplane through the window, listening to the drone of the generator. His eyes blinked slowly, as if the movement of his lids had been calculated according to some formula; faint stubble was on his face because this morning there had been no time to shave.

"It's easing," Moran said.

The light was a brighter yellow in the windows. Crow looked up; he had been thinking of the green leaves and the stream. He wondered where Bellamy was; then he heard the generator.

The cable had stopped twanging; the wing was still. They waited until the sand stopped pattering against the hull. Blue sky was in the windows and the world outside was gold.

Moran took the crates away from the door and heaved it open. Stringer was first out, the knotted handkerchief already on his head.

"The canopy's gone," someone said.

Crow went round to the leeward side of the wreck and saw that the parachute silk had gone for good, somewhere across the north dunes. They'd miss the shade, the rest of the day; and if there was a dewfall they'd get a gallon or two less water from it, without the big silk; but you wouldn't walk out there a mile and get back alive. It was three days since they'd had their last full ration and that was only a pint.

He made for the shade of the wing where the others were sitting. Towns had found sand in the air intake: the rags he'd stuffed there were blown away. Stringer came down from the aft cradle; when the storm began he had tried to cover the tail-unit control linkage with pieces of fabric but he'd lost his grip and fallen. He spent ten minutes examining the skid clamps, wing rigging, cowlings and pilot's controls, then came under the shelter of the mainplane.

"She stood up all right." There was no pride in

his tone; there was never anything in Stringer's tone. "Fore and aft control linkage is jammed with sand stuck to the grease points. We shall have to wash out with petrol and regrease. The air intake has to come off again."

Towns said, "Then we do it tonight. We do everything tonight that has to be done."

"Of course. There's no problem." He went into the hull.

Bellamy said, "Albert. Feeling strong?"

"Strong as a mouse—what's on?"

"Got to set up the distillery again."

They fetched fabric for a wick and bashed out a new burner from the wreck metal, rigging the jerrican and bottle under the tail unit this time, away from the wing tanks. Watson polished a new solar reflector for them because the other had blown away. They worked slowly, resting every few minutes, exhausted by even these small tasks; when they had to leave the shade they made straight for the next patch, reeling through the heat.

Moran fetched paper and a pencil from his baggage, to sit again below the wing. Making a small cross to represent the wreck and sketching in the horseshoe of the dunes, he estimated the position of the three graves nearby, putting their names: *Sam Wright, Lloyd Jones, Otto Kepel.* On the other side of the east dunes he drew a skeleton and marked it: *Camel.* Near it he marked two graves:

Harris, Loomis. If they managed to get out, a team would be sent here to find the bodies and ship them home. If they got airborne and then crashed without any fire the map would be found on him, if ever he were found at all. He explained details on the back of the paper, adding: *Cobb and Roberts were lost somewhere south, within 100 miles of base. Not together. Not buried.*

He staggered through the direct noon sun to the hull. Inside, Stringer was sitting with a piece of sheet metal across his knees; on it were papers and sketches; some magazines and catalogues of some sort lay at his feet. He was too absorbed to notice Moran as he passed forward between the remains of the seats until he found the papers that Otto Kepel had left, and the letter: *Vater, Mutter und Inga.* The cigarette lighter, knife, and keys he put into his pocket; the family would need, in their grief, small things of his to touch and to keep; the knife had been cleaned and they would never know its last purpose. The letter and the flying-report sheets he put with the map he had made.

Stringer didn't look up as he went out of the hull.

The sergeant was asleep. Tilney was flat on his back with his eyes open, and said to Moran, "We're leaving tomorrow, aren't we?"

"Eight o'clock sharp, kid. Don't be late."

He noticed that there was no more fear in the boy's eyes, and wondered why this was. Because there was a limit to fear, just as there was a limit to grief: the spirit, like the body, was self-healing. Or because his too-easy faith in God—who had done nothing for Captain Harris—was now placed in Stringer, who might save them all. Or one of a dozen things; maybe it didn't matter, so long as the fear had gone.

"Lew." Towns hadn't slept, though he'd worked harder than anyone last night. "There's a thing on my mind. We should put the cartridges back in the Coffman."

Moran looked at the old-man's face with its reddened eyes. There was nothing wrong with Towns now. "We should?"

"You might forget where they were put. Or it might be too hot for them there. Wherever it is, it's not the place for them. They should be where they belong, in the Coffman. We need them tomorrow." He looked away.

His eyes were all right, red with incipient desert blindness, but steady. His voice was all right, slurring over the words only because of thirst. He was all of a piece again, all Frank Towns. And it made sense: they had six more hours of this heat to live through, and the long work of the night, with nothing but a mouthful of water they would almost rather not drink because it would make them mad for more. By morning anything could be forgotten, even important things; by morning the plane might be ready to fly but without the cartridges they couldn't even start the engine. It made sense, but it wasn't Towns' reason for speaking; it must have been difficult to speak about this; it would be impossible for him to say, Look, I know Stringer's in charge and I still accept that. But I'm the pilot and tomorrow it's all going to depend on me—and how I feel. I can't feel much respect for myself with those things hidden away like you hide matches from a kid because they're dangerous. Give me this break.

Made sense again. Their pilot would need their confidence and his own. There was no risk.

"Tell you the truth, Frank, I'd forgotten we'd ever taken them out. You'll find them in the mail locker."

As Towns moved, Moran said, "Wait for the cool of the night, it's hell out there."

"I need to do it now. And thanks."

He wished he'd waited as Moran had said, because the sun hit him like a blow and he hadn't the strength to hurry; but it was true: he needed to do this thing now, and then he could forget the mad screech and the smashed light bulb, and later the worst thing of all, the bang of the gun in Moran's hand.

They were where he had said, in the mail locker, seven of them, safe in his hands: passports for seven men.

Stringer was working at something in the hull,

with papers balanced on a metal sheet—Towns could see a couple of air-frame designs he'd sketched in pencil; there were some colored catalogues with a name on them in big letters: KAYCRAFT. It was a name Towns had heard of somewhere.

The kid hadn't heard him come into the hull; he was unaware of him now as for these few seconds he stood looking down at him; and suddenly he came to know Stringer and what made him tick— he was a dreamer, as many scientists are dreamers; he could concentrate on his obsession to a degree where nothing else existed for him. Planning to build an airplane from wreckage and with worn-out tools in the killing desert heat, he could say, "I see no problem." Hearing that scream of pain from Otto Kepel when the hull had shifted, he could say, "There is no damage." Goaded to a brainstorm by opposition, he could recover and resume his work and say, "I haven't got time to die!"

Nothing existed—pain, heat, thirst, the desert, even the fear of death—nothing was real to him except his dream; and only a brain like his could build a machine like the *Phoenix* in this region of hell and give them all a chance of getting out. Student's glasses and schoolkid haircut, pencil in hand, the designer sat absorbed in his designs.

Towns turned for the doorway of the hull, and stopped dead as if he had hit a wall. He shut his eyes. Panic was in him, crying *no . . . no . . . no . . .*

Elleston Trevor

A simple thing had happened. In a city street, one carries in mind for a minute—unconsciously—the name of the product advertised on the bus that has just gone past. The visual impression fades, unless there is a link that makes conscious sense of it. Turning away from Stringer, Towns had carried a visual impression of the name: *Kaycraft*. The name on the catalogues. And there were two links: the sketched designs in which Stringer was absorbed and his resemblance to a schoolkid. The three images came together, making a pattern.

The shock and the panic were already over; but he stood stunned, knowing that the seven cartridges in his hand were useless now. Their chance of getting out of here alive hadn't gone: it had never existed. It had been a dream.

CHAPTER
23

MORAN HAD SHUT HIS EYES BECAUSE THE GLARE was bad even with sunglasses. Their bodies were being slowly dehydrated and the tear sacs were emptying, so that it was painful to blink. He heard someone moving and opened his eyes and looked into Towns' despairing face.

"It's no go," Towns said, crouching under the wing and doubling on his haunches. He covered his face with his hands and spoke very quietly through them so that no one but Moran would hear. "It's no go." He wouldn't have let himself tell even Moran except that he had to tell someone, make someone else share it. "It's no go."

The cartridges were in his pockets; Moran could see a glint of brass there. He asked, "What's happened?" The dread came back: Stringer was in the hull and Towns had just been there and he could mean only that they'd had another bust-up and the flight was "no go." "What's happened, Frank?"

"The flight's off." He took his hands away and

stared into Moran's face and the surprise was still in his voice, the surprise that for three weeks they had all been living a dream and never suspected it. "You know what Stringer is?"

Moran felt the dread tighten his scalp. So it was Stringer. Stringer and Towns. Again.

"You know what he is, Lew? He's a designer. He designs aircraft. Model aircraft. Model planes. Toys." The words came shivering softly out.

"I don't understand." The noon heat flowed under the mainplane, drowning them, burning them; he couldn't make his brain think clearly. "What happened in there?"

Towns had his hands round his legs and his head was lowered until his peeled brow rested on his knees. He wished now that he'd had the strength not to tell even Moran.

"Frank, have you had another fight?"

"No. No. It was just a quiet conversation."

And every word that Stringer had said had sounded so normal, so reasonable. It was the worst aspect of lunacy: its semblance to sanity.

He didn't know how long he'd stood there in the doorway, his back to the kid; it had been long enough to make Stringer aware of him.

"What are they, Mr. Towns?"

The light impersonal voice didn't rouse him from his nightmare.

"Mr. Towns, what are they?"

When he turned he saw that Stringer was looking across at his hand.

"These?" The kid's question itself was mad, irrelevant. "Cartridges." He forced himself to remember what he was doing with them. "Out of the Coffman starter."

"Why did you take them out?" The mild eyes blinked at precise intervals.

"They were taken out for safe storage."

"Then you must put them back now. We shall need them in the morning. We don't want to lose them."

"No. That's right. I'm on my way there now, to put them back."

Stringer nodded and turned again to the airframe sketches. Towns could see only the bright color of the catalogues and the name in big letters, Kaycraft.

"Is that your outfit, Stringer? Kaycraft?"

The kid looked up, looked down at the catalogues. Maybe he'd only just realized they were there and that he should have hidden them from sight.

"It's the name of my company, yes."

"I've heard of them. They make model planes, don't they?"

"Yes." Stringer seemed neither impatient nor worried about this. He sounded interested. "They make the best."

"I didn't know they designed big stuff, too."

"The biggest we make is the Albatross—a six-foot wing span parasol model—but it's not my own design because it's a glider, and I work on the power models." He opened one of the catalogues and showed it to Towns. "The biggest I've ever designed is the Hawk Six—this one. She took the Stevenage Cup last year in the Power Class under full FAI rules. The radio control was my own design, too."

The catalogue floated under Towns' eyes. Everything had become unreal.

"That's very good. Stevenage Cup. That's a fine little plane. But I meant big stuff, I meant I didn't know you designed the real thing, that carries people, a plane like the Skytruck. Like the *Phoenix*."

"No, Kaycraft are model-plane builders." He was turning the pages of the catalogue, as a gardener admires his prize roses.

"And you're one of their designers?"

"I've been their chief designer for two years." He turned the book toward Towns. "This one's the Ranger," he said. "The Mark I had shallower tip dihedrals, the II was a shoulder wing, and the III has all the stability factors of the first two and none of their tendency to stall in still-air conditions."

Towns said, "You've never designed a full-size aircraft. Like the Skytruck."

Stringer looked surprised. He had been talking about the Ranger. "Full size? Oh, no."

"Except this one. The *Phoenix*."

"This one?" He sat back, folding his thin hands. "I haven't *designed* it. It's been a question of adapting and improvising." He seemed puzzled by the turn in the conversation. Towns said groggily:

"I may be wrong, I may be wrong, but do you think a toy-plane designer is capable of building a full-size aircraft? I just want to—to get it right, in my mind." He felt the terrible urge to shout, *Tell me you're kidding, for Christ's sake, tell me it's just a big spoof to scare hell out of me!*

The kid's face was the most serious he had ever seen.

"A *toy-plane* designer? Mr. Towns, a toy plane is one of those metal machines that are wound up and placed on the floor. The clockwork motor connects with the wheels to make them move. Kay-craft makes scale flying models, which of course is a different thing."

Towns nodded, beaten. "Yep. I get that. I just wanted to have it right, in my—"

"As for my being capable of building a full-sized aircraft, Mr. Towns, I think you should appreciate two very important things. Precisely similar principles of aerodynamics apply to both scale and full-size aircraft—airfoil surfaces, lift and drag coefficients, weight-thrust equations, and the whole pattern of heavier-than-air construction—they are all precisely similar." The thin hands were folded in composure: a monitor was instructing his pupil. "In the year 1852 they installed a steam engine in a gas balloon, and it flew; but in the same period Henson and Stringfellow built a rubber-powered model airplane that was of course heavier than air—and it was for that reason much more advanced than the steam balloon. Model airplanes were flying successfully more than fifty years before the Wright brothers left the ground. They were not *toy* airplanes, Mr. Towns."

"No. No, I—didn't realize—"

"The second thing you should realize is that a model airplane has to fly itself. There is no pilot. In an air pocket or a shift of wind it has to maintain stability. The design must be even more efficient than that of a full-sized aircraft. I know the pilot's expression about a machine—'she'll fly hands off.' Take your hands off the controls and the machine will continue flying steadily. This doesn't apply to many full-sized machines, as you know—but *all* model planes must be able to do this or they couldn't fly at all. I expect you grasp this, Mr. Towns."

The bright glasses observed him.

Towns nodded and said, yes, he understood. He didn't want to hear any more. Stringer was on his subject and he could talk for hours like this, for days, for years, because he was an authority on this subject, probably the best man in the game.

He nodded again and said he understood; then he pushed the cartridges into his pockets and went through the doorway, plunging into the heat shock of the sun, lurching across the sand and dropping below the mainplane, to tell Moran because he had to tell someone.

After a time Moran asked, "Was that all that was said between you?"

"All."

"You didn't accuse him of holding out on us, or—"

"Lew. Get this. He wasn't holding out on us. You know the people who think they're Napoleon? Stringer thinks he's an aircraft designer. You've only got to listen to him to know just how far round the bend that kid has gone. Maybe he's more human than we thought—I could believe more things about him now than I could ten minutes ago, I could believe he's so sick-scared of dying that he had to dig up this dream and play it out rather than face the idea of death by thirst. And the dream is real to him. I wish to Christ I'd never found this out, then we could've started up and taken off and crashed, and got it done with." He cupped his skinned hands over his eyes to shut out the glare. "Maybe that's what we've got to do anyway."

Moran said in a while, "We don't tell the others, Frank."

"No."

"And we've got to forget it ourselves."

Towns squinted at him. "We can try."

"If we can't forget it we'll have to live with it. Look at it this way: for a model-plane designer he's not bad at big-plane theory. He's talked my head off, yours too, and we couldn't trip him. Look at his control linkage—he's got optimum leverage on every quadrant—he knew about the inverse tapers on the wing-root attachments—he hasn't pulled a single trick that made us doubt him—"

"His theory's fine. We've got to fly out on facts."

He couldn't talk any more, didn't want to think any more; all he could hear was the monotone . . . "She took the Stevenage Cup last year in the power Class." Stevenage . . . dear Christ. This was the Sahara.

Moran sat in the waves of heat, turning his face away from them as one turns away from a fire; but here the fire was everywhere and he was burning in it. He could think of no comfort: he'd been afraid that Towns and Stringer had come to grips again; they hadn't. He'd thought it was the worst thing that could happen; it wasn't.

*   *   *   *   *

The coolant bubbled.

The reflector beamed a pool of light on the sand. Bellamy saw it and did nothing about it. The sun's rays were being gathered in the reflector and projected, so that the pool of light was formed on the sand. Nearly a minute passed before the warning reached his consciousness; then he crawled from the shadow of the tailplane and turned the reflector so that the light hit the jerrican as it should. There were marks on his fingers: lines of blisters made by touching the reflector frame; he hadn't noticed the pain.

"Dave. There any water, is there? Dave?"

There was no need to touch the bottle, to feel its weight; each drip made a pinging sound inside the bottle; it sounded about half full.

"Not yet, Albert." His watch said just gone four; the shadows of the wreck and the plane were growing long. He couldn't let Crow have any water without a proper share-out: that was the rule; and in three hours the bottle would be full, so they'd wait until nine or ten o'clock when the heat would be gone and the water would taste cool and do more good; there'd be a mouthful each for the night. He knew that Crow was half asleep or had just woken, to ask a thing like that.

Someone was turning the generator inside the hull. It wasn't the usual steady moan; every half minute it stopped, then took up again unevenly. Whoever was in there hadn't much strength left; none of them had.

"I didn't want any," Crow said, and sat up, his red eyes still full of sleep. "I jus' wanted to know if it was workin' all right." He swung his skinned nose and looked at Bellamy to see what sort of condition he was in. " 'Ow you feelin', my ole mate?"

"All right." Ought to make a joke, say Top o' the world, something funny like that, but too much effort. "You?"

" 'Ckin' 'orrible," said Crow. "Summink I must've ate."

Bellamy narrowed his eyes and looked across the sand; Towns and Moran were sitting together under the wing, with their heads on their chests, asleep on their haunches. Tilney, flat on his back. Watson, near him. It must be Stringer in there with the generator. It was terrible to hear that even Stringer was weakening.

Shadows were passing over the sand, wings motionless, five or six of them. Impossible to look up into the glare and see where they were: and pointless. They were here.

The calves of his legs felt as if they'd been beaten with rods. Heat cramp. Have to ignore it.

"Where you goin'?"

"Gen'rator." Got onto his knees; sand was sharp, hot.

"Someone's at it."

"Take turns, Albert, watch the can."

"Eh?"

"Can. Jerrican. Don't let it go out." He moved

into the sun's direct heat and staggered under it, loping toward the hull door.

Stringer was sitting with his eyes shut, thin body swaying as he turned the handle. The noise filled the caved-in compartment and when Bellamy spoke to him his eyes jerked open, just like Bimbo's.

"Taking over," Bellamy told him. The kid's face was a blur and the dials of the instrument panel merged and spun in the heat that assailed his eyes.

"Half an hour," Stringer said, and got up. "We don't need more—it's the last night."

"Is it?" He tried to get the drawn white face into focus. "We fly out tomorrow?"

"Of course." The magnified mud-brown eyes were disapproving. "In half an hour I want you all outside." He eased past Bellamy and went down the aisle of the hull. Bellamy's question had worried him; he thought that everyone knew that the plan was to fly out tomorrow. Mr. Towns had worried him, too—he didn't think a "toy-plane" designer was "capable" of adapting a crashed machine and making it fly again. He hadn't thought of this before, and any new idea was interesting to him; but surely Mr. Towns overestimated the difference between a model plane and a full-scale one: it was a difference simply of size.

He had put away the Kaycraft material in case

anyone else should see it. He was not prepared to discuss the Ranger and the Hawk Six with people who regarded them as toys.

The generator had begun droning away, and the sound pleased him. He went outside, nearly falling over as he dropped to the sand from the doorway; the heat was very trying. Towns and Moran were sitting under the mainplane and he thought of going over to them but they looked as if they were asleep. He could speak to them later. With his handkerchief on his head he began walking round the *Phoenix,* checking the work they had done last night. Once, during the next half hour, he found himself unaccountably lying on the hot sand with colors flashing across his eyes; he picked himself up and decided to ignore the occurrence: after three weeks without food this kind of thing was bound to happen.

When the sun was low in the western sky he summoned the others and called for Bellamy to come outside. They stood together in the shadow of the plane.

"In an hour we shall begin work again. Before then, if anyone wants to take anything with him on the flight, he should see to it now. Nothing cumbersome, of course—all the baggage will be left behind—I am talking about things like private papers and small possessions. Also, I want to make sure the cradles are suitable, so each of you will now climb in, as if we were about to take off."

They said nothing. Bellamy put his foot in the wire stirrup and swung up, getting there before he had time to doubt if he had the strength. Crow followed, lying flat in the cradle, hands forward to grip the front rib, his heart still thudding from the effort. The rest of them took their positions, with Stringer watching them from near the wing-tip. The shape of the plane was now spoiled by the men who lay like bundles lashed to the fuselage. The parasite drag they would create was enormous but there was no way of stowing them inside the fuselage because it was one of the original Skytruck booms and very narrow; and to cut openings in the stressed skin would weaken the whole construction. The machine would fly with almost fifty percent more efficiency without them on board; but they had helped to build it so they had a right to be there.

He called them down. "There doesn't seem to be any problem. During the flight nobody must move about in his cradle because stability factors are critical. Now you can collect any small thing you want to take with you—we shall start work when the sun goes down." He climbed into the pilot's seat and began inspecting the control linkage.

Moran went to talk to Towns, because he'd looked on the point of refusing Stringer's order to climb into the cradles just now.

He was leaning against the fuselage, staring across to the dunes; the light of the dying sun turned them into reefs of smooth red coral, and above them two of the vultures were still wheeling, driven away—though not far—by the movement of the men.

"It's the last night here, Frank."

"I'd sooner stay, and do it the way Kepel did. Go out decent. You can't tell what's going to happen in a crash, might not be conclusive, and Watson's only got three rounds left."

Moran leaned one hand against the fuselage and looked into his face. "Whatever he is, and however good or bad he is, he's been three weeks building this thing, as well as he knows how. Tomorrow you're taking over. If you can get her off the ground there'll be a chance for us, a chance in a thousand, but a chance. If we stay here we'll be vulture meat by this time tomorrow. So if she flies at all, Frank, she's got to be flown with everything that's in you, and you can't do that unless you've worked up some faith in her. So start now, and don't stop. If we crash, you've got to go out knowing that it wasn't pilot error."

CHAPTER
24

WHEN THEY WERE TOLD, THEY WERE NOT READY
to be told. By these two words, everything was
changed. It frightened them.

Until it happened, just before five in the morning, they had worked without talking very much.
The gyrocompass was unshipped from the
Skytruck's flight deck and installed in the pilot's
seat of the *Phoenix*. The airspeed indicator also
was transferred. With these two instruments they
would be able to fly approximately straight and to
measure—with the help of a wrist watch—the distance covered. The rough position of the wreckage
and the graves could thus be given to the search
team who would go out to examine the wreck and
bring home the dead.

Towns had put the cartridges back into the Coffman starter, trying to do what Moran had asked
him: to work up some faith in the machine before
morning. These cartridges at least were real; they
would turn the engine, and the engine would run.
Maybe at full revs the big Thorne and Crossley

prop would somehow manage to drag the whole heap of junk across the sand on its skids until they ran into a water point. He'd asked Stringer, "Why do we have to risk getting airborne? We could just taxi out, all the way."

"I don't think you mean it seriously, Mr. Towns. I should remind you that the coolant system is designed to operate chiefly at cruising airspeed, therefore the engine would overheat and seize-up within ten miles or so, leaving us a hundred and fifty miles short of the nearest oasis. Also the skids wouldn't stand up to the continuous shock; I have designed them to withstand one take-off and one landing, and their calculated life is approximately one minute. There are in any case rocks and boulders on the desert floor and the first one we hit would smash the undercarriage and then the propeller. This airplane has been designed to fly, Mr. Towns. It isn't a toy to be wound up and sent along the floor."

There had been a moment during the long night when Towns had let himself believe that the *Phoenix* would really fly and that they would all get through alive; and he had thought about the future, his own future. He would put up no defense. Flying on without radio contact with ground was something a pilot occasionally did when he had faith enough in his familiarity with the route and terrain; but it was never an acceptable excuse. His license was already gone—he might just as well throw it onto the sand here—but there was something even more important than the ending of a lifetime in the sky. He had so far killed seven men, and even if he were allowed to keep his license he would never take life in his hands again. At the age of fifty you didn't shrug off a thing like that and put it down to bad luck and a bum weather report.

His last flight would be made tomorrow, if there was a flight at all.

By the early hours they had taken petrol and washed away the sand that the storm had plastered across the control linkage. The air intake was removed, cleared and replaced. Stringer had no further work for them, nor any time for them; he examined each part of the new machine and checked every modification they had made; sometimes he stood motionless for minutes deep in thought; no one disturbed him.

Bellamy kept the distillery burning, his hands moving by habit. Crow made a fabric bag for the monkey, with air holes in it, stitching it with wire. Sergeant Watson, unskilled, set himself to comb the sand immediately in the path of the airplane, clearing it of the small rocks and meteorites that littered the basin of the dunes. Alone for most of the night, he heard sometimes the voice of Captain Harris, as clearly as if that man were still alive. He would hear it again, at Aldershot, if he ever got out of here. *Refusing to obey an order to support your officer in circumstances of imminent danger to life.* What would you get for that? Peacetime, a stretch in the Glasshouse and reduced to private. No, it wasn't going to be so rosy. There'd be nothing to hate, nothing like Harris; plenty more of his kind but they wouldn't really be Harris, the genuine article. He'd miss that. Not so rosy, no. Better off here, better to stay behind, lie down and shut your eyes and think about a woman, a millionaire on holiday with a bit of skirt till it got too bad, then pull the bloody trigger and Amen, Watty, my old son, Amen.

He combed the sand for rocks, knowing that if that thing ever got up and flew, he'd fly with it, and never know why.

At four o'clock the moon rose and the naked bulb looked feeble as if it were dawn come. No one was working now except Stringer; they sat on the sand, their backs to the light, the chill air keeping them awake. They had no more strength with which to move and try to warm themselves; they sat in silence in the winter of the moon. And when they were told, they weren't ready to be told. Only one of them—Tilney—saw Stringer coming, a thin figure moving across the circle of light to stand looking down at them, the glint of his glasses masking his face. He said:

"She's ready."

And everything was changed, because it was all over now and there was nothing else to do except hope; and hope had been easier when they'd had to work for it.

Moran looked up at Stringer and saw him suddenly as a man on trial. The verdict was for the morning. He wondered if he could get the word out of his shriveled mouth. He must try.

"Cong'at'lations."

They wandered in the dawnlight as far as the mouth of the dunes, stooping to pick up a stone and throw it aside, stooping again, like beachcombers picking for a living, the rags of their clothes hanging from their bones. Before the sun's whole disk was above the earth they had cleared a pathway for the plane.

Stringer had gone into the hull to switch out the lamp; now he plugged in the shaver and leaned against the bulkhead, shutting his eyes because the skin of his face was peeled raw and the pain was a nuisance. The shaver felt very heavy. He tried to think clearly. The airplane was finished and all the delicate decisions had been made and acted upon. Now the *Phoenix* must fly; and the thought was a worry because he had been more concerned with the building of it than with the ultimate test of the design in the air. There were so many things he might have got wrong; he had never built a full-sized airplane before.

The sound of the shaver had hypnotized him and in falling he caught his head against something and lay for what seemed a long time. The plug had been pulled out of the socket and the shaver was not running. A voice said, "We're about ready, Stringer," and he got to his feet, saying, "Yes? Yes?" and opened his eyes and saw Moran in the doorway and said, "I'm coming. I was shaving. I'm coming." Blood on his hand from his sore face where he had knocked his head, not important. Annoyed, very annoyed. "Water?" he asked, but Moran had gone away. He hadn't meant to say "Water" like that. He put the shaver into its case and took it with him, because he always traveled with it, everywhere.

Mr. Towns. Where was Mr. Towns? Pilot.

They stood in a group near the tail unit. There was a bottle and a half, the half still warm from the distilling plant. The sun shone on their faces. They looked dead.

"Bottle and half," Moran said, trying to sound pleased. All through the night the air had been calm and there was no dew. "Share full one, Frank have other all himself." He spoke very good pidgin English, desert English. "Needs it, pilot."

They shared the full bottle, using the tin measure, helping one another to tip the mouthful in so that none was spilled. Stringer came out of the hull, blood down the side of his face; he stood, as they had stood after taking the water, closing his eyes, experiencing the strangeness: one didn't have time to swallow; the water was already gone, absorbed by the swollen tongue. Then the terrible need began—the need of more; and they moved away from Towns when he pushed the half-bottle into his mouth and drank.

The sun was already hot on their faces.

"Mr. Towns. We will take off as soon as the engine is warmed."

Towns looked at the puckered face and the twitching of its mouth; sometimes the expressionless eyes squeezed shut behind the glasses, then flickered open again. The little robot was running down at last. "As I have said before, this machine has a high aspect ratio, and very limited maneuverability at low speeds. There will be a tendency to yaw on take-off because of the single propeller; you must remember this isn't the Skytruck. Owing to the high span, rolling tendency will be slight. If you feel that you can keep control at a hundred feet there is no point in going higher; on the other hand, you must leave yourself room to correct any marked effects of instability."

Watching them, Moran was too jaded to worry. Towns stood there, an old man, his gray head heavy on his shoulders, his eyes sunk in his face, looking down at the kid who was telling him how to fly. Moran didn't know what Towns was thinking, or what he would say when Stringer had finished. It was going to be Towns' first and last flight in a prototype that would never go into production; he would be the only pilot ever to fly a *Phoenix,* the only one of its kind. If these things still mattered to him, there was a chance.

"The controlled slots are now fixed, as you know, in the open position, and with the crew on board there's a tail-heavy moment, so that she'll fly tail down all the way. Allow for that. I estimate cruising airspeed at a hundred and fifty to two hundred miles per hour, so that we should sight water points within two hours at the most. If the controls respond well enough, make a wide turn to the west and then keep straight and concentrate on maintaining level flight. It is all you have to do, and there should be no problem."

Towns saw the eyes flicker shut behind the glasses; the robot had switched off. He had listened very carefully to all that it had said, because today they were all going to live or die, and it depended on what he did with the controls.

"Thank you," he said.

Moran knew suddenly that he had been worrying very hard about how Towns was taking this; his whole body sagged with relief. Towns was going to try.

"Lew, we're starting up. Keep 'em clear of the down-wash."

"Okay." He led the others along the wing to where they had dragged the toolboxes and trestles and anything that would foul the tail skid. Stringer went with them but stood apart. Their shadows were long across the sand. They watched Towns climb the trailing edge and heave himself into the pilot's seat; for a minute or more he just sat there recovering from the effort; then he opened the cocks and pressed the Ki-gas, giving it a dozen, screwing it home. His hands were working from habit and he knew it, and let them: then for the first time he consciously allowed for the special circumstances here, and snapped the switches down in case there was a chance of the engine's firing on the suck-in cartridge. Habit again made him turn his head to see that they were all beyond the wing-tip, with no one near the prop.

Coffman.

The three blades swung to the explosion and oil smoke gushed from the exhaust but she didn't take. He noticed how the wings had flexed and wondered how the three-ton freight-loading cable would stand up in flight.

Number two cartridge.

The prop kicked and banged back on the reduction gear, spun on, kicked, and swung still. Somewhere an exhaust valve was a thou' open and the compressed gas hissed into the pipes. Five cartridges left in the Coffman. The fuel was there; the mags were firing; compressions were strong; there was no reason why she shouldn't start once the cylinders were cleared of oil and condensation.

Three.

A spinner but she kicked and blue smoke curled away in the sunshine; the reek of unburned fuel was on the air and he set the mixture to weak and shut the throttle a degree and pressed the tit, hoping that if flame started coming from the pipe someone would have the strength to beat it out for him.

Four.

A dead run and he began to be afraid because she had to start in the next three or it was no go, after twenty-six days, no go. Risk the next cartridge on clearing the pots—she was too rich, stank of the stuff. Mixture weak, switches *off,* throttle wide open and risk it.

Five.

Steady and no kick, a clearer, with black-and-blue muck curling out of the pipe; he shivered in the heat with two to go and the fear of Christ in him.

Six.

A spinner and she kicked, banging on the gears with the air frame shaking, blue smoke curling, clearing—orange flame and the big prop spinning at a run and settling, putting out a roar from the pipe that drowned the sound of the sobbing in his throat as he eased the revs up and sat like a sack listening to the cylinders beating, hunting, one of them choked still but picking up—then she was running with a will and in the long sweet sound he heard another, faintly, and turned his head and saw them standing there with their mouths open, cheering. His cracked lips hurt him and he knew that he smiled.

For a minute Moran couldn't move because the waking nightmare had left him weakened: the fear had come to him that Towns had waited for this moment with the cunning of the mad, to sit up there alone and flood the cylinders so that she wouldn't start, so that he used up all seven cartridges and sentenced seven men to death, to prove that Stringer was wrong and he was right: they should have made a test run, earlier.

But she was running. He moved, forcing his legs to work.

"Okay—get on board while she's warming up!"

Tilney's cradle was the aftermost on the starboard side and Crow helped him to reach it, bracing his foot in the wire stirrup and pushing him until he could get a purchase and haul himself forward, to lie prone with his hands on the grips, shutting his eyes against the haze of sand the prop was sending back.

Crow climbed next, and when he was settled Bellamy passed him the fabric bag with the air holes, and Crow took it gently, calling above the beat of the engine, "Bimbo . . . come on along o' me, Bimbo, you'll be all right."

Watson climbed and settled into his cradle on the port side with Bellamy in front of him. Moran walked across to Stringer.

"Will you be okay?" He knew Stringer had passed out when he was shaving in the hull this morning, and might be glad of a leg up into the forward seat.

"Of course." Stringer turned away, rounding the tail unit through the rush of sand, his clothes flapping against his thin body. He waited until Moran had settled into his cradle, then climbed the starboard wing and got into the makeshift seat, buckling the safety belt they had taken from the Skytruck.

"Running-up," he heard Towns call.

The revs rose and the image of the prop blades merged and hazed; the whole of the air frame began shuddering; the downwash sent a sand cloud streaming out behind the tail.

Tilney, his elbows braced forward of a cradle rib, felt the heat of the engine against his face, and shut his eyes.

Crow had an arm hooked round a strut and held the monkey against him. "You'll be all right, Bimbo, you'll be all right," talking to Bimbo all the time, because this was the voice that had given him water to drink, a voice he could trust.

Watson lay prone, waiting, thinking, Not so rosy, Captain Harris, sir, you bleeder, not so rosy.

Moran had his hands locked against the forward strut of his cradle and he lay listening to the fierce rise of the revs. *No one I'd sooner fly with, Frankie, no one.*

Bellamy felt the bulge of the diary against the ribs. He had put: *Sunday. Plane finished, hope to fly out. Wish us luck.*

The engine was howling at half throttle and when the skids began sliding on the sand Towns eased off and let her idle. Through his smoked glasses he could see the far shimmer of the desert. The sun was molten in a blinding sky. He tested the tail control surfaces and looked across at Stringer.

Stringer nodded.

CHAPTER
25

THE SAND BILLOWED IN A LONG CURVE AS THE tail skid began jockeying badly with the front skids plowing through the soft ground as the full power came on and pulled the machine forward a foot at a time, swinging to the left, all the time to the left, until the skid cage cleared and the run grew smoother; but even with the rudder hard over she moved in a curve, the left skid rail dragging until Towns used the ailerons and got the port wing rising, lifting the skid cage level; she began running straight but she'd moved in a half circle and the north ridge of the dunes was now ahead of them and close and she wouldn't get up, wouldn't get up—three hundred yards and closing to two with the power full on and the column hard back and the skid cage hammering under the weight. The dunes were close, at a hundred yards too close.

He eased back the throttle and let the speed die, waiting till the port rail began dragging again, correcting with the rudder, letting her swing in a wide curve with the starboard wing-tip brushing the flank of the dunes before he put the power full on again and used the ailerons to lift her on the left side and send her straight. The skid came up and she began her run from a quarter way across the basin, going straight now but headed too close to the wreck of the Skytruck and the litter of boxes and trestles. He tried to correct and felt the rail dragging, corrected again and lifted it, got her running straight.

There would have to be luck. If she hit a rock she'd run amuck and smash into the wreckage; there wouldn't have to be a rock in the way; he couldn't see the ground through the whirling cloud of sand the prop was fetching up, and if a rock was there he wouldn't see it, couldn't avoid it; there wouldn't have to be one. On this line they'd clear the wreck and head for the low south dunes with a run of four or five hundred yards with room to spare if she ever got up at all, if she ever got up.

The basin of dunes was filled with the sound of her. Sand marked her wake as she ran. The wreck of the Skytruck was slipping past on the starboard wing-tip, the bones of a nightmare littering the ground, passing from sight as she made her run across smoother going, wings flexing under the span of the big cable, skid cage hammering, tail yawing from left to right to left and setting up a dangerous pendulum swing that brought the wing-tips skating across the sand with a series of shocks that sent the cable twanging a single musical note that sounded above the engine's din until Towns got the stick back and held it against him, feeling the lift come into the wings; and the hammering of the skid cage eased; and the yaw went out of her; and all that was left of her on the sand was her shadow, falling away below.

She is not a toy, Mr. Towns, she is an airplane.

Her shadow crossed the dunes, smaller now. Ahead lay the south desert, limitless. Soon she turned slowly, with the sun swinging across the port wing-tip, and headed west as they had planned.

Two army officers of the El Araneb garrison were sipping a gin on the terrace of the old fort, in the shade of the awning. It was eleven in the forenoon. They heard an aircraft approaching; it sounded to be very low; then they sighted it, and put down their drinks, because there was no airfield at El Araneb and the machine seemed about to make a landing.

"My God, what an extraordinary shape the thing is, old boy—you see it?"

"Yes. Got chaps clinging all over it, very rum indeed."

They stood up. Below the terrace the Arabs were jostling together, pointing to the sky.

"No doubt about it, you know. She's coming in to land."

"Better get down there."

They were walking smartly side by side, leading the Arabs and a couple of British privates who had fallen in to see what was going on; they left the shade of the palm trees and made across open sand. The machine had landed not far away, and people were getting off. They looked rather groggy but they were all on their feet now and making slowly for the trees.

Out of the desert there came seven men, and a monkey.

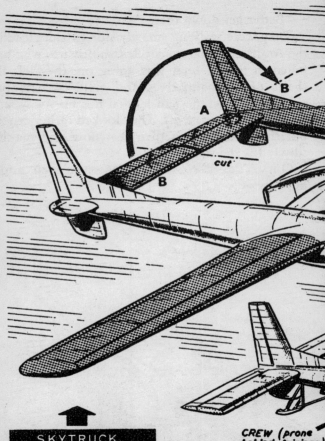

A

B

cut

B

B

CREW (prone
behind fairings)

SKYTRUCK

SHADED AREAS
= PHOENIX

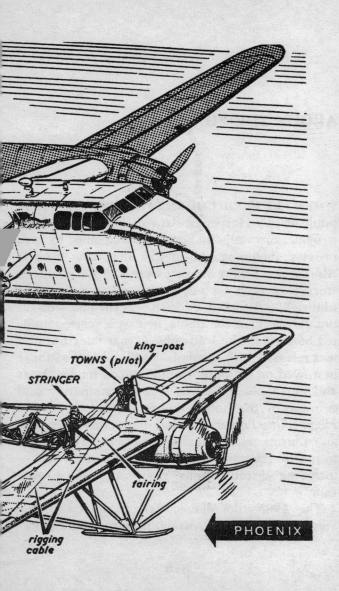

king-post

TOWNS (pilot)

STRINGER

fairing

rigging
cable

PHOENIX

ABOUT THE FILMS

WHEN *THE FLIGHT OF THE PHOENIX* WAS FIRST published by Harper & Row in 1964, this tale of struggle, survival, and hope was welcomed by rave reviews, including one in *Life* magazine. Robert Aldrich and Jimmy Stewart were so inspired by the story they each set out separately to pursue the film rights. Although Aldrich was the one who ultimately secured the rights, he cast a very committed Stewart in the lead role. A year later the film was released with accolades as impressive as those bestowed on the book—nominations for an Oscar and two Golden Globes. The determination and courage of the human spirit so evident in *The Flight of the Phoenix* is what makes this story such an enduring tale. It's a story whose truth continues to inspire readers more than three decades later—including director John Moore (*Behind Enemy Lines*).

The 1965 film classic, which starred Jimmy Stewart, Sir Richard Attenborough, Ernest Borgnine, George Kennedy and Peter Finch among others, was distinctive for featuring an all-male cast. Moore's film, by contrast, adds a female element to the ensemble, with Miranda Otto (*Lord of the Rings: The Return of the King*) joining Dennis Quaid (*The Day After Tomorrow, Far From Heaven*), Tyrese Gibson (*2 Fast 2 Furious*), Giovani Ribisi (*Cold Mountain, Lost in Translation*) and others. Not wanting to make Otto "just one of the boys," her character, named Kelly, serves as a friend and advisor offering friendship to her fellow survivors.

In the new film, John Moore and screenwriters Scott Frank and Edward Burns expand on the original's themes. Their survivors are castoffs from society who will never be missed. As they attempt to build a new plane from the wreckage of the old one, in hopes of flying back to civilization, they experience a rebirth of their own.

The success of 1965's *The Flight of the Phoenix* is due, in part, to the detailed research for which Elleston Trevor was known. Having served in the Royal Air Force during World War II as a flight engineer, Trevor had the technical expertise to make the story come alive. Moore, an airplane aficionado himself, has stayed true to the details, scouring the globe for an air-worthy C-119 to use in the film. The unique engine design of the C-119, a plane which was employed from World War II through

Vietnam, makes the escape depicted in the film fully plausible. But Trevor possessed more than technical knowledge—he understood human nature. As Moore explains, "The *Phoenix* can only be built if [the survivors] can get the hope they need. They have the tools. They have the expertise. But until they commit the hope to it, it will never fly."